MAGGIE CHRISTENSEN

Second Chances in Bellbird Bay

Cover and interior design: J D Smith Design
Editing: John Hudspith Editing Services

Dedication

To Jim, the love of my life.

Also by Maggie Christensen

Oregon Coast Series
The Sand Dollar
The Dreamcatcher
Madeline House

Sunshine Coast books
A Brahminy Sunrise
Champagne for Breakfast

Sydney Collection
Band of Gold
Broken Threads
Isobel's Promise
A Model Wife

Scottish Collection
The Good Sister
Isobel's Promise
A Single Woman

One

Greta Roberts hummed to herself as she opened the door to her boutique and breathed in its familiar fragrance, a mixture of new clothes and the scented candle she kept behind the counter, and which was always lit when the shop was open. Apart from her daughter, *Birds of a Feather*, situated on the esplanade in the small coastal town of Bellbird Bay was the most important thing in her life, and the coming Easter weekend promised to be one of the busiest in the year.

The boutique had saved her life when her divorce had followed by the death of her parents in the Bali bombings twenty years earlier when her daughter, Jo, was only fourteen years old. She still felt their loss keenly each year on the anniversary of the bombings, tortured by thoughts of *what if*. Last October had been the twentieth anniversary, and the pain was still as sharp as it had been on the day she heard the news.

It was a sad quirk of fate that it had been the inheritance from her parents which had enabled her to buy what was now a flourishing boutique known for its upmarket clientele and brightly coloured creations.

Another cause for her excitement today was the news Jo would be coming home. Greta's daughter had moved overseas to teach soon after finishing university, and Greta despaired of her ever settling down. She'd dearly love a grandchild or two – having given birth to Jo when she was only nineteen, Greta had expected to be a grandmother by now. But marriage and children didn't seem to figure in Jo's plans.

The email with the news she was coming home to Bellbird Bay came as a surprise, and Greta couldn't wait to see her daughter again.

She was about to put a match to the candle when her phone rang. 'Mum?'

'Jo, darling. Where are you?'

'I just got into Brisbane. I'm pretty tired but I'll hire a car and drive up. Should be there in a couple of hours. Can't wait to see you.'

'I could…' But Greta looked across the shop at the rows of summer clothes, the display of jewellery and accessories and thought of the prospective customers arriving in town for the surf carnival which always took place on Easter weekend.

'It's okay, Mum. I know you can't leave the shop. I'll go straight home. I just want to crash.'

Greta stared at the now silent phone feeling dissatisfied with the exchange. She hadn't seen Jo for over five years, not since she settled in England, excited to be in what she called the country of her ancestors – her grandparents had emigrated from there soon after their marriage. Had she imagined the hint of sadness in her daughter's voice?

Jo hadn't explained why she was choosing to come home in the middle of the school year. Her excuse she was suddenly homesick didn't ring true, coming from the girl who had set off on her great adventure, her eyes glowing with excitement at the prospect of travelling the world. She'd travelled across Asia and Europe, before reaching England and deciding to stay there.

'That's the beauty of teaching, Mum,' Jo had said at her graduation, proudly clasping her academic transcript, 'You can go anywhere in the world and find work.'

But Greta had often wondered if her parents' divorce following so quickly after her grandparents' deaths, had damaged the young girl in some way, making her want to leave the town she'd grown up in. She could remember how, for years after the divorce, Jo had pleaded with her parents to make up, had tried everything she could think of to bring them back together, to become a family again, to no avail. *Was that what had forced her to leave?*

Jo had only made a few brief trips home; her letters and phone calls had been full of the wonderful things she was doing. Until recently, Greta realised, when her communications had become farther and farther apart… until the one announcing her return home.

Putting her worries aside, Greta continued with her morning routine, happy in the knowledge Jo was back in Australia and would be there when she got home.

As she expected, the morning was busy, the brightly coloured display in her window attracting customers, many of whom were visiting Bellbird Bay for the first time. It was a relief when the rush died down around lunchtime and she was able to take a short break.

'Got a minute?'

Greta glanced up from her lunchbox to see her friend Cassandra at the door. 'Just taking the opportunity to have a quick bite before the rush starts again. You?'

'Same. Rushed off my feet. If it goes on like this all weekend, I'll be a mess by Monday.'

Greta laughed. She and Cass had opened their shops at much the same time and, while she stocked outfits suitable for every occasion, Cass, whose shop was called Sassy's, catered in everything for the beach.

'Coffee?'

Greta noticed the two takeaway coffees Cass was holding. 'Thanks. I was planning to duck out later.' She accepted the cup and took a gulp. 'Mmm, it's so good,' she said as the jolt of caffeine hit her system.

'When does Jo arrive?'

Greta checked her watch, as if she hadn't been doing that every spare minute. 'She should be home by now. I wish...'

'She'll be tired after her flight. Better she's fresh when you see her. Tomorrow's a holiday. You'll have the whole day together.'

'You're right,' Greta said. 'I wish I knew what's prompted her to come home at this time.'

'Man trouble,' Cass said. 'Isn't it always?'

'I don't know. She didn't say... and there's been no mention of a man in her calls or emails.'

'Did you always confide in your parents?' Cass asked. 'I know I didn't.'

Greta tried to remember. She'd already been married with a teenage child at Jo's age. But when she was younger? 'Probably not,' she sighed. But she hoped that, if Jo did have problems, she'd feel she could confide in her mother. She was looking forward to cosy evenings, sharing a glass of wine and learning more about her daughter's life.

But first there was the weekend to get through – and the surfing carnival. Every year at this time, she wished she was pulling on the red and yellow uniform of a surf lifesaver again, helping out her fellow lifesavers at the beach. But she had a living to make, and this weekend was one of the busiest in the year as the town filled with participants and sightseers all intent on having as much fun as possible.

'Earth to Greta.'

Cass's voice brought Greta back to the present. 'Sorry.'

'Where were you?'

'I was remembering the old days, when Easter weekend was spent surfing...'

'...and checking out the guys,' Cass laughed. 'I seem to remember...'

'Don't!' Greta put her hands up defensively. 'We were young and silly back then.'

'But it was fun, wasn't it... before life got in the way?'

'Mmm.'

'Will you be watching the carnival?'

'I'll try to duck out for a bit, but you know what it'll be like once everyone hits town.'

Cass nodded. It was the same every year during the surfing carnival and later in the year when the triathlon took place. The population of Bellbird Bay more than doubled in size. It didn't used to be like that. When they were growing up, Bellbird Bay had been a sleepy seaside town. It still was for most of the year... and Greta loved it.

The door burst open to admit a group of chattering women – tourists – and Cass said, 'I should go. They'll be at Sassy's next.' She gave Greta a grin and picked up their empty coffee cups before leaving.

'How can I help you?' Greta moved graciously towards the newcomers, her habitual smile on her face.

*

It was after six before Greta made it home, stopping briefly on the way to pick up the *Kaa Na Moo Khob* that had been Jo's favourite from the local Thai restaurant. She hoped her tastes hadn't changed.

As she turned the key in the front door of the old family house she'd inherited from her parents, situated in a quiet part of town, Greta could hear the sound of music coming from the kitchen. 'Jo!' she called, dropping her bag on the hall table and making her way through the house.

'Mum!' A whirlwind of blonde hair ran to greet her in a warm hug. 'It's good to be home.'

'Let me look at you.' Greta placed the takeaway on the benchtop, then feasted her eyes on the daughter she hadn't seen for so long and had missed so much. Jo's hair was longer, her skin pale from the English winter and there were a few lines around her eyes that hadn't been there before, but it was the troubled expression in her daughter's eyes that made Greta want to hold her tight and keep her safe. Something had happened to put that expression there, and Greta wouldn't settle until she discovered what it was.

It was Jo who broke eye contact first, moving away to lean against the sink. 'You look just the same, Mum. Elegant as ever. Bellbird Bay looked just the same, too, when I drove in.'

'It doesn't change much, though it's busier than usual this weekend.'

'I know. Easter. The surf carnival. How could I forget?'

Greta looked at her daughter affectionately, remembering the Easter weekends when Jo had been one of the young people intent on proving their prowess in the surf. She'd never been among the winners but had always enjoyed participating.

'I suppose all the guys I was at school with have left like I did,' she said, gazing down at her bare feet. She was wearing a pair of old shorts and a tee-shirt Greta remembered from before she left. She must have raided her wardrobe to find them.

'Not all of them. A few are still around. I don't know if you remember Owen Rankin. He was a few years below you in school. He's taken out the championship three years running and is in line to do it again this year. He has his own business now, designing and making surfboards.'

'Will Rankin's son? Is Will still around? He was a good teacher.'

'Still around and still running his surf school.' Will had been one of Greta's heroes when she was growing up. Will and his mate, Martin Cooper.

Growing up in the town of Bellbird Bay on Queensland's Sunshine Coast, like her daughter, Greta had fallen into the surfing culture early, starting with joining Nippers in primary school and graduating to become a fully qualified surf lifesaver in her teens. These were heady days, every moment out of school spent on the beach, her heroes, local surf champions Will Rankin and Martin Cooper, both a couple of years older than she was and who seemed like gods.

Now they were all in their fifties and life had taken over any earlier yearnings. But the memories were still there.

'Dinner?' Greta asked. 'I picked up your favourite Thai on the way home. And I'll open a bottle of bubbly to celebrate.'

'Thanks, Mum, but you don't need to make a fuss.'

'Of course I do. I haven't seen you for so long. It's a cause for celebration, and it's Easter.'

To Greta's disappointment, Jo didn't say much during dinner, excusing herself as soon as she finished eating with the explanation she was jetlagged. Saying she would feel better in the morning, she disappeared into her room leaving Greta with the dirty dishes and an almost full bottle of sparkling wine.

She washed up, then refilled her glass and took it outside to sit in the courtyard. It was pleasant out there, the only sound the distant roar of the waves. She gazed up at the stars trying to stem her disappointment, reminding herself that Jo was an adult, and would no doubt confide in her mother when she was ready. But it had hurt to see Jo's closed expression when Greta asked if everything was okay.

Two

Sitting in his Sydney office, Leo Carlson smiled as he hung up the phone. After more than two decades running the company, Leonard Holdings, he could still get excited about a new project.

He was due to travel to Fiji in a few days' time to oversee the redevelopment of a resort his company had purchased there, when he'd heard this hotel had come on the market. It was situated in a town of which he had fond memories, where he'd spent the summer between school and university. Bellbird Bay wasn't in his normal orbit, being too small to be considered as part of his growing empire of world class hotels and resorts, but it piqued his interest. And the news the present owner was in prison only added to his curiosity.

Checking his calendar, Leo calculated he could allocate a few days to investigate the property, to decide if it was worth adding to his portfolio. He picked up the phone again to ask his PA to book a flight and accommodation. If the place was still operating as a hotel, it might be useful to see it as a guest before making any decisions. It was Easter weekend so room availability would be a good test of the viability of the project.

He had barely put down the phone when the petite dark-haired woman who had been his assistant for the past ten years tapped on his door before coming in. Referring to her iPad she said, 'I've booked you on the nine-forty-three flight on Friday morning. It will arrive at twelve-ten, and I managed to secure a cancellation at the hotel. Is there anything else?'

'No thanks, Philippa. I'll pick up a rental car at the airport. A return flight?'

Philippa looked confused. 'You didn't specify so I left it open. If you wish, I can...'

'No, it'll be fine.' It wasn't often he set off with no specified return date. It could be interesting.

Now the booking was made, he was able to put it to the back of his mind and concentrate on the day ahead which consisted of a number of meetings with senior members of his staff and a lunch date with his ex-wife which he'd have preferred to cancel. He still gelt guilty each time they met. He knew it was his fault their marriage had fallen apart. Too caught up on the adrenaline rush the purchase of each new hotel brought, he and Zoe had grown further and further apart as he spent more time away than at home. It should have been no surprise when she found other men to spend her time with, younger men who flattered her and were willing to make her the sole focus of their attention.

When Leo glanced around Café Sydney, he spotted Zoe right away. She was seated at a window table and was checking her phone. The restaurant, on the rooftop of Custom House overlooking the harbour and the Sydney Harbour Bridge, was a favourite of hers. The woman he'd married in his early thirties and divorced a decade later looked as elegant as ever, her glossy dark hair cut into a geometric style that suited her sharp features perfectly. From this distance she looked barely older than the day they married, but Leo knew she'd never see fifty again and her hair colour relied on the efforts of her hairdresser.

As he drew closer, the lines around her eyes and mouth told their own story. He leant over to give her a peck on the cheek, inhaling the expensive scent which hadn't changed in the years they'd been apart. Feeling the familiar tug of guilt, he pulled out a chair. 'I hope this is important, Zoe. I don't have much time.' He bit his lip, knowing this was the wrong thing to say, but she always managed to get under his skin – even before she opened her mouth.

'Let's eat first and talk later,' she said, opening her menu. 'The food here is too good to spoil it with arguments.'

They ordered their meals, Zoe choosing half a dozen Sydney rock oysters followed by salad, while Leo decided on grilled swordfish. He ordered a bottle of the Pouilly-Fumé he knew Zoe favoured. There was no sense in antagonising her. He noticed she gave a small nod as he placed the order.

'Now,' he said, when they had graduated to coffee, 'What's up?' He'd already spent more time here than he intended or could afford.

'I need an increase in my allowance,' Zoe said, her gaze meeting his.

Leo groaned. He should have known. While her divorce settlement was generous, it was never enough to satisfy Zoe's insatiable appetite for travel and her predilection for impecunious young men. As his empire grew, so did her demands, and he'd learnt over the years that it was simpler to agree than to suffer the angst of a long drawn-out court case which would end in the same result. 'Who is it this time?' he asked, wondering why she'd insisted on this meeting when any negotiations regarding money could be – and usually were – handled by his accountant.

'Joel is an artist.' Her eyes became softer and took on a glazed expression. 'We want to travel to Southeast Asia. It's where his inspiration lies.'

More likely where he can buy cheaper drugs, Leo thought, amazed how such a sharp and usually intelligent woman could be taken in by these charlatans. But he'd tried to reason with her in the past and knew there was no point.

'I'll have Ken look into it,' he said, knowing the reference to his finance controller would raise her hackles, but also knowing he had no option. Since his business had grown, he no longer had control of his own finances, leaving it all to the professional he'd hired to do just that.

'Ken!' She sniffed. 'He doesn't understand.'

'I doubt anyone does, but I'll instruct him to look seriously at your request. Now, if that's all?' He leant over to kiss her cheek again, 'Stay safe, Zoe,' he said, before picking up the bill and making his way to the counter where he paid and left without a backward glance. He would never admit it, but he often worried about Zoe and her habit of picking up struggling young men. It was so risky. Anything could happen. But at least he'd be there to pick up the pieces.

Outside, Leo took a deep breath before heading back along Circular Quay and up George Street to his office, situated on the tenth floor of a glass-fronted office block. He had a business to run and, if he was to spend the weekend in Bellbird Bay, he needed to clear his desk before he went home today.

*

It was late when Leo opened the door to his apartment in one of the high-rise buildings on Sydney Wharf he'd purchased on his divorce, happy to let Zoe keep the family home in St Ives. At the time, he'd hoped she'd be satisfied by that plus a generous annual allowance. How wrong he'd been. It seemed these days, her one aim in life was to bleed him dry. But he could afford it, and it was one way to assuage his guilt.

As he stepped into the large open-plan apartment, his eyes, as always, were drawn to the view of the harbour and he felt a sense of peace envelop him. He was glad he had this to come home to after the day he'd had, though it had not been unlike every one of his days. Apart from the lunch with Zoe, today had mirrored every other day in Leo's life.

He poured himself a glass of scotch and went out onto the balcony. The sounds of revellers on the wharf filtered up to him, the lights of the ships docked there reminding him this was a bustling harbour. He leant on the balcony rail and remembered the summer of long ago, when he was eighteen and anything seemed possible. Bellbird Bay had been an oasis after the stress of the leaving certificate and the end of year celebrations. There had been a girl, too, a girl with long, blonde hair, tanned skin and a sweetness he'd never been able to recapture. Leo wondered what had happened to her.

Three

'What would you like to do today?' Greta asked Jo. They were enjoying a leisurely breakfast of toast and marmalade in the courtyard. Jo had only just appeared while Greta had been up for ages, unable to settle to anything, wondering if she should wake her daughter before deciding to let her sleep.

'I don't care.' Jo took a bite of toast and a sip of the lemongrass and ginger tea which had become a favourite of Greta's. She gazed into space.

Greta winced, willing her daughter to say more. But Jo remained silent and continued to gaze into space. Greta took a deep breath. 'How about we go to the beach? We could take a picnic. It's a lovely day.' She looked out at the clear blue sky with only a few clouds.

'Okay.' There was no energy in Jo's voice. It was as if she was permanently exhausted.

Greta tried to tell herself it had been a long trip and sometimes it took time to recover from jetlag, but she sensed it was more than that. Sighing, she cleared the table and set about making sandwiches with the sourdough bread and ham she'd bought the day before. She packed them into her old picnic basket along with a couple of bottles of ginger beer and two bananas, then looked across at Jo who hadn't moved. 'Ready?'

'In a minute.' Jo slid out of the chair to disappear in the direction of her bedroom. When she reappeared ten minutes later, she was wearing a pair of loose three-quarter grey pants with a blue shirt tied at the waist. 'I'm ready,' she said.

'Right.'

They drove in silence for a while until, looking out the window, Jo asked, 'Are we going to Dolphin Beach?' showing the first bit of interest Greta had heard since she arrived.

'You remember?' It was the beach where they'd spent a lot of time when Jo was small. Greta had liked it because it was quiet, away from the main beaches frequented by tourists… and it held good memories for her. She was glad Jo had fond memories of it, too.

'I used to think about it,' Jo said, 'when it was wet and cold in London, and I was waiting for my bus in the morning. It was as if Dolphin Beach was a dream, a mirage. But I knew it was real.' She hugged her arms around her. 'Thanks, Mum,' she said with the hint of a smile.

There was a strong breeze when they got out of the car, but by the time they made their way down to the beach, set in a sheltered bay protected by two outcrops of land, they were able to find a spot where they could be out of the wind.

'This is magic.' Jo stretched out her arms to encompass the pristine white sand, the gentle waves lapping on the shore and the seabirds diving around just above the ocean with its changing hues of blue and turquoise.

Greta smiled to herself. Maybe here, in the ambiance of this special spot, Jo would unburden herself.

'I'm going to have a swim,' Jo said. 'You?'

Greta shook her head. It hadn't occurred to her to wear her swimmers. But Jo quickly pulled of her shirt and stepped out of her pants to reveal a sleek one-piece bathing suit. She ran down to the ocean and was swimming strongly out to sea before Greta could speak.

This beach held special memories for Greta. It was where she'd lost her virginity many years before, where she'd enjoyed secret trysts, where she'd found a love she thought would last for ever.

'Mum?'

Greta came back to the present with a start.

Jo was staring down at her, dripping onto the sand. 'I forgot to bring a towel.'

Greta chuckled and rose. 'I have one in the car. I'll…'

'I can get it.' Jo picked up the keys and ran up the slope to the car much faster than Greta would have been able to do. She was back in a few seconds rubbing her hair with the old towel Greta kept in the car boot for emergencies.

'Hungry?'

'Mmm.'

Greta opened the picnic basket, and they unpacked the sandwiches and ginger beer.

After eating and a short rest, Jo, who seemed unable to keep still, asked, 'Fancy a walk along the beach?'

'Sure.'

They strolled along in the shallows, Jo as silent as before until she suddenly said, 'It's good to be back. I missed all this.'

'But you seemed to be enjoying your travels... London.' Greta gazed at her daughter, surprised to see tears in her eyes and wondered if she was ready to talk.

'I was... It's just... being back here... It almost feels as if I've never been away. Sorry,' she sniffed, 'I don't know what came over me.'

'You know you can talk to me, tell me what's bothering you, don't you? Whatever it is, I'd never judge you.'

'I know that, Mum. Thanks.' Jo fell silent again, then said, 'I spoke to Dad.'

Greta stopped in her tracks. Although she and Mick had been divorced for years, they were still good friends. Mick ran the whale watching tours out of the bay, had done for years. They'd met in their late teens, married early and had grown apart over the years, culminating in their divorce when Jo was in *her* teens. She ran into Mick regularly, but he hadn't mentioned speaking to Jo. 'When?' she asked.

'Last night, when I went to my room. I wanted to let him know I was back.'

'Oh!'

'You two still talk to each other, don't you?'

'Of course we do. We have you in common.' Greta threw her arm around her daughter and gave her a hug. 'And in a town this small, it would be difficult to avoid each other. We're still friends. Why?'

'No reason.'

But Greta could see Jo had something on her mind. She'd just have to be patient. She remembered when Jo was little, how she'd bottle things up – an argument with a friend, a poor grade at school – then it would all come out, usually when they least expected it. Hopefully the same would happen this time. Greta wondered if Cass was right, if there was a man involved. She gazed at her daughter's face as if she'd see the answer written there, but Jo appeared as implacable as she had since she returned home. The only sign was the slight darkness in her eyes when she thought she was unobserved.

Jo was chattier on the drive home, asking about Greta's boutique, her friends and what had been happening in Bellbird Bay, but to Greta's sharp mind there was something forced about all her questions. It was as if she was trying to stave off any questions Greta might have, determined to keep her own life secret.

On an impulse Greta took a detour along the esplanade on the way home, hoping the sight of the familiar scene might prompt more confidences.

The beach was almost deserted, set up for the carnival next day. At the sight of the flags and stands, Jo did exhibit some interest, twisting around in her seat. 'Things never change here in Bellbird Bay,' she said. 'I wish…'

But Greta didn't discover what Jo wished, because at that moment a couple of teenagers on electric scooters flashed across the road and she had to brake suddenly, throwing both of them onto the dashboard. The two boys didn't even seem to notice.

'I don't know why they allow those things on the road,' Greta said, shaking with relief.

'Oh, Mum. They're a great way to get around. Get with the times.'

'Hmm.'

The remainder of the journey passed without incident and when they reached the house, Jo disappeared into her room again, leaving Greta thinking how much Jo had changed from the happy-go-lucky girl who had left Australia to go on her big adventure over ten years earlier.

*

Although Greta's divorce was amicable and she and Mick remained friends, they never chose to socialise, both realising their differences were too great and they could never recapture the past. So it was a shock when she answered the door later that day to find him standing there with a bottle of wine in one hand, an esky in the other.

'Mick, what are you doing here?'

'I thought we could have dinner together with our girl.' He looked down at his feet, perhaps realising he should have called first, or arranged to meet Jo elsewhere.

Greta stared at him in surprise. 'Our girl is thirty-four,' she said. 'She's hardly a girl any longer. She said she called you. Did she suggest this?' she asked, suddenly suspicious.

'Dad!' Jo appeared at her shoulder. 'You came!'

Greta stood aside while the two hugged, her suspicions confirmed. *What was going on?*

'Did…?' she asked Jo.

Her daughter looked shifty. 'I thought it would be nice if we all had dinner together,' she said. 'I haven't seen either of you for such a long time.'

'Lighten up, Greta,' Mick said, his customary laid-back attitude reminding her of one of the reasons for their split. 'Jo wants to be with us both. Where's the harm in that? I brought some fresh prawns, straight off the boat. One of my mates went out early this morning.'

'Prawns. Yum,' Jo said, leading Mick through to the kitchen.

Greta followed reluctantly. This was her house. Why did she suddenly feel as if she was the interloper? She took out three plates, napkins and glasses and followed the other two who had already made their way outside and were seated on one of the benches at the long wooden table she'd purchased when she moved in.

Despite her misgivings, Greta enjoyed the prawns with buttered brown bread she rustled up along with a tomato, cucumber and red onion salad, all washed down with the Oyster Bay sauvignon blanc Mick provided. The meal was followed by slices of Ruby Sullivan's strawberry torte Greta had bought from *The Pandanus Café*. Jo was more animated in her dad's company and even managed to share some anecdotes from her travels. Though Greta noticed she steered clear of talking about her time in London and her reasons for returning home.

'Thanks, Greta,' Mick said as he left, giving her a peck on the cheek. 'It was all Jo's idea, but it was a good night, wasn't it? Good to spend time together again as a family.'

Greta merely nodded, forbearing to mention they hadn't been a family for years. But the evening had been better than she expected.

Alone again with Jo, Greta began to clear up, only to have Jo say, 'It was good to see you and Dad together again.'

'We're not together, Jo,' Greta said. But it had been nice. Greta couldn't remember when the three of them had last sat down to a meal together. Maybe now Jo was home, they could do it more often. Greta wondered if she'd like that.

Four

Rising early on Good Friday, Leo drove to Sydney airport through streets empty of traffic. It was a holiday weekend and most people – sensible people – would be sleeping late, preparing to meet family or friends for a barbecue or some other entertainment. Instead, he was flying off to investigate the viability of one more project.

Sometimes Leo wondered if this was all there was, if the rest of his life was going to be consumed with meetings, travel and the urge to purchase and renovate one more property.

The excitement he used to feel, the anticipation of adding yet another hotel to his portfolio, had diminished over the years. Maybe it was time for a change, time to retire. Although only in his early fifties, he could easily afford to retire and live in comfort for the rest of his life, but what would he do with his time if he no longer had the office to go to each day?

Leo thought how far he'd come from the twenty-year-old who discovered the magic of working in a hotel. Unlike others who saw their hospitality jobs as a means of funding their studies, deprived of the university opportunity he'd expected, Leo discovered he loved the atmosphere and had been filled with the urge to own the hotel. And he had. He now owned not one hotel, but an entire chain of hotels, and Leonard Holdings had become a well-known brand.

He used the flight to check up on the progress of the hotel in Fiji, the one he was to visit the following week, satisfied to see everything was on target. Closing his laptop, he gazed out the window, the sight of the coastline below him taking him back to that summer before his life changed for ever.

'I love you,' Leo yelled as he picked up the girl and swung her around and around, till she begged him to stop. Then he'd let her down gently, their feet sinking into the wet sand at the edge of the ocean. It was a moonlit night, and the beach was deserted, the only sound the gentle lapping of the waves on the shore. 'Promise me you won't forget me,' he said, burying his face in her hair.

It had been a magical summer. Arriving in Bellbird Bay with his mates ready to party their last summer of freedom before the serious business of university began, they'd been determined to enjoy every minute. He'd gone along with the gang for the first few days then, one day coming out of the surf, his surfboard under his arm, he'd met the girl, her long blonde hair blowing in the breeze, her tanned legs seeming to go on for ever.

She had just finished school too but, unlike Leo, she lived in Bellbird Bay so knew all the secret spots where they could be alone. He hadn't spent much time with his mates after that, preferring to spend his days with her, surfing, lying on the beach and talking about what they intended to do with their lives. At that time Leo had plans to study law, to become a lawyer like his father. She was unsure what she wanted to do, apart from leaving Bellbird Bay.

At the end of the summer, they vowed to keep in touch, sure their love would last for ever. They planned to meet up in Bellbird Bay again in the Easter holidays. But everything changed a month later when his dad had a heart attack, and his mother needed him to stay close to home.

Suddenly, the love he'd found on the beach seemed less important than his mother's grief. The discovery his dad had left a host of debts meant they had to move house, and in the confusion, he lost the address and phone number of the girl in Bellbird Bay. When he tried to find her, contacting everyone he could think of, he heard she was seeing a local guy, one she'd dated before he came on the scene. He was devastated but as time went on, forced into the workforce, his plans to study law abandoned, his mother's failure to come to terms with both his father's death and their new circumstances, sent it from his mind.

Now, seeing the familiar coastline, Leo remembered those halcyon days when anything seemed possible.

*

'Your key, sir.' The smartly dressed receptionist handed Leo his key and he turned towards the lift, noting the large foyer, the carefully placed seating. On the right was the entrance to the restaurant which he planned to check out for lunch before heading into town. So far, his impression was favourable.

Once in his room, Leo checked out the ensuite and the tiny fridge to find the former satisfactory but the latter sadly lacking. He wondered who was in charge now the owner was locked up. It was a different situation to any he'd encountered before. Hopefully there would be someone in town who could enlighten him as to what had happened, help him decide if it was worth pursuing.

The lunch menu was predictable, the chicken salad nothing out of the ordinary. He could visualise how the room would appear in the evening with the lights dimmed and the piano he could see in one corner being played softly. From what he'd read in the brochure he picked up in his room, the hotel prided itself on its upmarket appeal and its potential as a top of the range wedding venue.

Finishing lunch, he wandered outside to inspect the grounds to discover a large pool area and a stretch of grass which was presumably designed for the wedding venue. Leo's imagination started to go into overdrive. Clearly the current owner wanted to appeal to the upper end of the market. But how viable was that in Bellbird Bay? Why not capitalise on the nature of the town as a holiday spot and run it as a family hotel? The grassed area was a perfect spot to set up a variety of child-friendly activities and he could picture the large foyer filled with family groups and the sounds of children's laughter.

Fired up with enthusiasm for the hotel's potential, he decided to walk into town. Another plus was the hotel's location on the edge of town, close enough but a distance from the main street and esplanade which he remembered.

As soon as Leo reached the esplanade, the smell of the sea met him, reminding him of how much he missed it. It wasn't often he took time to spend by the ocean. Even when he visited coastal towns, he was always too busy with meetings and contractors to enjoy the simple pleasures of the beach.

But this was different. As he wandered along the esplanade, the shops on one side, the ocean on the other, memories flooded back, memories of a girl with blonde hair, memories of his first love. He wondered again what had happened to that girl, if she had fulfilled her dreams.

He noticed a lot of activity on the beach, then signs advertising the surf carnival which was happening the next day. A man erecting a stand reminded Leo of someone from that long-ago summer, with his faded blond hair tied back in a straggly ponytail. As he watched, a strong breeze almost capsized the structure. He rushed onto the beach to help.

'Thanks, mate,' the blond-haired man shook his hand. 'Almost lost it.'

'Glad I could help.'

The man stared at him, his brow furrowed, then said, 'Don't I know you?'

'I don't...' Then Leo recognised him. It was the guy he'd remembered. What was his name again?

'Will Rankin.'

Of course. 'Leo Carlson. I spent the summer here back...'

'Hell yes. I remember. You were one of the group of schoolies who came up from Sydney. I don't usually remember faces but you... you dated a local girl, didn't you?'

Leo reddened. It was as if he was back there, trying to make excuses for stealing a local girl from the group of surfers she'd been hanging around with.

But Will didn't seem to notice. 'Do you still surf?'

'Not lately. You obviously do.' Leo gestured to the logo on Will's tee shirt which read, *Bay Surf School*.

'Yeah.'

'Hey, Dad. I told you to wait till we got here.' A younger man, looking exactly like the Will Leo remembered, came running up followed by another, taller, dark-haired young man.

'My son, Owen,' Will said, 'and his mate, Nate. This is Leo, guys. He spent a summer here long before you were born.' He chuckled. 'A lot of water under the bridge since then.'

Leo nodded, envy for Will sending an ache to his gut. How he'd love to have a son… a child to share things with. But Zoe had always refused to have children saying it would ruin her figure and she'd be a hopeless mother. It was one of the many things they'd disagreed about.

'What brings you back to Bellbird Bay?' Will asked, as the two young men finished erecting the stand.

'I'm in the hotel business these days and I heard there was one for sale here.'

'Yeah.' Will's face darkened. He appeared to be about to say something then stopped himself.

'Finished, Dad,' Owen called. 'We're off now. See you tomorrow.'

'Right. See you have an early night.'

'Sure thing, Dad,' Owen laughed.

When the two had left, Will turned to Leo. 'The club's closed today,' he gestured to the white building which housed the surf club, where Leo remembered spending many happy hours, 'but we're having a couple of friends round for a barbecue later. Why don't you join us? We can fill you in on what's happening in Bellbird Bay these days and give you a bit of background on the hotel.'

'Thanks, it's kind of you.' Leo was surprised but pleased to accept. From what he could remember, Will had been a champion surfer back then, one all the girls wanted to be with – all except one, Leo remembered, the image of the blonde girl forcing its way back into the forefront of his mind.

*

This must be it. Leo checked again the address Will had given him as he drew up outside the red brick bungalow. Then he caught sight of the van in the carport bearing the logo of the surf school. As soon as he got out of the car, he could hear the sound of voices coming from around the side of the house and wondered if he'd been right to accept. He was about to step back into the past, a past he'd long forgotten. But there was something about this little town that had stuck in his mind during all those years he was building his business. And from what he'd seen so far, it hadn't changed much since then.

'Hey, you made it.' Will came towards him, dressed much as he had been on the beach, a beer in one hand. 'Come and meet the others.' He led Leo into a backyard that seemed to be filled with people. 'Coop,' he yelled to a tall man with fading blond hair.

The man turned, and Leo was shocked to recognise Martin Cooper, the world-famous photographer, whose photos graced the walls of several of his hotels. Seeing him with Will, he remembered him from that summer he'd spent here. Why had he never made the connection before now?

'Remember this guy?' Will was asking his friend. 'He was part of that group of schoolies who...'

'Vaguely,' Martin said. 'I'd left by then and was only back for a few weeks. G'day.' He stretched his hand out to shake Leo's. 'What brings you here this time?'

Will didn't give Leo time to reply. 'He's looking at buying Harris's hotel.'

'Really?'

Leo wasn't sure why Martin's lips tightened. What was his problem?

'You belong to one of the big hotel groups?' Martin asked.

'Leonard Holdings.'

'I've heard of them. Isn't Bellbird Bay a bit small for you? I thought you were more into the luxury resort market, large cities.'

'Usually, yes. But this place has some good memories for me, so I decided to check it out.'

'We don't need people like you bringing their fancy ideas to our town,' Martin said, before turning away to join a group by the barbecue.

'Sorry about that,' Will said, staring after his friend. 'Coop's sister had a run in with the current owner. It's nothing personal against you, but...' he scratched his head, 'Bellbird Bay isn't ready for the sort of transformation you might have in mind.'

'The current owner... I heard he was in prison?'

'Yeah. Long story, but the gist of it is, he was found to be bribing local officials to get his plans through the council. You can see how Martin might resent someone else trying to do the same.'

'I can assure you...' Leo began, shocked anyone might think he would be party to nefarious dealings.

'No worries. But maybe don't mention too much about your plans, eh?'

'Sure.' Leo allowed himself to be led to where a garbage bin filled with ice held a variety of cans and bottles of beer. He accepted a can of Four X, and was introduced to a number of Will's friends, but noticed Martin Cooper kept his distance.

By the time the barbecue was over, and people were beginning to leave, Leo had discovered a bit more about Milton Harris, the man who, on paper, was still the owner of the hotel in which he was interested. From what he'd heard, the guy had been no better than a common criminal, having eluded justice for years until it finally caught up with him here in Bellbird Bay. He could understand why many in the community might be wary of his intentions and made a vow to ensure he consulted widely before making any decision regarding a purchase. During his conversations, he'd learned Will Rankin was a well-respected member of the community and a member of the council, expected to become mayor in the upcoming local elections. He was obviously someone to cultivate.

As Leo left, after shaking Will's hand and promising to return his hospitality, he wondered again what had become of the girl he'd spent that summer with. Then he remembered her determination to leave Bellbird Bay. He had no reason to suppose she hadn't done that.

Five

Jo was still in bed when Greta left for work next day. She'd peeked into her room to ask if she wanted breakfast, but her daughter was still sound asleep, so Greta closed the door again gently. Jo looked so innocent lying there asleep. It was difficult to believe she was in her thirties, the age Greta had been when her marriage had fallen apart. Greta wondered again what had happened to bring her home – and to contact Mick and invite him to drop round for dinner. What was that about? No doubt she'd find out in good time. Meantime she had a shop to open.

The morning passed quickly. As Greta predicted, she was flat out until it was time for the carnival to start, when things slowed down sufficiently for her to risk closing up for the duration of the competition.

Watching the young men and women vying for the championship always took Greta back to her own teenage years, to the years when she'd have given anything to catch the eye of Will Rankin or Martin Cooper. But, two years older than she was, they didn't know she was alive. She did have a few dates with Mick Roberts who was on the outskirts of the group. And, when Mick returned from his gap year, he was the one who found her on the beach one night, drunk and in tears when she hadn't heard from Leo for weeks and her letters had been returned. He'd taken her in his arms and comforted her, his obvious attraction to her a balm to her soul, helping her forget the magical summer when she'd lost her virginity to the boy from Sydney, the boy who had disappeared from her life as suddenly as he'd arrived, the boy she'd never completely forgotten.

This year, the contest was close, but it was no surprise to the onlookers when Will's son, Owen, took out the championship again – for the fourth consecutive year. There was a huge roar from the crowd when the announcement was made, and a young girl Greta recognised as the daughter of Neil Simpson, the new owner of *Bay Books*, rushed to throw her arms around him. Greta smiled at this display of young love, wishing for the hundredth time that Jo could find herself a nice man and settle down. Maybe, now she was back here in Bellbird Bay, the town could work its magic on her, though it hadn't done much for Greta since she and Mick parted ways.

Thinking of Mick reminded her of the previous evening, the first they'd spent in each other's company since she could remember. Then there he was, standing with Will and Martin congratulating young Owen. Greta turned away before he caught sight of her, and went back to reopen the shop, knowing that now the winner had been announced, people would start drifting back to the esplanade, to the cafés and shops. Her break was over.

Greta was surprised when the shop door swung open, and Jo walked in. Dressed in a strappy sundress and wearing a wide-brimmed straw hat, she could have stepped out of one of the fashion magazines Greta loved to peruse.

'Jo, I didn't expect to see you here,' she said, going forward to give her daughter a hug. Fortunately, she was between customers and was taking the opportunity to replace garments left in fitting rooms back onto the racks.

'I decided to come into town to watch the carnival. I had lunch with Dad and a couple of his mates at the surf club,' Jo said. 'It was like a big party. Pity you couldn't join us.'

'Some of us have to work,' Greta said, but she managed to inject a note of regret into her voice. 'I saw Will Rankin's son won again.'

'Yes. He was in the club too, surrounded by well-wishers. He seems to be as popular as I remember his dad being.'

'He's a chip off the old block. Did you know he designs surfboards these days? Has built up a pretty good business.'

'You said. Been busy?' she asked, looking at the pile of garments still lying on the counter. 'Need a hand?'

'That would be good, honey.' Greta was reminded of the days when she started the boutique. Jo had been in her teens and had loved coming to the shop with her mum and helping out. But the task had soon palled when Jo discovered boys and decided it was more fun to spend time on the beach or in one of Bellbird Bay's many cafés.

They worked comfortably together for a bit, Greta pausing only when a customer walked in, and soon it was time to close up. 'Fancy having dinner out tonight?' Greta asked, hopefully. Maybe Jo would open up if they were in a neutral location.

'Mmm. Sounds good. Is the little Italian restaurant still open?'

'*The Firenze*? Yes. If we go now, we can probably get a table before it gets busy.'

'Let's. There was an Italian restaurant close to where I lived in London. We ate there a lot.'

Greta glanced at her daughter out of the corner of her eye. This was the first time Jo had mentioned her life in London since she returned. It wasn't much, but it was a start.

*

If Greta had hoped Jo might reveal more about her life in London over dinner, she was disappointed. The meal was delicious – garlic prawns followed by spinach and ricotta cannelloni and washed down with Greta's favourite lambrusco, but it didn't elicit anything further from Jo about her reason for her sudden trip home. Instead, to Greta's surprise, Jo wanted to talk about her dad and how he was planning to expand his business.

Finally, when Greta could stand it no longer, she asked, 'Is this to be a short visit?'

Jo looked down, replaced her fork several times before replying, 'I think I may be home for good.'

A warm glow enveloped Greta. She hadn't expected this. 'In Bellbird Bay?' she asked stupidly.

'Maybe… if I can find work. I re-registered with the education department before I left London and plan to see if there's any casual work going to start with.'

'Oh!' So, Jo's decision to come home hadn't been as sudden as it seemed. Greta felt deflated. Had she been the last to know? 'Bellbird Primary?'

'Where else? I did one of my pracs there. Remember?'

Greta did. It had been in Jo's final year at uni, and Greta had harboured hopes she'd come back to teach here, too. But she hadn't counted on her daughter's love of adventure, her desire to travel, to see the world. And that was exactly what she'd done.

'Tom Douglas is principal there now, and Joy Pardon is infant mistress. They're both very approachable. I can…' Greta bit her lip. Jo was an adult. She didn't need her mother's help.

'Thanks, Mum. I think I can contact them myself. I may drop into the school tomorrow to see if there's anyone around. I know it's the holidays, but I know teachers, too, and the early bird…'

Greta felt a weight falling off her shoulders. If Jo found a teaching position right here in Bellbird Bay, there would be all the time in the world for her to share what was bothering her, the reason she was back here and not still in London, or heading off to some other part of the world.

Six

Leo felt satisfied when he sat down to his second meal in the hotel. He had spent the day exploring the town including watching the surf carnival. Seeing the young surfers battling it out for the championship took him back to that magical summer he'd spent here. Not a lot had changed, except for the crowds. He didn't remember Bellbird Bay being so busy. It was a good sign, evidence there was a thriving tourist market.

Tonight, the hotel restaurant was busier than on the previous evening. He was surprised to hear a few foreign tongues among the other diners and tucked away the knowledge that Bellbird Bay didn't only cater to the domestic market. The meal was better tonight, too, he noticed, cutting into the wagyu steak he'd ordered, and which was served with tiny, buttered potatoes, asparagus, and garlic butter mushrooms. As he sipped the Elephant in the Room merlot, chuckling at the name, he was making a mental note of his impressions of both the hotel and the town. So far, all were favourable, though he knew, if he went ahead with the purchase, there were several things about the hotel he'd change.

Once again Leo experienced the familiar surge of excitement a new project always engendered. He could already visualise how this place could become part of Leonard Holdings. He was mindful of what Will Rankin had said, of his warning that Bellbird Bay didn't need a fancy resort. He agreed. What he had in mind was something completely different to what he'd done elsewhere, and he couldn't wait to share the concept with his team.

It was still early when Leo finished his meal, so he decided to go for a walk. Earlier, when he was watching the surf carnival, he'd noticed a boardwalk stretching up from the esplanade and was curious to discover where it led. This time, he hopped into his car, parked it close to the surf club and started up the boardwalk.

As he made his way towards what looked like a headland, he admired the homes situated on one side. The small houses which appeared to have started life as beach shacks had now been turned into comfortable homes, most boasting a deck overlooking the ocean which tonight roared on the other side of the boardwalk. It must be nice to live here, he thought, passing one deck from which came the sound of happy laughter. His high-rise Sydney apartment seemed very far away and sterile in comparison.

As he expected, the boardwalk ended at a headland from where, even in the gloom, he could see right out to sea where a couple of ships were anchored. Below, the surf battered against the rocks. It was high tide.

Leo was about to turn and retrace his steps when a beam of light shone across his path. Almost blinded, he blinked to see an elderly woman standing at a gate and holding a torch.

'I thought I heard someone,' she said. 'It's late for anyone to be up here, so I came out to check.' She peered at him.

'I'm not about to jump if that's what you're thinking.' Leo was amused, wondering how this frail old lady could have prevented anyone intent on suicide, the thought of being dashed to the rocks below making him shiver.

'No, I can see you're not the type to take your own life. You have too much to live for. But take care. Don't allow your arrogance to let you ignore what's right in front of you. The universe has given you a sign. Be sure you make use of it and correct the mistakes of the past.' She wagged a finger in his face before disappearing as quickly as she'd appeared, leaving Leo staring into the darkness where her torch had been.

What the...? Had he imagined the apparition, the strange words which didn't make any sense. Leo shook his head as he walked back down, his feet moving faster than on his way up, his mind reeling from the encounter.

Back in his hotel room, Leo opened one of the tiny bottles of scotch from the mini bar and poured it into a glass. He sat at the small table and opened his laptop, intending to record his impressions of Bellbird Bay and the hotel. But he found the face of the old woman kept insinuating itself between him and the screen, her words replaying in his head. What had she meant? Was he arrogant? He'd been called many a thing over the years, but arrogant? And what did she mean about the past?

He closed his eyes, intent on clearing his head, but his mind wandered to that glorious summer between school and university when he'd fallen in love for the first time.

It had been a day like all the others. He and his mates had spent the morning surfing, trying to outdo the locals but failing miserably. The guys were a few years older and had much more experience than Leo and his friends who were only in Bellbird Bay for the summer to celebrate the end of school. It was their last summer of freedom before university.

When he saw the girl step out of the ocean to carry her surfboard up the beach, her blonde hair flying in the breeze, her tanned body glistening with seawater, he felt his breath catch and his heart leapt. She was unlike anyone he'd ever met before, and she was looking straight at him. Somehow, he summoned the courage to approach her, and she laughed up at him, sending a host of unfamiliar longings through him.

'I'm Leo,' he said.

'Greta.' She swept a strand of hair from her face.

Leo thought it was the sexiest thing he'd ever seen. She was the sexiest girl he'd ever seen. His throat constricted.

She laughed. 'Are you one of those schoolies?' she asked with a grin. 'I saw you earlier.'

It hadn't taken long. In only a few days they were inseparable, and he couldn't imagine a life without her in it. Their stolen hours on a deserted beach fulfilled all his teenage fantasies. And it seemed she felt the same way.

Leo's phone rang and he opened his eyes with a start, surprised to find himself in the hotel room. What had possessed him to think back to that halcyon time? It had been over thirty years ago… a lifetime. He picked up his phone. 'Carlson.'

By the time the call was over – and he'd managed to reassure Ken that he wasn't on a wild goose chase, that this hotel in Bellbird Bay held some promise – the memory of the long-ago heavenly summer had faded. But when he closed his eyes to sleep, the image of the young girl with blonde tresses and the long, tanned legs returned to taunt him, the memory of her soft skin and sweet lips against his making sleep difficult.

Seven

It was two weeks since Easter, and Jo had found work in the local school replacing a teacher who was taking maternity leave. 'I know it's only temporary, Mum,' she'd said, 'but it'll give me time to work out what I want to do next.'

While glad to have her daughter home for at least a few months, Greta worried about what was going to happen when her contract was over. Jo had still given no indication of her reasons for leaving London.

Greta sighed as she dressed for another day in her boutique in one of the gaudy tropical prints for which *Birds of a Feather* had become famous and went to the kitchen to fix breakfast.

Jo was already there, drinking tea and eating toast spread with vegemite. 'I missed this when I was travelling,' she said with a grin. 'I should take a supply with me next time.'

Greta's heart sank. 'So, you intend to go off travelling again?'

'Maybe. I know I said I was home for good but the position at Bellbird Primary won't last for ever. Got to dash,' she said, finishing her tea and taking a last bite of toast before Greta could respond, 'I promised to help set up a reading corner before school today.' She stopped for a moment before adding, 'There's this delightful little girl in my class. She loves books so much and it's so sad. Her mother died.'

Greta watched her leave, her heart heavy at the thought her daughter was in her thirties and showed no sign of settling down, despite the fact she clearly loved children. It was such a pity she seemed destined to spend her life with those belonging to other people. It was so easy to compare her own life with Jo's, but she had to keep reminding herself that they were different people and that once upon a time, she'd wanted nothing more than to leave Bellbird Bay, too.

She'd been eighteen and eager to see the bright lights of the city, planning a future in which Bellbird Bay played no part. Then her dreams had fallen apart. She'd discovered she was pregnant, and Jo was the result, her lovely Jo. She could never regret the decision to continue with the pregnancy, to marry Mick, to make her life here in Bellbird Bay. Her unfulfilled dreams were the reason she'd encouraged Jo to set out on her travels, but she hadn't anticipated her daughter would still be intent on travelling the world at this age.

*

Now the Easter rush was over, Greta sometimes closed the shop at lunchtime, eating a packed lunch in the back shop or walking across to *The Bay Café* to eat there, either alone or with her friend Cass.

Today, Cass was busy, but Greta decided to go to the café on her own, in need for a cup of the strong variety of coffee they served.

She had just taken a seat and ordered a double espresso along with a slice of sweet potato and fetta bake, when a familiar voice said, 'Greta, didn't expect to see you here.' Turning, she saw Mick grinning at her.

'Mind if I join you?' He didn't wait for her response, pulling out a chair at the sun-bleached wooden table she'd chosen outside the café.

'How's life? And how is Jo enjoying teaching at Bellbird Primary? I haven't seen her since school started. I keep meaning to call, but…' he spread his hands to indicate his frustration.

Tempted to tell him it took no time to pick up a phone, Greta merely smiled and nodded. Mick was looking good today. He'd lost a bit of weight and had done something different with his hair. She hadn't noticed the evening he came to dinner, too irritated by his unexpected presence.

'What's the matter? Have I got something on my face?' Mick swiped his face with one hand.

Greta blushed, realising she'd been staring. 'No, nothing. Jo seems to be enjoying teaching here, but…' she paused as her coffee was served, '… I worry about her, Mick.'

'Worry? She seems to be doing all right. She fell right into a job as soon as she arrived in town. Always falls on her feet, our girl does.'

'That's the problem. She's not a girl any longer. She's thirty-four, Mick. It's time she thought about settling down, starting a family.' Greta felt her eyes moisten and blinked rapidly. She didn't want Mick to see her in tears.

But he knew her too well and handed her a paper napkin.

Greta wiped her eyes.

'We never thought, did we,' he said, when she put the napkin down again, 'thirty-four years ago, when Jo was born, we'd still be worrying about her all these years later? But she's her own woman, has been for some time, and all the worry in the world isn't going to change her.'

'Thanks,' Greta said, as her lunch appeared, and the waitress placed a plate containing a vegetable salad in front of Mick. She remembered how health conscious he'd become since the heart scare six years earlier. Then she asked him, 'Has she said anything to you about why she left London, about what brought her back home?'

'No.' Mick appeared puzzled. 'Should she have? I assumed she felt it was time. She's been gone a while.'

'But in the middle of the school year, Mick. Don't you think it's odd?'

'I think you're worrying about nothing. But, if you're so concerned, why don't you ask her?'

'Mmm.' Greta took a sip of coffee, forked up a piece of the slice and decided to do just that.

*

Greta spent the rest of the afternoon wondering how to confront Jo with the question which had been haunting her since she opened the email to say her daughter was coming home to Bellbird Bay. By the time she got home, she still hadn't worked out how to approach it, knowing Jo was likely to tell her it was none of her business and storm out of the room just as she used to when she was a teenager.

'I've made dinner, Mum,' Jo greeted her as soon as she walked in. 'Chicken curry okay?'

'Lovely. It's so good to have you here.' As she spoke, Greta realised how much she was enjoying having someone to talk to when she came home from work. She hadn't realised how alone she'd often felt over the years, attempting to disguise her loneliness with membership of a book club, yoga classes and outings with Cass and other friends.

Dinner over, Greta and Jo took their glasses and the remains of a bottle of wine through to the living room where Jo curled up on the sofa just as she used to do and recounted stories of the class she was teaching.

'They're such a great group of kids,' she said, 'so different to the ones I taught in London.' Her eyes clouded and, for a moment, Greta almost asked the loaded question. But the moment passed as Jo continued to talk about a little girl in her class – the one she'd mentioned before leaving that morning. 'She's such a cutie, Mum, and she's so bright. At show and tell this morning, she told the class she had a new grandmother. It brought tears to my eyes.'

'I saw your dad today,' Greta said, when Jo paused, trying to figure out if this was her chance to question Jo, to say she and Mick both wanted to know.

'You did?' Jo's eyes lit up. 'I've been meaning to call him, to arrange to meet up. How was he?'

'He's looking well. I'm sure he'd be pleased to hear from you.'

The conversation stalled, as Greta tried to find the words she needed, and a few minutes later, Jo rose, yawned and went off to bed, leaving Greta to regret her lost opportunity.

But the day hadn't been a complete disaster, she reflected as she removed her makeup and prepared for bed. It had been good to talk with Mick over lunch. His suggestion they do it again sometime – a planned meeting next time – had taken her by surprise, but after an initial hesitation, she'd agreed.

Eight

Leo was back in Bellbird Bay. After a hurried trip to Fiji to ensure all was going according to plan, he'd decided to take a break and leave the company in Ken's capable hands for a couple of weeks at least. The few days he'd spent in Bellbird Bay had certainly whetted his appetite and fuelled his desire to spend more time there.

He couldn't remember when he'd last taken time off, time for himself, time when he wasn't rushing from one project to the next. His PA had looked at him askance when he'd told her to cancel his appointments and not to contact him except in an emergency.

He chuckled now, recalling her shock when she'd asked him to repeat his request.

And now he was back, with two whole weeks of R&R ahead of him. Of course, it wouldn't be entirely a holiday. As he'd chosen to stay again at the property he had earmarked as his next acquisition, he'd still be able to check out both the hotel and the town, but there was no urgency.

The sun was shining when he opened the blinds in his five-star accommodation. Being out of season, he'd had his choice of rooms and had chosen one of the grand suites. It was perfect with its distant views of the ocean.

This morning he decided against breakfast in the hotel, choosing instead to sample one of the local cafés, many of which had sprung up since his schoolies trip. Casually dressed in jeans and a long-sleeved shirt, he popped his laptop into his canvas satchel, adding a sweater at the last minute in case it was cooler than it looked, and set off to walk to the esplanade.

By the time he got there, he was feeling hot and was ready for coffee and a hearty breakfast. He took a seat on one of the sun-bleached tables outside *The Bay Café* he'd noticed on his previous visit and ordered a long black and the delicious sounding smoked hog hash, a combination of potato hash, smoked hog, baby spinach, poached eggs, hollandaise sauce and grain mustard.

While he was waiting for his order to arrive, Leo opened his laptop to check his emails. Even on holiday there were some things he couldn't ignore.

*

Breakfast was as delicious as it sounded, and Leo was on his second cup of coffee when a blonde woman walked past. He did a double-take; she looked so familiar, the hair and profile. Suddenly he was back with the scent of the sea and the feeling of the sand beneath his feet, and the blonde girl with the surfboard, flicking her hair. Then he returned to the present, his heart racing as the girl walked off. He reminded himself the girl he'd met all those years ago would be in her fifties, the same age as he was. This one was much younger, probably in her thirties. As he watched, she entered a dress shop. From where he was sitting, Leo could just make out the name – *Birds of a Feather*. It looked like the sort of place Zoe loved to frequent. He hadn't heard from his ex since the lunch prior to his first trip to Bellbird Bay, but Ken kept him informed of her movements. He knew she and her current partner were now ensconced in a villa in Thailand thanks to a large injection of funds from him. Hopefully it would be enough to keep her off his back for the foreseeable future.

Dropping a few notes on the bill, he packed up his laptop, deciding to investigate the shops, starting with the bookshop. He always loved poking around bookshops when he had time, and *Bay Books* looked interesting. In another life he'd have owned a bookshop, though he doubted it would have brought him as much pleasure or been as much of a challenge as his hotel chain.

He pushed open the door to the bookshop, stopping for a moment to breathe in the scent of books and something unidentifiable but familiar. Then he made his way to the central table on which there was a display of recent releases, one of which caught his eye.

Adam Holland was one of his favourite authors and it seemed that, when he'd been too busy to keep up with his reading over the past year, the author had produced two books in a new series. There was also a copy of the first book in the series with which Leo was familiar alongside a card which advertised it as the book on which the TV series was based.

'You're a fan?' The man who'd been behind the counter when Leo walked in smiled at him.

'I am, but I'm afraid I'm behind the times. I wasn't aware of the new series or that there was a TV version of the Phil Hanlon books.'

'The pilot was released a few months ago and was a huge success. I understand Adam's in negotiation for the TV rights to the entire series – perhaps his new series too.'

'You know him?' Leo was surprised the man referred to the author by his first name.

'He's a local, one of the many locals who are household names. Bellbird Bay is a haven for artistic types, most of whom prefer to remain incognito.'

'Hmm.' Leo tucked away this piece of information for future reference. He'd be interested to discover what other famous characters chose the seclusion of Bellbird Bay. 'I'll take these two,' he said, picking up both books in the new series which appeared to be set in a coastal town not unlike Bellbird Bay.

'Thanks. Anything else I can help you with today?'

'I don't think so.' These two should keep him occupied for a while and would help him relax.

He was leaving the shop when he almost bumped into Martin Cooper. The other man glared at him for a moment and was about to move out of his way when Leo put a hand on his arm. 'Martin, I think we got off on the wrong foot last time we met. Will mentioned something about the current owner of the hotel where I'm staying. I feel I need to explain...'

Martin folded his arms. 'Say your piece,' he said.

'I understand what you were thinking. Leonard Holdings has built its reputation – *I've* built my reputation,' he corrected himself, dragging a hand through his hair, 'on providing luxury accommodation, much like the one the Harris guy set out to build here. But that model doesn't suit Bellbird Bay.'

'No?'

Leo felt an easing of the tension which had been between them. 'No. I want to turn the place around, make it into a family hotel, transform what the current owner was setting up as a venue for upmarket weddings into a family friendly space – putt putt, tennis courts, paddling pool, climbing wall – something more in keeping with the place I remember, with a modern touch. I'm sorry this Harris guy caused your sister so much angst – Will told me about it – but I'm not him.'

'So you *are* going to buy the place?'

'I am.' Until he said these words, Leo hadn't been totally convinced he would. Despite spending time there, listing his impressions, he had still been wavering. It had taken this conversation with Martin Cooper to bring him to a decision.

'Well then, I wish you well. If there's anything I can do to help...' Martin reached out his hand and Leo shook it, glad he'd managed to turn him into, if not a friend, someone who wasn't about to scupper his plans. 'Will said you were okay,' Martin admitted. 'I just didn't want to see Bev shafted again. She's been through a lot... and I haven't always been here to support her... but I am now.'

'Right.' Leo didn't remember Martin's sister. He guessed she'd been part of the beach crowd that summer, part of the group of surfers, maybe even a friend of the girl he'd spent so many hours with. Once he'd met her, he had no eyes for any other girl.

They shook hands again and Martin went off. Watching him go, Leo wondered what had brought the world-renowned photographer back to his hometown, wondered if the girl he'd never forgotten had returned, too. It suddenly occurred to him that Will and Martin would know her – or know of her. He should have asked them. Next time he saw them, he would.

Nine

It was Monday and *Birds of a Feather* was closed for the day. Glad of the respite, Greta dressed in a pair of jeans and pulled on a long-sleeved cotton sweater. Sometimes it was nice to forgo the elegant image she was careful to portray at work for a more casual one, and to exchange the brightly coloured garments that were her signature for more subdued ones. As she closed the door and set off for the library, she forced herself to put Jo out of her mind and concentrate on the task at hand. It was her turn to choose the book for the book club she belonged to, and she wanted to take time to select one which would appeal to all the members of the group.

As she drove across town, she thought about the various members of the group. Only one, Cass, was a close friend, but they'd all been meeting on a monthly basis for several years, led by Dot who tried to keep them on track and at whose home they often met. Tomorrow would be the first time they were to meet in the house where Ailsa Cooper lived with her new husband, Martin, the same Martin Cooper who had been one of Greta's teenage heroes.

When Greta entered the library, she was struck by the buzz of children's voices and, glancing across the room to the children's section, she could see what looked like an entire class of children pushing and shoving each other as they found places on the floor. In the midst of them, organising the seating, was her daughter. Jo hadn't mentioned coming to the library this morning. But neither had Greta. They had been too busy chatting about various items on the news.

Now Greta stood and watched as Jo managed to settle the noisy group before taking a seat in front of them, along with one of the librarians.

Jo loved kids, Greta could see that, and they loved her too. She should have one of her own – or more. But the five years she'd spent in London was the longest time she'd spent in any one spot since she graduated. At thirty-four, it wasn't too late for her to have a child of her own, but where was she going to find the right partner if she kept moving on?

'Greta?'

Greta turned to see Grace, another member of the book club, one who often selected their books as she worked in the library. 'Sorry, Grace. That's my daughter with her class.'

'I heard she was back. You must be pleased to have her home.' Grace smiled. 'I remember how it was when Mel arrived in town. We never quite let go, do we? Does she have children of her own?'

'No.' Greta couldn't hide her regret.

'She still has time.'

'Maybe. She's thirty-four, Grace.'

'Lots of women are having their children later these days, Greta. You may be a grandmother yet.'

'Mmm.' Grace had never said much, but Greta knew she'd had a few problems with her daughters. But she was now grandmother to two little girls. How Greta envied her. She gave herself a mental shake. 'I need to choose next month's book for us,' she said. 'Dot would never forgive me if I turned up empty-handed.'

They both chuckled at the prospect of Dot's fury if one of the group failed to keep to her rigid standards. She could be officious at times, but her heart was in the right place, and she was really a kind woman.

Moving off with the promise to catch up again sometime outside the book club, Greta got down to the serious business of choosing a book which would promote discussion and meet the different tastes of the group, finally deciding on Di Morrisey's latest book set on Sydney's Pittwater.

Before leaving, she tried to catch Jo's eye, but her daughter was too engrossed in the story she was reading to the children to notice her.

Outside the library, Greta decided it was too nice a day to go straight home so, once she'd stored the books in her car, she wandered along the street. As she passed the art gallery, she caught a glimpse of someone inside who sent a shiver down her spine. The tall figure standing there with the gallery owner, gesticulating towards the photographic exhibition of Martin Cooper's latest work was frighteningly familiar. It couldn't be him. He turned and Greta's heart leapt; she felt the blood drain from her face; she began to tremble as her eyes fell on the profile of the man she'd never expected to see again. Dizzy, she stumbled away.

Five minutes later, she was sitting in *The Greedy Gecko* her hands clasped around a cup of camomile tea, trying to suppress the trembling that had overtaken her entire body. It had been thirty-five years since Leo Carlson had disappeared from her life, since she'd waited in vain for the promised letter. The young man who'd meant so much to her, who'd promised to love her for ever, had disappeared without a trace leaving her to pick up the pieces of her life.

It was Mick who rescued her, who gave her a reason to live. When he returned from his gap year working on boats in the south of France, he had taken her under his wing and comforted her. In his arms, she'd begun to live again, to believe that the future held something for her. But her dreams of travel, of leaving Bellbird Bay had come to nothing. She was still here. But, she reminded herself, she had Jo, she had *Birds of a Feather*. She had made a life for herself in the town she'd once been so determined to leave.

Greta spent the rest of the day wondering what had brought Leo Carlson back to Bellbird Bay, eventually deciding he must be here on holiday. It wasn't unusual for families from New South Wales to visit out of season and *The Bay Gallery* with the current exhibition of Martin Cooper photographs was an obvious spot for a tourist to visit. There had been no sign of a wife, but she'd been too traumatised to notice anything other than the never forgotten features – the aquiline nose, high forehead and wide mouth couldn't belong to anyone else, could they?

*

By the following evening, when Greta was on her way to her book club, she still hadn't fully recovered from the shock of Leo's presence in Bellbird Bay. But, she decided, as she unloaded the books from the car, even if it was him, it was unlikely their paths would cross.

After the usual pleasantries, the meeting began with each contributing their thoughts on the previous month's book. When the discussion was over, Ailsa disappeared into the kitchen to reappear with a trolley containing tea and cake, and the conversation became more general. Greta blanked out for a few minutes, glad no more was expected of her. She came to with a start at the sound of a name she recognised.

'And Martin says he plans to turn the place into a family friendly hotel,' Ailsa was saying.

'Sorry, who are we talking about?' Greta said, sure she'd misheard, that Leo was so much on her mind she was imagining things.

'Leo Carlson... Leonard Holdings. He's buying the hotel Milton Harris owns. Haven't you heard? Everyone's talking about it.'

Not quite everyone. This was the first Greta had heard about it. So it really was Leo. She'd been trying to pretend she'd imagined seeing him.

When she went to bed that night, after pleading a headache on her return from the book club, the past flooded back into Greta's mind. It had been a magical summer. After their first meeting on the beach, she and Leo had spent every day together. Somehow, he'd managed to access a motor scooter and the pair of them would ride out to Dolphin Beach. It became their special spot, somewhere they could be alone, the protected bay with its white sand and calm sea adding to the feeling they were in a magical place.

All too soon, the summer had come to an end and Leo left with promises to contact her, to make arrangements for her to join him in the city. Greta had waited and waited but there had been no letter, no phone call. When her letters to him had been returned, she'd fallen into a depression, only surfacing when Mick Roberts returned home.

Mick and she had dated a couple of times before he had left so it was easy for them to fall back into seeing each other and to be accepted as a couple. After that first night when he'd comforted her and they'd made love, when all she wanted was to forget Leo Carlson and his promises, they'd started to see each other. It was good not to be left out, to have everyone wondering what had happened to the boy from Sydney. Then, when Greta discovered she was pregnant, Mick had insisted they marry, and all her dreams of travel had taken a back seat to the serious business of marriage and a family. When Jo had been born a bare seven months after the wedding, everyone had accepted it as a premature birth, only Greta was aware of the possibility that Mick wasn't her father. It wasn't till some years later, when Jo needed a blood transfusion that she discovered the truth.

Ten

Having made the decision to purchase the hotel, Leo couldn't wait to set things in motion. As soon as he returned to his room, he opened his laptop and sent emails to Roy, the company solicitor, Ken and his PA. Despite being sure he wanted to go ahead, he knew he still had to follow the protocols he'd set up to ensure there were no obstacles and there could be a smooth transition. He'd been caught out before and, although he didn't expect any problems – the guy was in prison for goodness' sake – it was always best to be sure.

For the next few days, he was on tenterhooks waiting for a reply, some indication there were no obstacles to purchasing this hotel which Leo now realised he wanted more than any of the fancy resorts he'd purchased in the past. There was something about Bellbird Bay that pulled at his heartstrings, and he was sure it wasn't only the memories it held for him. Though that was a big part of it.

He hadn't bumped into either Will Rankin or Martin Cooper again so, on Sunday evening, he decided to dine at the surf club. Maybe he'd see them there and he could casually bring up Greta's name, find out what had happened to her, perhaps even where she was living now.

He whistled to himself as he showered and dressed in a pair of chinos and a blue long-sleeved shirt and pulled on a pair of shoes rather than the sandals he'd been living in since he got here. Then he hopped into his car to drive to the club.

To his delight, the first people Leo saw when he reached the top of the stairs were Will and Martin. They were standing at the bar chatting with the barman, a young dark-haired man they seemed to know well, and who Leo recognised from the beach. As he was debating whether or not to join them, Will turned and caught sight of him. He smiled and waved him over.

'Still here?' Will asked.

Martin merely smiled.

'As you see,' Leo said. 'I've set things in motion for the purchase of the hotel. My team is working on it now. If things work out, you may be seeing a lot more of me.'

Leo saw the two men grin at the mention of 'his team' and wished he'd chosen to express himself better. He didn't want to alienate them. He realised this was one project he intended to see through himself which would mean he would be spending a lot more time here, and it would be good to have friends – especially Will who was on the council.

'We've just been talking about you,' Will said. 'Martin tells me you had a chat.'

'Yeah.' Leo smiled at Martin. 'We're good now.'

'We're having dinner here. Cleo and Ailsa are already at a table on the deck. Why don't you join us?' Will asked.

'It's good of you, but I don't want to intrude.'

'Not at all. I'm sure they're both eager to meet the man who intends to remodel Milton Harris's hotel.'

'If you're sure?'

'You'll have a beer?' Will asked. 'Nate,' he called to the barman.

When Leo had been served, the three men carrying their beers, Will and Martin also carrying glasses of white wine, headed out to the deck where the two women were waiting for them.

Leo didn't remember sitting out here before. He guessed when he used to come here, he and his mates had been intent on seeing how much they could drink at the bar... then he'd met Greta, and the club with its bar ceased to have any attraction.

They reached the table which was at the edge of the deck overlooking the beach. The sea was calm this evening and there were a few brave people walking along the edge of the water, their figures shadowy in the darkness. Out at sea, Leo could see the lights of a ship. He wondered if it was the same one he'd seen from the headland, remembering for an instant the words of the weird woman he'd met there.

'Cleo, Ailsa, this is Leo Carlson, the guy who's buying Harris's hotel. Leo, my partner Cleo and Martin's wife, Ailsa,' Will said.

'Pleased to meet you both,' Leo said, 'Will has been kind enough to ask me to join you for dinner.'

'Welcome to Bellbird Bay,' the small woman with a cloud of dark hair around her shoulders said. Leo thought she was Cleo.

'Welcome,' the other repeated. 'It's always good to see a fresh face, and the hotel needs something done about it. Martin says you intend to turn it into a family friendly resort?'

'That's the plan.'

The conversation which ensued focussed on Leo's plans to remodel the hotel, only ceasing when their meals arrived. On Will's recommendation, Leo ordered a burger with chips which was the best he'd tasted.

It was only when their meals were finished and they had graduated to coffee that Will said, 'Leo was here at schoolies one year. It must have been thirty-odd years ago, Leo?'

'Thirty-five.' The summer was etched in his memory.

'Way before we came to town,' Ailsa said, smiling at Cleo.

Leo saw his opportunity. 'About that,' he said, taking a deep breath, 'I met a girl that summer.'

Will chuckled. 'Didn't we all?'

'I've always wondered what happened to her,' Leo said, trying to sound nonchalant.

'A local girl?' Will asked.

'Her name was Greta... Greta Henderson.'

There was a pause, then Will snapped his fingers. 'I remember. She was younger than us. She's Greta Roberts now.'

Leo's heart dropped. Of course she'd be married. What had he expected? But it sounded as if... 'She still lives here?'

It was Ailsa who replied. 'I know Greta. We're in a book club together. She owns the boutique *Birds of a Feather*. You may have seen it on the esplanade.'

Birds of a Feather! That was the name of the shop he'd seen the young woman enter, the one who'd reminded him so much of the girl who... 'Does she have a daughter?'

Ailsa gave him a strange look. 'She does have a daughter. Jo only returned home at Easter after working overseas for a number of years. Why do you ask?'

'I saw her. I thought it was Greta before realising it couldn't be. The woman I saw was younger… thirties.'

'That would be right,' Ailsa said. 'I think she's around thirty-three or four.'

Leo's stomach churned. An uneasy feeling blanketed him as he thought back to how many years it had been since schoolies. He did the maths. If Greta's daughter was thirty-four, he could be her father. She could be the daughter he'd always longed for. But surely Greta would have contacted him? Then he remembered how he had failed to communicate till it had been too late, how he and his mother had moved. His tongue stuck to the roof of his mouth. He must have turned white because, as if from a distance, he heard Will's voice.

'You okay, mate?'

'Sorry, just had a moment.' Leo took a gulp of beer, trying to block out the possibility which had taken hold a moment ago. But what if it was true?

The conversation around him continued, but he was immune to most of it. All he could think was that Greta had a daughter… and she could be his.

Eleven

Greta was still reeling from the discovery Leo Carlson was in town when the weekend came around. Jo had planned a beach picnic with her class. She was excited about it and had been talking about it for days, planning different activities and arranging for several parents to come along to help.

As the morning progressed, Greta was busier than she'd expected. Now Easter was over, most of the tourists had gone, leaving only her regular customers. She hoped she'd manage to find time to make good her promise to Jo to check out the beach to see what was happening with her class.

Fortunately, there was a lull just after lunchtime and Greta took the opportunity to put up a *Closed – back in 10 minutes* sign on the door and duck out to pick up a coffee from *The Bay Café*. She strolled across the road with her coffee to watch Jo with the children. She chuckled as she saw Jo set up a couple of games and organise some mothers to supervise. A tall young man approached the group. Then a little red-headed girl ran up to him and pulled him over to where Jo was standing. The two talked for a few moments before he headed off again.

Greta wondered who he was. She didn't recognise him, but why would she? If he was new in town, a man his age would have no reason to visit *Birds of a Feather*. His wife would be a different story. Thinking of stories reminded her of the strange story she'd heard about Bev Cooper and her long-lost son. There had been a daughter too, hadn't there? A granddaughter for Bev. Lucky Bev! For a moment, Greta wondered if the young man talking to Jo had been Bev's son. Then she shook her head. It would be too much of a coincidence. But she did remember Jo talking about the little girl in her class who'd lost her mother and who had a new grandmother.

Just then, Jo looked up and Greta waved to her. Then, her promise to her daughter kept, she finished her coffee, dumped the empty cup in a garbage bin and headed back to the shop. At least watching the episode on the beach had taken her mind off Leo Carlson for a while.

*

After a busy afternoon, Greta was looking forward to a relaxing evening with Jo. Too tired to contemplate cooking, she picked up a lasagne from *The Firenze* on the way home. The little Italian restaurant which had been an institution in Bellbird Bay for as long as Greta could remember, and which was now managed by the grandson of the original owner, had recently instituted takeaway service which Greta regularly took advantage of.

'From *The Firenze*?' Jo asked when Greta unpacked it in the kitchen. Jo was sitting at the table staring at her phone, something Greta had noticed she did a lot, as if searching for a message.

'Yes. I had a full-on afternoon and thought it would save us cooking.'

'I'm for that,' Jo said, closing her phone. 'Wine?'

Greta nodded, noticing her daughter already had a glass. She wondered how long Jo had been sitting there.

'Looked like the kids were having fun on the beach,' Greta said, when the lasagne had been served, along with the salad she'd quickly thrown together.

'I hope so. They're a great bunch, and the mothers who came to help were amazing. We're going to do it again in a couple of months.'

'Who was the man I saw you talking to?'

Jo reddened. 'He's Mia's dad. She's the little girl I told you about, the one who lost her mum.'

'You hadn't met him before?'

Jo shook her head. 'He starts work early on school days at the local nursery.'

'*The Pandanus Garden Centre?*'

'That's the one. Why?'

'I think I know who he is.'

'What do you mean?' Jo forked up the last of her pasta. 'I told you. He's Mia's dad.'

'He's Bev Cooper's long-lost son. Bev owns the garden centre. You must remember her – Martin Cooper's sister.'

'Mum! They're your vintage, not mine. Though I know who you mean. How can he be her long-lost son?'

'I don't know the whole story, only what's been said at my book club.'

'Your book club? Honestly, Mum, do you ever talk about books or is it the local gossip mill?'

Greta bridled. 'We don't gossip. Far from it. But there was some talk at the time. It was last year, and Bev, and Mia's grandfather…'

Jo put her hands over her ears. 'I don't want to hear any more.'

'Fine. If you're finished, let's leave the dishes for now and take the rest of the wine through to the living room.'

'Good idea.'

Once there, the conversation focussed around Jo's experiences at Bellbird Primary and her hope she might be able to find more permanent work there.

'So you do intend to stay around?' Greta asked, a warm glow enveloping her at the thought of having her daughter nearby. 'Your dad would like that, too.'

'Maybe. Perhaps it's time I put down roots and Bellbird Bay is as good a place as any.'

Emboldened by Jo's words, Greta took a deep breath and said, 'I don't understand you. You love children. Don't you have any desire to find someone, settle down, start a family? At your age I…' Greta bit her tongue, knowing she'd gone too far and expecting a sharp retort from her daughter, but none came.

Struck by the silence, Greta turned her head to look at her daughter, shocked to see tears streaming down Jo's cheeks. 'Oh, my darling, what's the matter?' She set down her glass and took Jo into her arms, hugging her like she had when Jo was a child, and wishing a kiss could make whatever it was better as it had back then.

'Oh, Mum,' Jo sobbed. 'I thought I had. I was living with someone in London. Damien.'

Stunned, Greta said, 'You didn't tell me.'

'I wanted to, but... I don't know why I didn't. I guess I was afraid to talk about it in case... Well, I was right. When I became pregnant...'

Greta gasped. Her daughter had been pregnant, and she hadn't known?

Jo scrubbed her eyes and continued. 'Damien didn't want a baby. He was delighted when I miscarried. That's when I decided to come home.'

'Oh, my darling!' Greta hugged Jo tighter. The thought of her daughter suffering a miscarriage alone in London with a partner who was pleased about it didn't bear thinking about. 'You did the right thing... coming here. I wish I'd known.'

'I didn't want to tell you,' Jo sobbed. 'I felt such a fool. Damien...' she broke down again, '... he couldn't understand why I wanted to leave. He's...'

'Has he been contacting you?' Greta remembered all the times she'd seen Jo gazing at her phone.

Jo nodded. 'He doesn't understand it's over. I never want to see him again.'

Greta stroked her daughter's forehead and pushed back a strand of damp hair. She wanted to tell her there were plenty of other men out there, but knew it was too soon. She could only hope Jo made a swift recovery. Surely the fact she had come home, found a job and was thinking of the future was a good sign?

Jo's tears finally subsided, and she agreed to the cup of tea Greta offered to make.

As Greta boiled the kettle, she reflected that she was becoming like her mother for whom a cup of tea was the cure for all ills. But she knew tea couldn't cure what ailed Jo. It would take time.

'Thanks for listening, Mum,' Jo said, clasping the cup of hot, sweet tea in both hands, her face streaked with tears.

'I'm so glad you finally told me. It's not good to keep these things bottled up. I've been worried about you.' Greta peered at her daughter to see the shadow which had been in her eyes since she returned was beginning to fade.

'Thanks, Mum. Will you tell Dad for me? I can't face going over it all again.'

'Of course, my darling.'

'I think I'll go to bed now. I have school tomorrow. Goodnight.' She kissed her mother on the cheek.

'Goodnight, sweetheart.' Greta kissed her back.

Left alone, Greta collected the cups and glasses and the empty wine bottle and took them into the kitchen. Once there, she stood at the sink staring out into the darkness, her thoughts in a whirl both about the news Jo had shared and her request that Greta tell Mick. Greta had all but forgotten Mick's suggestion to meet again. He hadn't pursued it and may have changed his mind. Now it was Greta who would be contacting him to arrange a meeting.

Twelve

Now Leo knew where Greta was, he wanted to see her, talk to her, but hesitated. She was married now, and his memories might be deceiving him. He wondered what his life would have been if his father hadn't died, if he'd been able to keep his promise to write, to see Greta again, to study law. By the time they'd moved, and everything had been settled, it had been too late. The news she'd moved on had been like a knife turned in his heart. He'd persuaded himself to put the magical summer to the back of his mind, only to be taken out and mulled over when he was feeling nostalgic.

Then he'd met Zoe and thought she was the woman he'd spend the rest of his life with and raise a family. Now he found himself beset with memories of the golden girl he remembered and who was only a short distance away. And there was her daughter... the young woman he'd already seen.

It would be easy to walk into the shop Ailsa had mentioned. *Birds of a Feather* wasn't far from *The Bay Café* where he enjoyed his coffee, and often had breakfast. He could see it from his favourite table there. Given the proximity and the size of Bellbird Bay, it was surprising he hadn't bumped into Greta by now.

According to what Ailsa had said, Greta's daughter must have been born less than a year after that summer. She could be his – unless Greta had found someone else as soon as he left town. They'd pledged their love to each other, promised they'd be together for ever. But he hadn't kept his promise. Why should he feel betrayed if she hadn't either? He'd heard of girls marrying to give their baby a name, to avoid the stigma of being a single mother. Was that what Greta had done? He ached to find out.

*

As chance would have it, the opportunity to meet, not Greta, but her daughter, came earlier than Leo expected.

He was enjoying an afternoon coffee in *The Bay Café*, reading an email from his solicitor which listed a number of issues relating to his proposed purchase of the hotel, and an offer they'd had to purchase the entire hotel chain which he immediately dismissed. He had just come to the part where Roy suggested it might not be a viable project when someone bumped his table, sending his coffee flying and spilling across the table to drip onto his pants.

'Oh, I'm so sorry.'

Leo looked up to see the young woman he'd last seen walking into *Birds of a Feather*, the young woman who might be his daughter. Close-up she was the image of her mother, apart from her eyes which were the same brown shade as his own. Leo's heart lurched.

'No worries,' he said, brushing off the drips with a paper napkin and wondering if he could prolong the conversation long enough to discover more about her and her mother.

'But I've spilled your coffee and sent it all over you. Let me buy you another. It was black, right?' She disappeared before Leo could reply, to return a few minutes later carrying a mug for him in one hand and balancing two takeaway coffees in the other. She placed the mug on the table. 'For me and Mum,' she added, indicating the cardboard cups. 'She owns the boutique over there. I'm Jo,' she said with a friendly smile.

'Leo.' He held out his hand.

Jo placed the two takeaway cups on the table and shook his hand. 'Are you visiting Bellbird Bay?'

'I'm here on business. I'm guessing you live here?'

'For the moment.' She frowned. 'I only came home recently. I have a teaching position for this term. After that, I'm not sure. What sort of business?' she asked, reaching for the cups she'd placed on the table.

'International hotels. I'm looking to buy one here.'

'Interesting. I've often wondered if I should have stayed in hospitality. I did a bit of it on my travels when I couldn't find a teaching job. Would I know any of your hotels? Maybe I've even worked in one.'

To Leo's surprise, she sat down and, leaning her elbows on the table, cupped her chin in her hands. He swallowed. It could have been thirty-four years ago with Greta facing him over the table. She used to sit exactly like that. Of course, Jo was older than Greta had been then, but they were like two peas in a pod. 'My company is Leonard Holdings,' he said after a pause. 'Leonard Hotels.'

A wide grin spread across Jo's face. 'I have. I worked on reception in your Paris hotel for several months. I had to brush up on my French,' she chuckled, 'but most of the guests were British. Very upmarket. Is that what you intend to do here?' Her forehead creased.

'No. Bellbird Bay is quite different and needs a different style of hotel.'

'Good. Well,' she picked up her cups and rose, 'I'd better take Mum's coffee to her before it gets cold. Nice meeting you.'

And she was off, leaving Leo staring after her, wondering how he could have handled the conversation better to get answers to the questions he had about Greta and her.

*

'Guess what?' Jo rushed into the boutique and handed Greta a takeaway coffee. 'Hope it's not cold.'

'Why would it be cold?' Greta asked.

'I met this man at the café. Well, actually, I bumped into his table and spilled his coffee over him. But you'll never guess. It's the guy everyone's talking about, the one who's planning to buy the hotel.'

Greta felt the blood drain from her face. 'Leo Carlson?' she managed to say through tight lips. 'You met Leo Carlson?'

'That's who he said he was. Owner of Leonard Holdings… and… I even worked in one of his hotels when I was in Paris. How cool is that?'

'You talked?'

'Of course. I apologised; bought him another coffee; we introduced ourselves. I asked what he was doing here, and he told me. No big deal,' she added, as Greta reached for the counter to brace herself. 'He's a good-looking man for... Must be around the same age as you and Dad.' Jo took a sip of her coffee. 'Ugh it is cold. Sorry, Mum.'

'It's okay.' Greta didn't feel like coffee anyway. Jo's news had thrown her. Her daughter was full of surprises.

Thirteen

Greta couldn't dismiss the picture of Jo and Leo together. She wanted to ask her daughter more about him. How had he looked, exactly what had he said, but to do so would be to give away the fact she knew him – had known him – had known him well. But the image of them together was burned into her brain and refused to go away.

Also, after her shocking revelation, Jo said no more about her pregnancy, much to Greta's frustration. Now she knew what had prompted Jo's sudden return home, she wanted more details. How long had she and Damien been together? Had she wanted the baby? What about her job? But having briefly opened up, Jo didn't choose to elaborate. She had gone to bed immediately afterwards and next morning, acted as if nothing had happened. For Greta, on the other hand, it was as if a cloud of uncertainty had been lifted. She wanted to comfort her daughter but didn't know how.

Cass noticed Greta was distracted when they met for a meal in *The Firenze* the day after Jo had met Leo. It was their custom to do this after their weekly yoga session, effectively ruining the benefits of the exercise.

'What's up?' Cass asked. 'Is Jo okay?'

'I'm worried about her. You were right when you said it was about a man, but it was more than that.' Greta proceeded to share what Jo had told her.

'Poor Jo,' Cass said when Greta had finished. 'But she did the right thing, coming home. Now she just needs to meet someone else to get over it.'

'It's not that simple, Cass. A miscarriage can be devastating, especially combined with the end of a relationship. I wish she'd talk to me about it.'

'I thought you said she did?'

'Only the bare facts. I'm her mother. I want to know more. She's surrounded by children every day. I don't know how she can cope.'

'Maybe it is her way of coping,' Cass said gently. 'I know it wouldn't be yours, but we are all different and deal with grief differently.'

'Mmm.'

'Oh, look!' Cass nodded through the window to across the road where a man was striding along in the direction of the esplanade. 'Isn't that the guy who's planning to buy Harris's hotel? I heard he was a looker.'

Greta looked across to where Cass was indicating. Her heart leapt. Bellbird Bay was such a small town, they'd be bound to meet sooner or later. Jo had already met him. He may already know Greta was still living here, know about *Birds of a Feather*. Then a dreadful thought struck her. *What if he knew Jo was her daughter?* Greta felt dizzy. She thought she was going to faint.

'Are you okay?' Cass's voice seemed to come from a long way off. 'You've gone quite pale.'

'I... I'm sorry Cass. I...' Greta rose and stumbled to the ladies' room where she held on to the sink and stared in the mirror at a face she barely recognised. No wonder Cass had asked if she was okay. Her face was devoid of colour, her eyes glazed. *If the sight of Leo Carlson across the street through a window could do this, what would it be like if she met him face to face, as she was bound to do if he stayed in town?*

Cass was still looking worried when Greta returned to the table. The half-eaten plate of spaghetti carbonara which was one of her favourite dishes, now appeared unappetising, congealing on the plate. 'I'm sorry, Cass. I think I need to go home.' She opened her purse and took out a fifty dollar note. 'This'll more than cover my share. Sorry to do this to you. Don't...' she said as her friend started to rise. 'Enjoy the rest of the meal – and the wine. See you tomorrow.'

Cass stared at her dubiously. 'Are you sure you'll be okay?'

'I'm sure.' Greta just wanted to leave before she was actually sick. 'Jo's at home. I'll be fine after a good night's sleep.' A good night's sleep? When would she ever have that again? Ever since she'd been aware Leo Carlson was in town, her moods had seesawed between excitement and unadulterated terror. Right now, terror was winning.

*

Greta did feel slightly better when she awoke next morning. Dressed in one of her brightly coloured outfits, as she applied her usual makeup ready for the day ahead, she determined she wouldn't allow herself to get into such a state again. Leo Carlson was part of her past, a past she'd always remember fondly, but the past, nevertheless. They were both different people from the foolish young things they'd been back then. He was no doubt married with a family of his own. Why did she imagine he'd want to see her again any more than she wanted to see him? The trouble was… she knew, if she was being honest with herself, she'd love to recapture those magical days when the sun always seemed to shine, and the world was their oyster.

'What happened last night, Mum?' Jo asked when she entered the kitchen. 'You got back early. I heard you come in. Did you go straight to bed?'

'I didn't feel well, must have been something I ate.' Greta couldn't face Jo's questions when she came home the night before so, hearing the television blaring in the living room – the theme tune of one of Jo's favourite soaps – she had slunk off to bed, relieved to close the door and be alone.

'Feeling better now?'

'Yes, thanks.' Greta fixed herself a bowl of muesli and a cup of lemon and ginger tea, before joining her daughter at the table.

'Thanks, Mum,' Jo said after a long pause.

'For what?' Greta asked, mystified.

'For not subjecting me to an inquisition about Damien and London. I may feel like talking about it sometime, but not yet. It's all too raw.'

'I understand.' Greta glanced up to see Jo looking embarrassed. 'But when you're ready, I'm happy to listen without judgement. I love you, honey.'

'Thanks, Mum,' Jo repeated. 'Have you seen Dad again?'

The words were barely out of her mouth when Greta's phone rang, and she saw Mick's number on the screen. Glaring at her daughter who she suspected of being complicit with her dad, Greta picked up the phone and answered.

'What did Dad want?' Jo asked when, with a bemused expression, Greta ended the call.

'He invited me to lunch on Monday.'

'I hope you said yes,' Jo said, even though she must have heard Greta's side of the conversation. 'I'm really glad you two are seeing each other again.'

'We're not... It's only lunch,' Greta said, flustered, remembering how she had enjoyed his company when they met for coffee.

'Will you tell him?'

'Tell... oh, about you? You're sure you don't want to yourself?'

'Please. It was hard enough telling you... but Dad...' Jo rolled her eyes. She'd always been her dad's blue-eyed girl – despite the fact her eyes were brown – and Greta could understand her reluctance to share this with Mick.

'Okay.' At least it would be something to talk about. She and Mick would always have Jo in common. What was she thinking? They'd never found conversation difficult. That hadn't been the problem. It had been Mick's liking for other women that had been the death knell of their marriage. And, as far as she knew, that hadn't changed.

Fourteen

For the next few days, Leo was busy checking paperwork relating to the hotel purchase. Now it was common knowledge he was the new buyer, the staff regarded him differently. He was treated with even more courtesy than before and was aware of the barely disguised comments when he appeared in the dining room. It was the reason he often chose to eat elsewhere, in one of the many cafés or restaurants in Bellbird Bay.

But regardless of how busy he was, at the back of his mind was the possibility he had a daughter. It took a bit of getting used to, after all those years wishing for children, to suddenly find she'd been there all the time. He knew he wanted to get to know her better – and to see Greta again. But he didn't want to make a fuss. What if Jo didn't know about him? He'd thought long and hard about how to handle the situation and couldn't come up with an answer, other than to walk into Greta's shop and confront her.

Sunday was a glorious day. Looking out of the window of his hotel room at the blue sky and the swell of the ocean in the distance, Leo could imagine himself back in Bellbird Bay as a teenager, preparing for one more day on the beach with the girl he'd fallen in love with. He pitied those people who dismissed the idea of love at first sight. He knew it to be true. The strength of his feelings all those years ago had never left him. And now he was back where it had all begun, and the memories threatened to overwhelm him.

Dressing in jeans and a tee-shirt and pulling on his denim jacket,

Leo made his way across town to the esplanade, the part of town that seemed to draw him. Perhaps it was the knowledge Greta was there, inside her shop, that he could walk in, say hello and it would be as if he'd never left. Who was he kidding? It was thirty-five years since he left, since he broke his promise to keep in contact, for her to join him in the city. How would she react to seeing him now?

This time, he sauntered down to the beach and, taking off his sandals, began walking along the edge of the water. It was pleasant here. The beach was almost deserted. Only a few families were seated on the sand, their children engaged in digging holes or building sandcastles, a few swimmers braving the waves and, of course, the inevitable groups of surfers sitting out on their boards. At one end of the beach, he could see Will Rankin's van with its sign waving in the breeze. It was no doubt a typical Sunday in Bellbird Bay.

Here on the beach, the memories came thick and fast, memories he'd managed to stifle for over thirty years. Had he made a mistake coming back here? Would it have been better to let sleeping dogs lie? Somehow he couldn't believe it would.

Having walked the length of the beach with his mind filled with that summer all those years ago, it was a shock to see Jo Roberts coming towards him. For a brief moment, he thought he'd conjured up the Greta he'd been remembering. He blinked.

She spoke. 'We meet again,' she said, pushing her wet hair out of her eyes and smiling up at him. 'It's Leo, isn't it?'

'Jo, good to meet you again.' Leo thought quickly. 'I was about to have lunch in the club. Join me?' Then, seeing her frown, added, 'Take pity on a stranger in town?'

She hesitated for a moment, stared at him, then said, 'Okay. I'll get my gear.' She gestured to the bundle of clothes on the beach.

Ten minutes later they were walking into the surf club.

*

Conversation during their meal of what Leo realised now was the inevitable burger and chips washed down with a beer for him and a glass of lemon, lime and bitters – 'I don't drink during the day' – for

Jo, was lively. Jo shared anecdotes about her travels and teaching, while Leo answered her questions about his hotel chain.

During a lull in the converstion over coffee, Leo said, 'I used to know your mother.'

'You did?' Jo's eyes widened. 'You were here before?'

'A long time ago. My friends and I spent a summer here between school and university.'

'Oh, schoolies,' Jo dismissed him. 'They usually only come for a couple of weeks, not the whole summer. Must have been before I was born.' She chuckled.

Leo suppressed the urge to ask her exactly when she'd been born. He cleared his throat. 'Your mother… she's on her own?'

'At the moment, but I'm hoping… I know Dad wants to get back with her. It would be good for both of them.'

Leo's heart dropped. This wasn't what he hoped to hear. Perhaps he needed to make a move, talk to Greta soon, rather than leave it to fate for them to bump into each other. 'You said she owns the boutique on the esplanade. Is it open seven days?'

'No, that would be too much, even for Mum. She closes the shop on Mondays.'

Leo made a mental note. He'd go to see Greta as soon as her shop opened on Tuesday. He needed to apologise. She deserved an explanation. And he needed to know if Jo really was his daughter.

*

Greta was tired when she arrived home from the boutique at five on Sunday. She'd been on her feet all day and couldn't wait to have a seat, put her feet up and pour herself a glass of wine, not necessarily in that order.

Jo was waiting for her in the kitchen, a bottle of chardonnay and two glasses on the table.

'Oh, thanks, darling. I've had a hectic day. How did you guess?'

Jo didn't reply immediately, pouring Greta a glass of wine before saying, 'Why didn't you tell me you knew Leo Carlson?'

Greta took a shaky breath. 'How did you…?'

'We met on the beach and had lunch together at the club. He told me you knew each other, that he'd spent the summer between school and uni here in Bellbird Bay. When I told you I'd met him, why didn't you say?'

'It was so long ago,' Greta tried to prevaricate. 'I didn't think…'

'What were you hiding? It must have been before I was born.' A puzzled expression flitted across her face, as if she was trying to work something out. 'You were only eighteen when you became pregnant, weren't you?'

Greta felt her stomach churn. She held her breath.

'Is… is he my real dad?'

'No!' Greta said, shocked. 'No,' she said again more calmly. 'Why would you think that? Mick's your dad.' Her voice quivered.

'What year was it?' Jo persisted. 'You must remember. Was it before Dad…' Her voice trembled on the word.

'It was the year before you were born. Your dad was on his gap year. Leo left. Your dad came home. We married. You were born. You've heard our story before.'

'But not about Leo Carlson. How well did you know him? My birthday's in October. Were you and he…?'

Greta was too distraught to reply. Ever since she knew Leo was in town, she'd been afraid of this. 'You were a premature baby. You've always known that.'

'It's what you always told me. Now I don't know what to believe.' Jo stormed out leaving Greta to finish her wine on her own and wish it would all go away, to wish Leo Carlson had never come back to Bellbird Bay.

Fifteen

Greta had arranged to meet Mick on Monday in *The Greedy Gecko*. As she walked along towards the café, she couldn't help remembering the last time she'd been there. It had been just after she'd caught sight of Leo Carlson in *The Bay Gallery*. She glanced around carefully to ensure he was nowhere in sight this time, shivering at the memories his presence had evoked.

People were talking about him, about the wealthy entrepreneur who was rescuing the hotel from the clutches of the criminal who had bribed members of the council to get his development plans passed, and about how handsome he was. They had no idea she knew him, that she had once imagined spending the rest of her life with him. He'd planned to become a lawyer. Greta wondered what had happened to make him change direction and build a hotel empire.

It worried her that Jo had met him, had even worked in one of his hotels. But even more, it worried her that she was bound to meet him again, too. She found herself beset with these contradictory emotions every time she thought about Leo Carlson. She was glad when she reached the café and saw Mick already sitting there. Mick might be many things – and she'd called him most of them over the years – but she knew exactly where she stood with him, while with Leo... She shuddered at the prospect of meeting him again after all this time.

Mick rose to greet her with a kiss on the cheek that effectively dislodged thoughts of Leo as she breathed in the familiar aroma of salt and oil that always surrounded her ex-husband.

'Thanks for coming,' Mick said, more unassuming than she remembered. 'I wasn't sure you would.'

'When have I ever reneged on an agreement?' It was Mick who'd broken their marriage vows, not her.

'How's Jo?' Mick asked when they'd been served, each ordering grilled fish with a rocket, pear and blue cheese salad, accompanied by a glass of white wine for Greta and a beer for Mick. His healthy lifestyle didn't exclude the odd glass of beer.

'You haven't spoken to her?'

'She's called a couple of times but hasn't been very forthcoming. She's not my little girl anymore.' Mick sighed.

'She's thirty-four, Mick,' Greta reminded him again.

'I know, I know.' He held up his hands. 'I just thought. Last time we met you said you were worried about her. Has she told you anything about why she left London so suddenly?'

Greta laid down her knife and fork, took a gulp of wine. 'She has. She wants me to tell you.'

Mick raised one eyebrow. 'Sounds serious.'

She took a deep breath and started to repeat what Jo had said about Damien, and her reasons for leaving. As she spoke, she could see Mick's face turning red.

'The bastard,' he exploded, when she had barely finished. 'I'd like to get my hands on him. I'd…'

Greta laid a hand on his arm. 'There's nothing we can do, Mick. It's over. At least she had the sense to come home to us.'

'Hmm. She plans to stay in Bellbird Bay?'

'I get the feeling she'd like to. It'll depend on the school; if there's a job for her here.' It suddenly struck Greta as ironic Jo was here because she'd lost her baby, and she'd been able to find a job because someone else gave birth to one. Life could be bizarre, but things had a strange way of working out for the best. She gave herself a mental shake. She was beginning to think like Ruby Sullivan.

'Hmm,' Mick said again then, taking a swallow of beer asked, 'This guy who's looking to buy the Harris place – Leo Carlson – is he the same one who you…?'

Greta felt herself blush. How did Mick know Leo's name? Had she ever mentioned it back then when she'd been in such a state? She'd been stewing over Leo's betrayal, the complete absence of communication, when Mick had returned from his gap year. The young surfer she remembered had turned into a tanned man with broad shoulders, a man who'd offered the comfort she needed, and she'd been quick to fall into his embraces, to use them to forget the city boy who'd lied to her. But she hadn't forgotten him.

'He's the guy you helped me forget,' she said, taking a gulp of wine and almost choking.

'I knew that. Have you spoken to him?'

Greta shook her head, trying to stifle the apprehension which was never far from the surface these days.

'Greta...' Mick leant across the table. His face was so close she could see the lines around his eyes and the grey in his stubble. 'I'd like us to try again.'

For an instant, Greta almost asked, 'Try what?' Then she realised what he was saying. 'I don't think so, Mick.'

'Why not?' he persisted. 'We're neither of us getting any younger; Jo's back home. It's an opportunity for us to become a family again.'

'What brought this on?'

'I've been thinking, seeing my old mates getting married, and it struck me we are both still here, still single. We were good together, weren't we?'

'Until you decided to kick the traces.'

'It was a long time ago. I'm a reformed character these days. I haven't the time or the energy to run after other women, if that's what you mean.'

What else could she mean? Greta took a good look at the man sitting across the table. He'd aged well. In his mid-fifties, Mick Roberts was still a fine figure of a man. If she was looking to have a man in her life, she could do worse. But she wasn't looking. Unbidden, the image of Leo Carlson appeared in her mind's eye, Leo as she'd seen him through the window of *The Firenze*. She'd settled for second best once; she didn't intend to do it again.

'It's too late, Mick.'

'Will you at least think about it? Jo would be happy to know we were back together.'

Jo's thinly veiled comments about exactly that came back to Greta. 'Have you...?

'I may have mentioned the possibility.'

'Oh, Mick! It's not that simple. I've made my own life. It's what I want. I'm happy as I am.' Greta tried to forget the lonely nights she'd spent before Jo came home, would likely spend again. Jo wouldn't stay with her for ever. Even if she decided to remain in Bellbird Bay, she'd want her own place, her independence.

'Just say you'll think about it,' he repeated with the hang dog look she remembered him using when he wanted to get his own way.

'I'll think about it,' she said to please him.

Sixteen

Tuesday morning dawned, promising to be another glorious day. Leo was beginning to think it never rained in Bellbird Bay, but he knew it did. He remembered a horrific rainstorm when he was last here. The rain caught him and Greta on their special beach and they'd been forced to shelter under a tree. Greta had been worried about being struck by lightning and he'd held her tight to allay her fears.

How he wished he hadn't lost touch with her. If only his dad hadn't died, if there hadn't been the debts, if he hadn't lost her contact details. There would be no problem these days. With social media and mobile phones, it was difficult to lose touch, but back then, her address and home phone number were all he had. He assumed she'd gone travelling as she planned. He imagined how different his life might have been if Greta had come to Sydney. Even the advent of a baby would have proven no barrier to their life together.

It was still early, so he headed out to *The Bay Café* for breakfast, choosing a table from where he could see *Birds of a Feather* and watch for Greta's arrival. As he tucked into the plate of eggs benedict and sipped his usual black coffee, Leo tried to work out what he was going to say to Greta. But no matter how hard he tried, everything he composed sounded crazy. He'd just have to play it by ear.

He'd checked the opening hours the day before and at just before eight, he saw a figure enter the shop. Nervously, he finished his coffee and went inside to pay. Then he made his way across to the glass-fronted boutique.

To Leo's surprise, when he looked through the glass, it was to see two women standing inside. He recognised Greta straight away. Dressed in a brightly coloured outfit, she was more elegant than the girl he remembered, and the long hair was now shorter, but she had kept her slim figure and her features were the same. He took a deep breath, and his hand reached for the door handle.

*

Greta was chatting to Cass about her weekend, including Mick's outrageous suggestion, when the shop door was pushed open, and a tall masculine figure filled the doorway. Her heart thudded so loudly she was sure both Cass and the man could hear it.

Cass gave Greta a strange look. 'Talk later,' she said as she scuttled out leaving Greta to face Leo on her own.

'Greta!'

'Leo?'

They stood staring at each other, drinking in the sight of the older versions of the youngsters they remembered. Greta was the first to find her voice. 'I heard you were in town. You met my daughter, Jo.' She hadn't meant it to sound like an accusation but knew it did.

'She's a lovely young woman, looks just like you did.'

'It was a long time ago, best forgotten.' Her heart was still beating madly, and she was trembling so much she was forced to hold on to the counter to remain upright.

'I've never forgotten.'

Why did he have to look so good? The sight of that well-remembered face, the sound of his voice... they still sent shivers down her spine.

'What are you doing here?' she asked.

'I'm here to buy a hotel.'

'No, what are you doing in my shop?'

'I came to see you, to apologise. I wanted to... I need to...'

Leo was interrupted by the door swinging open and three chatting women breezing in. His face fell.

'Not here. I have a business to run.' Greta turned to face the women who were fingering dresses on one of the rails at the side of the shop.

'Then where? Can we meet for dinner? I need to talk to you.'

Greta felt flustered. She wanted him to leave... she wanted him to stay. She was curious to hear what he had to say... she needed to take care of her customers. Could she bear to have a meal with him, to sit across a table from him, to... He was waiting for her answer. It would soon be all over town that Leo Carlson had been in *Birds of a Feather* to talk with Greta Roberts. She had to say something, to get rid of him. 'Okay.'

Leo's eyes lit up. 'Tonight at seven. The Italian restaurant across the way?'

Greta nodded and watched as he made his way out, before moving to help one of the women into a fitting room with an armful of garments.

A sudden influx of customers after the three women left, kept Greta busy till lunchtime. She was eating a sandwich and keeping an eye out for customers when Cass popped her head in to ask, 'Was that Leo Carlson? I didn't know you were friends.'

'We're not. But I did know him a long time ago.'

'He's an attractive man.'

'Yes.' Greta had no wish to discuss him with Cass or anyone else.

'I'm only saying... What did he want?'

Greta sighed, realising she wasn't going to get off this easily. 'He wanted to invite me to dinner.'

'Wow!' Cass's eyes widened. 'And...?'

'And nothing. I accepted. Tonight,' she added, seeing the question in her friend's eyes. 'Now, I have a lot to do.' She took a last bite of her sandwich and gestured towards the pile of garments which needed to be put back on the racks.

'I'm going, but I expect a full account later... and the story of how you know him,' Cass threw over her shoulder before the door closed behind her.

Greta bit her lip. She should have known Cass wouldn't leave it there. She'd have to figure out a good story before tomorrow when her friend would be back for more details.

The afternoon seemed to drag, with Greta alternately wishing she'd refused to have dinner with Leo, and eagerly anticipating spending the evening with him. By the time she put the closed sign on the door at five o'clock, she was a nervous wreck.

One thing she was sure of was that she intended to look her best, to show him what he'd missed by failing to contact her. She went into the back of the shop, to where she had hidden the garments she intended to use in her next window display. The black wide-legged pants with the wildly patterned tunic was the perfect outfit to set off her ash blonde hair. It was one of the signature outfits for which *Birds of a Feather* had become known and would give her the confidence boost she sorely needed to face Leo again.

*

'Going out, Mum? It's not your book club tonight, is it?'

Greta glanced into the kitchen where Jo was eating leftover chicken. She'd hoped to make it out without being spotted. 'Dinner with an old friend,' she said.

'You're looking pretty good for dinner with Cass so I'm guessing it's not her. Let me think...' She pretended to rack her brains. 'Who's in town that you used to know? Are you having dinner with Leo Carlson? Mum?'

'I might be.' Greta knew she'd taken more trouble over her appearance than she had for ages, certainly more than she'd taken for her lunch with Mick.

'Does Dad know?'

'It's none of his business.' Jo's question only reinforced Greta's suspicions her daughter and Mick were both working to get her back together with him. Greta could imagine his dismay if... when... he found out about her dinner with Leo. But it was just dinner; it wasn't as if she was going to sleep with the guy. As soon as the thought crossed her mind, she felt an ache she hadn't felt since... Damn! What had made her even imagine sleeping with Leo again – though there hadn't been much actual sleeping in their relationship.

'You're looking very nice, anyway. New outfit?'

'From the latest delivery.'

'Suits you.'

'Thanks.' Greta was pleased Jo approved of what she was wearing, even if she might not approve of her dinner companion.

As Greta drove across town to the restaurant, she tried to persuade herself she had only agreed in order to hear what Leo wanted to say. She'd eat dinner, hear him out and that would be an end to it. There would be no need for them to meet again. So why did a small part of her hope he'd want to see her again, hope that maybe, just maybe, he was free and would be interested in rekindling what they'd shared?

Greta was a bag of nerves, her stomach churning, when she parked the car. She took a deep breath and headed towards the restaurant.

*

Leo stared across the table, drinking in the sight of the face which had filled his dreams, older now, but still as beautiful as he remembered. He wondered how to begin. He cleared his throat.

'How are you finding Bellbird Bay?' Greta asked, while he was still working out what to say. He'd never felt so tongue-tied in his life.

'Full of memories. Greta... I know I treated you badly. I need to explain.' He leant forward.

'Your wine, sir.' The waiter appeared with the bottle of pinot gris he'd ordered. Bad timing.

'Thanks. No need for me to taste it.' Leo waited till the man had filled both their glasses and waved him away.

He could see Greta was waiting for him to speak.

She picked up her glass and took a sip of wine.

'I didn't forget you. I fully intended to be in touch but...' He saw her sceptical expression, wanted to dispel it, to make her understand. He pushed a hand through his hair. 'You have to understand, Greta, I loved you. I didn't lie to you. When I got home, I discovered Dad was sick. He died next day. Then his debts came to light. Everything else flew from my mind. I needed to help Mum. We had to sell up. There was nothing left. We moved and... somewhere in all this I lost your details. I realise now it's no excuse. but back then... I was only eighteen, a boy trying to deal with my parents' problems. I had to grow up very quickly. I had to find work, give up on the idea of uni and... I did try to contact you through one of the crowd we knew back then... and heard you'd moved on. I never forgot you. Not even when

I married Zoe. I soon realised it was a mistake. We've been divorced now for several years.'

He glanced at Greta to see she was listening intently. Encouraged, he continued, 'My work became my life. Building and renovating hotels and resorts went some way to filling the emptiness in my life. When I saw the hotel for sale here in Bellbird Bay, it was like a sign.' He remembered the strange words of the old woman he'd met and shivered. She'd spoken about a sign, too. 'Coming back here...' he spread his arms, '... it brought it all back. Then I discovered you were still here, that you had a daughter...'

'She's not yours, Leo.'

Leo felt his heart thud. He stared at Greta till she dropped her eyes. 'Are you sure? She's the right age. Unless you...' *Had she forgotten him so quickly?*

Greta took a gulp of wine, then, clasping her glass in both hands and staring down into it said, 'I waited for your letter. It never came. I wrote, but my letters were returned. I thought you didn't want to see me again. I was heartbroken. Everyone knew we'd been together. I hated going out, seeing everyone else part of a couple. Then Mick came home. We'd known each other before... I wanted to forget. He'd been overseas on a gap year. He was on his own too. We gravitated together. He comforted me. He wasn't you, but he was here and... one thing led to another...' She raised her eyes to meet his.

Leo felt a spurt of anger.

Greta didn't seem to notice. 'When I discovered I was pregnant, I did think the baby could be yours. But you were gone. Mick was there and asked me to marry him. All my dreams of leaving Bellbird Bay, of travelling, disappeared in the blink of an eye. I said "yes".'

'So Jo *could* be mine?' Leo's heart lifted.

Greta shook her head. 'When she was born in October, it was still possible. I told everyone – Mick included – she was premature and kept my suspicions to myself. She looked like me but with brown eyes. Mick has brown eyes, too. He never knew my suspicions. There was no need.'

'Oh! I'd hoped...' His stomach contracted.

'You have children?'

'No. After we married, I discovered Zoe had no intention of having the family I wanted. She valued her freedom too much to ruin her life with a child – her words.'

'I'm sorry.'

The arrival of their meals broke the tension which had built up through their revelations, but Leo was no longer hungry. Even though the *scallopini al funghi* he'd ordered looked delicious, he had to force himself to eat any of it. Greta appeared to be having the same problem with her *spaghetti arrabiata*.

'I'm sorry,' she laid down her cutlery, 'I seem to have lost my appetite.'

'Me too. Shall we go? I think we need to be somewhere away from people.' Leo gestured to the other diners, all of whom were chatting and laughing, enjoying their evening.

Once outside, without speaking, they headed for the beach, deserted at this time of night. Leo helped Greta down onto the sand and waited till she'd removed the high heels which would make walking on the soft sand difficult. Then they made their way to the hard-packed sand closer to the ocean.

It was a clear night, a full moon shining on the water and providing them with enough light to distinguish each other's features. The only sound was the soft lapping of the waves on the beach.

'I missed this,' Leo said after a few minutes of walking in silence. 'For months, I always thought I'd come back.'

'Why didn't you?'

Leo sighed. 'My mother. She took Dad's death badly, then the debts, as I said. Dad had always seemed so... so well-organised. It was a shock to discover the mess he'd left his finances in. We had to move into a tiny flat. There wasn't enough money for me to go to uni. I had to get a job. That's what introduced me to hospitality.' He looked up into the sky. 'I started off as a kitchen hand, gradually moved up to working the front desk at night. I discovered I liked the atmosphere. It's difficult to explain. I felt as if I'd come home. Anyway,' he bent down to pick up a piece of driftwood and threw it back into the sea, 'there was never any time to come back to Bellbird Bay. Then, I guess life took over... as it does. I can't tell you how much I regret it.'

He reached over to grasp Greta's hand, pleased she didn't pull away, realising for the first time, that he had no reason to blame her for meeting someone else.

'I wish I'd known.' Greta stopped walking and gazed up at him, her face glowing white in the darkness. 'I waited and waited to hear from you. I thought you'd abandoned me, that you'd never meant all those things you said. I felt such a fool. So, when Mick appeared, wanted to spend time with me, I was flattered. It meant I didn't need to be alone anymore. Mick was a good husband, a good father.'

Leo gazed down into her familiar face. In the dim light, she looked exactly like the girl he remembered. 'Can we start again, Greta?' he asked, his voice hoarse with emotion.

Greta's hand tightened in his. 'I'd like that,' she said, her voice barely audible.

Greatly daring, Leo leant down till their lips met. It was as if time stood still, as if the past thirty-five years had never happened and they were once again the two young lovers whose lives stretched before them.

Seventeen

Greta felt as if she was eighteen again. The touch of Leo's lips on hers took her back to those heady days, to that special summer. She clung to him, locked in a cocoon of happiness. She wanted to stay there for ever.

Slowly they drew apart. She could feel Leo's eyes on her in the darkness as the moon slid behind a cloud, his words and her reply at the foremost of her mind. Start again. If only life was that simple. She wanted to believe it, to imagine they could still have a future together. And for an instant, it was as if it was within her grasp.

But her life was here in Bellbird Bay. She had a business, a daughter with problems of her own, an ex who wanted to get back together. She was no longer the naïve young girl in the first throes of love. Leo was no longer the young man who promised her the earth. He was a successful businessman with a chain of hotels and resorts. His life and hers were poles apart.

Greta knew exactly when Leo sensed her withdrawal.

'What's wrong?' he asked.

'This. It can't work, Leo. No matter how much we might want it to. We're different people from back then. Look at you. I'm just a small-town shopkeeper, you... you're a wealthy entrepreneur.' She folded her arms around her body, as if to protect herself from the emotions which were whirling around inside.

'We're not so different, really. We both did what we had to do to keep going. For you, it was...' he choked, '... getting married, giving birth to your daughter. For me, it was building an empire, an empire I'd give away in the blink of an eye if I thought we could have a future together.'

Greta was glad it was dark, and Leo couldn't see her face clearly. She wished she could believe him. But how could he arrive in town and expect her to change everything she'd believed for the past thirty-five years? Suddenly the prospect of getting back with Mick seemed like a viable option. Mick was a known quantity, while Leo – this new version of Leo – was a stranger, a stranger who felt achingly familiar, she reminded herself.

A light flashed several metres in front of them. There was the sound of voices. Then a young couple appeared, arms entwined. They looked so like Greta and Leo had when they were their age, she was seized by a pang of regret. She hoped they were facing a better future than the one fate had handed out to her and Leo. Though it hadn't been all bad. She and Mick had been happy. She had Jo. It was only when he began to find other women attractive, to stay out later and later, come home with lipstick on his collar – such a cliché – that things had gone sour.

'We were like them once.' Leo took the words out of her mouth. 'We could be again, Greta.'

'No.' She pulled away from the hands reaching for her. 'It's too late, Leo,' she said, echoing the words she'd said to Mick only the day before.

'I'm sorry, Leo. I need to get home. Thanks for dinner, for apologising, explaining. There was no need, but thanks. I wish you well with your purchase of the hotel. I presume you'll be leaving Bellbird Bay soon.' She turned and made her way as quickly as she could across the beach, stopping only to pull on her shoes when she reached the esplanade, before heading to her car.

*

Stunned, Leo stared after Greta's slim figure as she disappeared into the gloom. The young couple had disappeared too, leaving him alone on the beach, unable to hide his disappointment. He'd been so overjoyed to see Greta again, harboured hopes she felt the same. They were both free and, while it was a blow to learn Jo wasn't his daughter, it didn't change how he felt about Greta.

He hadn't realised till now how much he'd hoped for a reconciliation. He'd thought their kiss signalled that. As an author once said, the earth had moved for him, and he'd thought Greta felt the same way. How could he have been so mistaken? In his business life, Leo was renowned for his ability to read people, to know exactly how they were feeling. He'd used the skill to good effect when dealing with difficult clients, with recalcitrant staff. Why didn't it work in this instance – with Greta?

Shaking his head in despair, Leo made his way back to the esplanade, the lights of the buildings seeming to mock him. There was no sign of Greta, but the window of *Birds of a Feather* glowed brightly, reminding him of her.

Although dispirited, as he drove back to the hotel Leo was determined not to give up. The words of the weird old woman he'd met on the headland popped back into his head. She had told him not to be arrogant. Had it been arrogance, his assumption Greta would be eager and happy to pick up where they'd left off, as if the years between had never happened? They'd both led full lives since then. She'd been married, had a child, a child who was now a grown woman. She was a businesswoman, no doubt a successful one. She'd remained in Bellbird Bay and appeared to be well-liked. What did he have to offer her?

What else had the old woman said? Leo racked his brains. There was the bit about the universe sending him a sign. Well, he knew all about that. It was what had brought him here. It was the other part he was trying to remember. He was pulling into the hotel car park when it struck him. She'd said something about correcting the mistakes of the past. Wasn't that what he was trying to do? He sighed. Maybe after a glass of scotch and a good night's sleep, he'd feel better, and it would all make more sense.

Eighteen

Greta didn't sleep well. She rose early and was already eating breakfast when Jo emerged, her eyes bleary with sleep, her blonde curls tangled. She looked about eighteen.

'You're up early, Mum. Good night?'

'It was okay.' Greta had no intention of describing her evening to her daughter. She was still trying to come to grips with it herself – with Leo's apology, his explanation, and the kiss on the beach. She'd lain awake for hours trying to analyse what had happened and her reaction. She'd enjoyed his kiss. His lips felt exactly as they used to, his nearness provoking the same desire which had been her undoing all those years ago. Back then it had resulted in her losing her inhibitions and with them her virginity.

Jo yawned, clearly satisfied with Greta's response. She made herself a cup of Greta's lemon and ginger tea and dropped a slice of bread into the toaster, waiting for it to pop up before taking it to the table and sitting down.

Greta loved their mornings together, loved seeing her daughter like this. It had been so long since they shared a house, she intended to make the most of it before Jo moved out as she inevitably would. No thirty-four-year-old wanted to live with her mother.

'Anything special on today?' she asked.

'Sports,' Jo mumbled through a mouthful of toast. 'I love getting the kids out of the classroom and letting them run around. I loved sports day when I was little.'

'You used to play netball,' Greta reminisced. 'I remember the uniform, and how you would panic if I didn't iron it properly.' She laughed. It had been a fun time. She had gone to every game to cheer Jo on, Mick too, when he could. They had been good times, when they were a family – a happy family. Could they be again if she agreed to what Mick wanted, or had too much water gone under the bridge? Greta suspected it had. As she'd told him, it was too late. They were different people, and Jo was grown with her own life to live.

'I'm teaching the girls to play netball,' Jo said in a dreamy voice. 'It's fun.'

'Aren't they a bit young?'

'Probably, but they love it. What about you?'

'What about me?'

'Your day. Are you seeing Leo Carlson again?'

'I doubt it.' After the way she'd left him standing on the beach, Greta couldn't imagine he'd want to see her ever again. Although she now regretted her sudden departure, at the time it had seemed her only option. She knew if she'd stayed, things might have escalated – and she wasn't ready for what might have followed. But there was a tiny voice – one which had niggled at her in the middle of the night – which told her she was a fool, that she'd been waiting for Leo Carlson to return for over thirty years. She stifled it now, as she had then. 'He's not the boy I used to know. People change. I've changed, too.'

'He's an attractive man, Mum. So, Dad shouldn't be worried?'

'What's your dad got to do with it? I've told you we're not getting back together.' Greta's lips tightened.

'So you say.' Jo didn't sound convinced.

'I'm going to have my shower.' Greta rose and put her dirty dishes in the dishwasher before heading to her bedroom and the ensuite. She'd heard enough.

It was a relief to Greta to walk into *Birds of a Feather*. This was where she belonged, she thought, as she opened up the computer and looked across at the racks of dresses which she'd carefully selected to reflect the style she'd chosen to market. She didn't need a man in her life – any man. They were all tarred with the same brush.

She was still telling herself that, while remembering how she had felt in Leo's arms, when he walked in.

*

After a sleepless night, Leo awoke determined to see Greta again. It might be a sign of the arrogance the old woman had mentioned, but he was sure he hadn't imagined Greta's response to his kiss.

After a quick shower to waken him up, he dressed in jeans and a long-sleeved tee-shirt in an attempt to avoid looking like the wealthy businessman Greta accused him of being. He knew that, inside, he was still the lovesick boy who had promised her the world. He wanted to show her that boy, to remind her how much they'd meant to each other, how he'd cared, still cared.

This morning he wasn't hungry, so decided to settle for coffee and a pastry in the hotel restaurant, nodding to the receptionist on the way. He was impressed by the staff and wouldn't make many changes there but would need to find a good manager. The last one had left when the owner was arrested.

He was soon on his way, wanting to catch Greta as soon as she opened.

Greta was standing behind the counter looking as elegant as ever. Her eyes widened when he pushed open the door. Her mouth opened, but before she could speak, Leo held up one hand.

'Greta, please hear me out. Last night... I may have acted precipitously. I thought...' He dragged a hand through his hair. 'I thought it was what you wanted.'

When Greta didn't immediately respond, his hope flared, only to be dashed when she said, 'Nothing's changed, Leo, has it?'

But he could see something in her eyes that belied her words, causing him to hope again. 'I may own a string of hotels, Greta, but I meant what I said last night. I've always regretted how I treated you. I want to make reparation, to atone for any hurt I caused. Will you at least let me have a chance?'

He could see she was debating how to reply and, glad there were no customers to interrupt them this time, he pressed on. 'We could have dinner again – or lunch if it works for you. I intend to be in Bellbird Bay for some time, for as long as it takes us to reconnect properly.'

'Then you'll be off again.'

'No.' Leo considered what he could offer Greta, what might

persuade her to give him the chance he so greatly desired. 'Once the hotel is up and running, I could stay.' He held his breath, wondering even as he spoke how he could run his empire from this small coastal town, surprised how the thought of it filled him with a sense of peace.

'Really?' Greta asked, her expression one of surprise. 'You'd stay here? For me?'

'If that's what it takes. If we can rediscover what we had.' A heady sense of joy filled him at the prospect of spending more time here, of getting to know this version of Greta, so different yet so much the same as the girl he remembered.

'Well… maybe…'

Leo could sense she was weakening and pressed his advantage. 'How about we start with dinner again – one we actually eat this time?'

Greta chuckled. 'We did leave rather abruptly, didn't we?'

Leo began to relax. 'Might be better we try somewhere else. Where do you recommend?'

Greta seemed to think for a moment before replying, 'Why don't I cook dinner for us. We can be private and talk uninterrupted.'

'Your daughter?'

'She's planning to see her dad later this week. We can arrange to do it then. I'm quite a good cook,' she added, as if he might doubt it.

'I'm sure you are. I'd be delighted to accept.'

'If you let me have your phone number, I'll text you the details.'

They exchanged numbers, then Leo looked around the shop for the first time, noticing the racks of brightly coloured clothes, the knick-knacks carefully positioned around. 'I like what you've done here,' he said.

The door opened and an older woman walked in. She appeared surprised to see Leo there.

'I should go. You will be in touch?' Leo asked.

'I will. I keep my promises.'

Feeling duly chastised, Leo gave a rueful grin and left.

*

Greta felt her heartbeat return to normal. All the time Leo had been there, it had been racing so fast, she thought she might pass out.

'Hello, Grace,' she said to the woman who had just come in and was watching Leo leave with interest.

'Was that...?'

'Leo Carlson? Yes.'

'I didn't realise you knew each other. When we talked about him at book club, you didn't say anything.'

'It was a long time ago. I didn't think he'd remember.'

'It looked as if you were close.'

Greta gave a heavy sigh. 'Oh, Grace, I think I may have just made a dreadful mistake.'

'Do you want to talk about it? Sometimes it helps to chat to someone who isn't involved. I'll quite understand if you don't. I realise this might not be the best time.'

'Thanks, Grace, but you didn't come in to hear my problems.'

'No. Mel and Aaron have decided to get married, and I came to find something to wear, but there's no hurry. They haven't set a date. It'll depend when they can book with *Pandanus Weddings*. I just thought I'd start looking early.'

'Oh, congratulations! You and Ted must be so pleased.' Greta knew how Grace had worried about her younger daughter who had arrived in Bellbird Bay pregnant. It had been such a relief to her when the girl formed a relationship with Aaron, the son of Grace's own new partner. The young couple had been living together for some time – and now there was to be a wedding.

'We are,' Grace said. 'It's all very well for Ted and me to decide we don't need marriage, but Mel and Aaron are younger and there are children to consider.'

'Children? You mean...?' Greta knew Mel had a daughter. Isla must be around three by now.

'Yes, she's pregnant again. We're going to have another grandchild.'

'How exciting.' While delighted for her friend, Greta again experienced the empty feeling she always did when her friends talked about their grandchildren. Would she ever have one of her own to brag about? Jo was already in her mid-thirties, and if there had been no miscarriage... But thoughts like that were pointless and didn't help Jo either.

'Anyway, enough about me. You don't seem busy this morning. Any chance you could duck out for coffee, and we can have a chat? Only if you feel you can confide in me. I promise nothing you say will go any further.'

'Thanks.' Greta realised a chat with Grace was exactly what she needed. She had always valued the older woman's opinion and knew she meant it when she promised their chat would be confidential. 'It's still early, I don't think I'm going to miss out on too many customers if we have a quick coffee. I'll just…' She took her *Closed – back in 10 minutes* sign from the drawer, ready to stick on the door and picked up her bag.

*

'So there you have it,' Greta said. They were seated at one of the bleached tables outside *The Bay Café* from where she could keep an eye on the shop, and Greta had just given Grace a potted version of the story of her and Leo.

'Well! That's quite some story,' Grace said, 'but why do you think you've made a mistake? It sounds to me as if you and he have a lot to talk about, and he's an attractive man. I do know what it feels like to be unsure of starting a relationship. When I first met Ted, I didn't want anything to do with him. But I'm so glad I gave him a chance.'

'That's what Leo asked for… a chance,' Greta said, remembering the pleading expression in his eyes. 'Maybe you're right. Anyway, it's too late to change my mind now. I just have to work out when Jo will be out for the evening.'

Greta was cooking dinner when Jo came waltzing in and threw her bag on the benchtop. 'You're looking happy,' she said, seeing the smile on Jo's face. 'Did something happen at school today?'

'The oddest thing. The infants were all having their sports afternoon. I was supervising a group of girls playing netball, when Mia – the little girl I've told you about…'

'The one who's lost her mother?'

'That's the one. She was running to catch the ball when she tripped and fell, twisting her ankle.'

'The poor little mite.' Greta paused, sensing there was more to come.

'Luckily it was close to the end of the session, so Gai – one of the other teachers – offered to take over while I drove Mia to Emergency.'

'She's okay?'

Jo nodded and continued, 'I called her dad to meet us there.'

Greta remembered the man speaking to Jo on the beach – the one who was Bev Cooper's son.

'He met us at the hospital, and we waited together while Mia's ankle was x-rayed and bound up. She'll be fine.'

'And?' Why did Greta feel there was more?

Jo turned red. 'Bryan – that's his name – suggested we all go for an ice cream afterwards – to help Mia feel better and to thank me for taking her to the hospital.'

'Oh?'

'He's nice, Mum. Not like Damien. He wanted to know what it was like growing up in Bellbird Bay, about my travels. He was a journalist, a sports reporter, in Sydney, until he lost his wife. The poor man. It must have been such a shock. He's working at the garden centre now, says he loves the manual work, being in the fresh air. I thought my life had been hard, but it must have been so much worse for him. His dad brought him and Mia here to get them away from their memories.'

'That's… lovely, honey.' Greta didn't know what else to say. While she was glad Jo had met someone she seemed to like, who might help her forget Damien, this Bryan was most likely still grieving for his wife. She didn't want to see Jo hurt again.

Jo was still standing there with an expectant expression.

'Is there something else?'

'He's asked me to go to a performance at the local theatre with him… on Saturday evening.'

Jo looked so excited, happier than she'd been since she came home, that Greta didn't have the heart to ask any more questions. 'That sounds nice.' *And it gives me the perfect opportunity to have Leo to dinner.*

Nineteen

When his phone pinged next morning and Leo saw Greta's number, he wanted to give a whoop of delight. Despite their exchanging numbers, he'd been afraid she might regret her invitation.

The text was brief, giving her address and suggesting seven on Saturday. He quickly accepted, grinning as he added a smiley emoji to his reply and hoping this could be the start of something special. There was a spring in his step as he headed out for breakfast at *The Bay Café*.

After a breakfast of eggs benedict with smoked salmon and two cups of coffee, Leo was ready to start the day. This morning, he was keen to satisfy his curiosity about the man Greta had married, had turned to so quickly after his own departure – and seeming abandonment, he reminded himself. He had already checked out the whale watching tours conducted by Mick Roberts, who appeared to be a well-known local identity, and although it was early in the season, discovered he could book into a cruise around the bay.

He'd booked before leaving his hotel room. Now he checked his watch, judging he had enough time to stroll along to the far end of the bay where the harbour was located.

There were only a few other passengers on this mid-week, off-season cruise, so it was easy for Leo to strike up a conversation with the skipper, a fit, tanned man in his fifties. It wasn't difficult to work out what had attracted Greta to him. He was personable, knowledgeable and possessed a good sense of humour which kept everyone interested and amused, even when the sea creatures failed to appear. When a large whale accompanied by her baby, finally did make an appearance, everyone cheered Mick as if he had personally delivered them to their audience.

On the way back to harbour, Leo made his way to the cabin and chatted to Mick, discovering he had spent a year crewing on boats around the Mediterranean before returning to Bellbird Bay to work with his father. That must have been when he and Greta had got together. A casual question asking about his family elicited the worrying response that although divorced, Mick and his ex had remained friends and he was optimistic of a reunion. At this news, Leo felt as if a hand was crushing his heart. It made him all the more determined to find a way to revive the love he and Greta had once shared.

'Join me for a drink?' Mick asked, when they had tied up, and most of the others had disembarked. 'I usually head to the surf club for lunch around this time to catch up with a few mates.'

At first, Leo wanted to refuse, but could think of no real excuse and it would give him the opportunity to learn more about the man he now regarded as a rival for Greta's affection.

On the way to the club, the two men chatted about how the town had changed – Leo having revealed he had visited previously, caught Mick glancing at him oddly making him wonder how much Mick knew about his connection to Greta.

Inside the club, both men were greeted at the bar by Will Rankin.

'So you two have met,' he said with a chuckle.

'Leo joined my cruise this morning,' Mick said, gesturing to the barman for a beer which appeared almost immediately. 'What'll you have, Leo?'

'Four X, thanks.' Leo had developed a taste for the Queensland beer when he was here before and had been pleased to renew it.

'So,' Will said, when the three of them were seated on the deck, 'you do know Leo here was a teenage heartthrob of your ex, Mick?'

'So I believe. Should I be worried?' he joked, nudging Leo.

Leo laughed but didn't reply. Will had answered part of his question.

'I guess the best man won,' Mick said, taking a gulp of his beer. 'You were out of the picture by the time I came back.'

'I was only here for the summer,' Leo muttered, wishing he'd refused Mick's invitation. The other two were discussing what to have for lunch when his phone rang. 'Sorry, I need to take this,' he said, seeing Ken's number on the screen. He moved away from his companions. 'Ken, what's up?' He had told his colleague only to contact him in an emergency.

'We have a problem,' Ken said, his voice serious.

'What?'

'The purchase of the Bellbird Bay hotel. It may not be as straightforward as we anticipated.'

Leo's stomach churned. Just as he was getting somewhere with Greta. 'Spit it out.'

'It seems the owner – a Milton Harris – is in prison.'

'We knew that.'

'Yes, but what we didn't know is that he has given his power of attorney to a woman called...' there was the shuffling of paper, '... Roslyn Portelli.'

'So?'

'She wants to meet you, to negotiate in person.'

Leo cursed silently. He didn't need this aggravation. It should have been a straightforward purchase handled by their respective solicitors. Who was this woman and what business did she have holding up the sale of the hotel?

By the time he returned to the table, Mick and Will had been joined by two others, Martin Cooper and a man who was introduced as Ted. This time, Martin greeted Leo in a friendly fashion.

'You all grew up here?' Leo asked.

'We all tend to come back. Isn't that right, Ted?' he asked the other new member of the group who seemed a few years older than the others.

'So you're the guy we've been hearing about, who's going to buy Harris's hotel. Will tells us you have plans to turn it into a family resort?' Ted said.

'That's right.' But Leo's was forehead creased. He was worried by Ken's call.

'Is there a problem?' Ted asked. 'I was a solicitor in a previous life. I know the setbacks that can arise with major purchases.'

There was a sudden silence. Leo saw the others staring at him. 'No, no problem,' he said with a forced laugh, hoping he was right, and this could be sorted out quickly. He hated having to leave town just as he appeared to be making headway with Greta. He picked up his beer and took a gulp of the icy liquid, glad when the conversation in the group resumed.

Leo listened as the talk swirled around him. It seemed to be about the forthcoming local council elections which they hoped would catapult Will into the position of mayor. He was receiving some good-natured ribbing from Martin Cooper who appeared to be his best mate, but they were all in favour of him in the role.

'It's about time an old surfer took charge,' Ted said, grinning. 'You stayed around when many of us went off to follow our dreams.'

'My dream was right here, always has been,' Will said.

Martin clapped him on the shoulder. 'You've done well for this town, Will. You deserve this. What does Cleo think of it all? Will the wedding be before or after the election?'

Will blushed. 'Before. *Pandanus Weddings* had a cancellation and, being on the spot, Cleo was quick to grab it.'

By remaining silent and listening, Leo soon discovered Will was widowed and this would be his second marriage. His new wife, Cleo, ran the café at the garden centre where *Pandanus Weddings* was located, the garden centre which was owned by Martin's sister. He was learning how closeknit the community of Bellbird Bay was and felt pleased he seemed to have gained entry to this group of men who were at its core.

The men ordered lunch, Leo happy to be included. During the meal, he learned that, apart from Mick, the men were all in happy relationships. It was a pleasant change from events he'd attended in the city where everyone seemed to complain about their spouses and be on the lookout for some extracurricular activity. It was all a far cry from the life he'd had with Zoe, and Leo liked what he heard. The longer he spent in Bellbird Bay, the more he liked it. He felt at home here. There was something about the town that tugged at his heartstrings.

Twenty

Saturday arrived at last. Greta had stocked up ready for the meal she planned to cook for Leo – poached salmon with baby roast potatoes, asparagus and a warm sweet potato salad. It was a meal she'd cooked often in the past, one which Mick had loved. She pushed down thoughts of Mick. Tonight was about Leo, her and Leo. It was to be their new start, and the butterflies in her stomach were doing cartwheels. It was fortunate the shop was busy all day. It prevented her from thinking too much about the evening ahead.

Jo was excited, too. She'd been unable to sit still at breakfast, bringing out garment after garment for Greta's opinion as to what she should wear, before finally deciding on a pair of casual pants paired with a long-sleeved, linen shirt.

Greta completed the preparations for dinner while Jo fixed a sandwich, saying she wasn't hungry. Then, when her daughter had left, threatening not to be late home, she dressed in an outfit similar to the one she'd worn when they last met. This time, the pants were cream and the top a shade of French navy covered with red poppies.

Sipping a glass of white wine to steady her nerves, Greta checked everything was ready. She had just popped the potatoes into the oven when the doorbell rang. Taking a deep breath, she went to answer it.

'Hello there.' Leo handed over a bottle of wine and a bunch of flowers before following Greta to the kitchen. He appeared to be as nervous as she was, but once seated on one of Greta's tall stools at the benchtop, he seemed more at ease.

'This is nice,' he said, looking around at the well-appointed kitchen which Greta had designed herself after her divorce. 'It has a comfortable feel about it.'

'Thanks – I think,' she said.

'Really. I spend most of my life in hotels and rarely get an opportunity for any home life.'

'Don't you have a home?'

'Home is an impersonal Sydney apartment in which I probably spend a few days a month. I travel a lot... too much,' he added with a sigh.

'I suppose you have to... in your position.'

'Yeah. I envy you.'

Greta stared at Leo in surprise. He owned a large hotel empire, spent his life travelling the world. She owned a small dress shop in a quiet coastal town. What was there to envy about her life?

Seemingly sensing her bewilderment, Leo elaborated, 'You have a home, a daughter, a business you enjoy and are well-respected in your community. I met your ex,' he said, by way of explanation. 'He speaks highly of you. In fact, he made it sound as if you two were getting back together.'

'In his dreams. Sorry, Leo, but it's a figment of Mick's imagination. Since the divorce, we've remained friends – impossible not to in Bellbird Bay – but that's all.' She bit her lip, knowing it wasn't quite true. 'Until recently, anyway, till Jo came back home. Now, he seems to think it's time we became a family again.'

Why was she telling him all this? The words seemed to be pouring out of her. Nerves, she decided, turning away to check the salmon which was poaching slowly in its bath of white wine and herbs.

When she turned back, Leo was checking his phone.

'Sorry,' he said. 'Business. One problem with having hotels in different time zones is that the business never sleeps. I'll turn it off now.'

'It must be exciting, though,' Greta said, trying to imagine what it might be like to own businesses all over the world. 'Jo said she worked in your hotel in Paris.'

'Yes, it was one of my earlier ones. It can be exciting, but the thrill wears off after a time and it becomes routine. Travelling from one place to another, one hotel to another; after a time, they all look the same. I've never put down roots the way you have. You seem happy here. I envy you that.'

'I am. Happy. Despite the fact I wanted to travel the world, Bellbird Bay satisfies all my needs. But you married, too.'

Leo gazed up at the ceiling. 'Zoe only wanted what she thought I could give her – wealth, travel, the kudos of being married to Leo Carlson of Leonard Holdings. I think she foresaw my success before I was aware of it myself,' he said bitterly.

'And now?'

'Now I'm tired of it all. Coming back here to Bellbird Bay has made me realise how sterile my life has become. Seeing you, Mick, Will Rankin… people who are happy and content with their lives, not always striving for more.'

'And yet you're here to buy one more hotel.'

'Enough about me. Something smells good.'

'Oh!' Greta realised she'd been ignoring her cooking. When she checked, everything was ready to be served. 'I thought we'd eat here,' she said, indicating the kitchen table which was set for dinner.

'Sounds good. More wine?' Leo picked up the bottle and, without waiting for a response, filled both their glasses while Greta served up the meal.

Greta had forgotten Leo's sense of humour, the way he'd always been able to make her laugh. That hadn't changed, and she found herself giggling like a teenager again as he described some of the things that had occurred in his hotels. He had listened avidly, too, when she told him about how she'd felt when her plans for the future changed rapidly with the discovery she was pregnant. 'But I could never regret Jo,' she said. 'She made up for everything.'

They were silent for a few moments as she silently acknowledged how Leo was part of that everything.

'Mick seems like a good guy,' Leo said. 'Do you want to tell me what went wrong?'

'Women… other women. I guess I always knew he had a roving eye. He had quite a reputation before he went overseas. But I was younger then, and when we got together again and Jo was born, I thought he'd changed, and for a time it seemed he had.' She sighed. 'I put up with it for a while for her sake, so she could have two parents, a normal family life, but,' she took a sip of wine, 'it got too much even for me. When my parents died, and I didn't need to pretend to them any longer, I left and filed for divorce. Jo was a teenager by then and could cope with having a part-time dad. That's when I started *Birds of a Feather*.'

'I'm sorry. You haven't had an easy life.' Leo put a hand on hers.

Greta blushed as his touch sent a wave of warmth through her, so familiar yet so different. 'It hasn't been so bad. And now Jo's back, things are even better. Speaking of which…' she checked the time, '… she may be back soon. She's on a date,' she explained seeing Leo's raised eyebrow, 'with the father of one of her pupils. I know he lost his wife not too long ago… and I'm not sure…' She bit her lip. 'I know she's old enough to look after herself, but I can't help but worry.' *Especially given her history*, Greta thought. 'I'd hate to see her being hurt.'

'I'm sorry I hurt you, Greta.'

'I didn't mean…' But had she? Was her worry about Jo a reflection of the way she'd been hurt all those years ago? 'I know I can't protect her from life. No one can do that. Didn't someone say life is what happens to you while you're busy making other plans?'

'John Lennon.'

'You always did know the answers.' Greta chuckled, remembering.

'I guess I should go, then. Thanks for a lovely evening. It reminded me of how we used to be, how easy it is with you.'

Greta accompanied Leo to the door where, with only a moment's hesitation, he leant down to kiss her. This time, when their lips met, they clung together, only separating at the sound of a car driving up.

'I want to see you again,' Leo said, 'but I need to go to Sydney on business. Can I call you when I get back?'

'Of course.' Greta nodded, embarrassed to see Jo stepping out of the car whose arrival had broken up their embrace, her heart dropping at the news Leo was going away again.

'Mum, this is Bryan,' Jo pulled forward the tall young man who was standing behind her. 'Bryan, my mum.'

'Mrs Roberts.' Bryan nodded.

'Call me Greta,' Greta said, wondering how much the pair had seen. Leo had driven off quickly, as soon as Jo exited the car. 'Would you like to come in for coffee?' She felt awkward. How did you behave with your thirty-four-year-old daughter's date who might have seen you in a clinch?

'Thanks, but I have to get back.' He shuffled his feet.

It was then Greta realised Jo was glaring at her as if willing her to disappear. 'Right,' she said, stepping back and going inside to leave the young couple together.

'Well, that was awkward,' Jo said when she came in some minutes later, but she was grinning. 'We'll need to coordinate better next time. I'm guessing your evening went well.'

So, Jo had seen them kissing. 'Yes, it did. Yours?'

'It was good. You mentioned coffee?'

'I did, but I think chamomile tea might be better at this time of night. I have the kettle on.'

'Perfect.' Jo kicked off her shoes and dropped into a chair, pushing away the dirty dishes.

'I'll clear those.' Greta picked them up, loaded them into the dishwasher and made the tea. Then she joined Jo at the table.

'Bryan seems nice, Jo,' Greta began.

'How can you tell, Mum? You barely spoke. But, yes, he is. The play was good, and he talked a lot about Mia. He's so fond of her. It's so sad.'

'Is… how…?' Greta didn't know how to ask what she wanted to know. How long since Bryan's wife died? Was he still grieving? Was this a romantic date or was he looking for a friend? She hoped he wasn't just looking for a replacement mother for his daughter.

'He came to Bellbird Bay with his dad and Mia last year. As I think I said, it was to get away from the memories Sydney held for him… with his wife. I think he's still grieving, Mum, so don't be getting any ideas. I'm not ready for another relationship yet, either. But he's good company and it's nice to have someone of my own age to spend time with, someone who doesn't ask any questions.'

Greta buttoned her lip, wondering if this was a shot at her… and Mick, who had no doubt interrogated Jo after learning about Damien and the miscarriage.

'And to answer the question I know you're dying to ask, yes, I'm seeing him again. A group of people he knows are going sailing tomorrow and he's invited me along – *as a friend*. Mia will be there, too, with a little friend who is a year ahead of her at school.'

'Right. Well, it sounds like a lovely way to spend a Sunday. I'm sure you'll enjoy it.' Greta seemed to recall Libby Walker's daughter lived with a guy who was involved with boats... and didn't she have a granddaughter around that age, too? It would be lovely if Jo was going to spend time with people Greta already knew. Anyway, it would be good for Jo to mix with a group of young people, people her own age. Surely if she made friends here, she'd be more likely to stay?

Twenty-one

By the time Monday came around again, Greta was ready for a break from work. It had been two days since dinner with Leo, and she could still taste his lips on hers, feel the flash of desire that had shot through her, only to be interrupted by Jo's return.

But Leo was now on his way to Sydney to take care of some business or other, and Greta suspected it would always be like that. No matter what he might say to the contrary, he was a hotelier first and foremost and he'd always be flying off somewhere to troubleshoot or whatever it was he did.

Today, she was determined to relegate him to the back of her mind and concentrate on Jo. Seeing the dreamy look in Jo's eyes when she returned last night worried Greta. She didn't want to think her daughter was heading for another disappointment. Without saying anything to Jo, she'd decided to try to discover a little more about the man who had put the stars in her daughter's eyes. Maybe Bev Cooper would be able to help.

Having made this decision, Greta waited till Jo had left for school, then, pulling on a pair of jeans and slipping a jacket over her tee-shirt, she drove to *The Pandanus Garden Centre and Café*, where she knew she'd find Bev.

It was still early when she arrived, and there were plenty of spots in the car park. Walking through the arched entrance, Greta reflected, not for the first time, what a success Bev had made of this place. She could remember when it had been a small family nursery. Then Bev

Cooper had bought it, and it had gone from strength to strength, now boasting a café and, more recently, becoming home to *Pandanus Weddings* which had proven to be very popular with both locals and visitors to the town.

Greta had patronised it several times over the years, when she wanted to replenish her garden, or to meet friends for coffee in the café. She didn't know Bev well; Bev had been a few years above her at school, was Martin Cooper's sister and had been part of the surfing crowd Greta had admired and longed to be part of. But in a town the size of Bellbird Bay, it was impossible to be strangers. Bev had visited *Birds of a Feather* on a few occasions and Ailsa, her friend and now sister-in-law, was a member of the same book club as Greta.

This morning she made her way to the shop where a couple of staff members wearing the unique green aprons bearing the pandanus logo were already serving some early customers. There was no sign of Bev.

'Can I help you?' a cheerful young girl asked, after farewelling an elderly woman pushing a trolley loaded with plants.

'I wanted to speak with Bev. Is she around?'

The girl glanced about then said, 'I think she popped over to the café. You might catch her there.'

'Thanks.' Greta made her way through the garden centre to the corner in which the entrance to the café was almost hidden by a high hedge. Once there, she scanned the tables which were set out around the huge pandanus from which the centre and the café got their name, finally catching sight of Bev seated at a table next to the kitchen. But she wasn't alone. She was speaking with a tall young man with reddish blond hair who looked familiar. As Greta approached, Bev looked up.

'Greta, what are you doing here? It's a bit early for coffee. Are you meeting someone?' Then, as if recollecting herself, she added, 'Have you met my son, Bryan? Bryan, this is Greta Roberts who owns *Birds of a Feather*.'

Bryan turned bright red. 'Pleased to meet you again, Mrs Roberts.'

'Greta,' Greta said automatically.

Bev looked from one to the other.

'I'll be getting on now, Bev. Catch you later.' And with a brief smile, Bryan walked off.

'You've already met Bryan?' Bev asked.

'Yes.' Greta felt awkward. This wasn't how she intended to broach the subject. 'I actually came to talk to you about him.'

Bev raised her eyebrows. 'You'd better take a seat. Coffee?'

'Yes, please.' Greta was glad of the respite as Bev disappeared into the kitchen. She hadn't expected to come face to face with Bryan.

All too soon Bev was back with a cup of cappuccino.

'Thanks.' Greta took a sip, the shot of caffeine strengthening her resolve.

'You've met Bryan?' Bev asked again.

'Yes… He and Jo… my daughter, they spent some time together on the weekend.'

'Jo… of course. Iain said Bryan had taken someone along yesterday when a group of them went sailing. And Mia said something about her teacher. Is that your daughter?'

'Yes.' Greta ran a finger around the edge of her cup. 'This is awkward, Bev. perhaps I shouldn't have come.'

'Well, you're here now, so say what you have to say.'

Greta blanched. She'd heard about Bev's bluntness, but this was the first time she'd experienced it herself. 'It's… she stammered, '… Jo… she only came back home recently having been hurt by a relationship that went wrong in London, and…' She bit her lip. Bev didn't need to know the details, about the miscarriage. 'She arrived home yesterday looking so happy, I… I don't want her to be hurt again.'

'And you think…? I'm sure Bryan would never hurt her… not knowingly, anyway. As you've probably heard, the grapevine being what it is, Bryan and I only found each other recently. I'm still getting to know him, but I do know he's a gentle, caring son and father, one who recently lost the wife he adored. *If*… and I do say *if*… anyone is going to be hurt, it will be him. But don't you think you may be worrying needlessly? One weekend… and she is his daughter's teacher.'

Greta swallowed, suddenly embarrassed. Had she been projecting her own past onto Jo? 'You may be right. I just wanted some reassurance. I didn't mean to insult your son.'

Bev suddenly smiled, her whole face lighting up. 'You don't know how wonderful it makes me feel to hear the words, "your son". For so long, I thought he had died… but you don't need to hear my story. I'm sorry your daughter has suffered. I guess we all have at some time or other. But, let me reassure you, I'm sure Bryan would never do anything to hurt her.'

'Thanks.' Greta exhaled. She had heard something about Bev's story, but the other woman was a very private person and the actual details had never been revealed. She had learned more in the past few minutes than the gossipmongers were aware of.

'I haven't met your daughter,' Bev continued, 'but I look forward to it. Mia talks a lot about her new teacher. I'm glad Bryan is making more friends,' she said. 'He was pretty much a loner when he arrived in Bellbird Bay. Then he met up with Will and Ailsa's sons and got caught up in training for the triathlon. It seemed to unlock some of the sorrow he was carrying. Maybe meeting your daughter will prove to be the next step in his recovery.'

'Thanks,' Greta said again, surprised to think Jo might be able to play a part in Bryan's healing process. 'I'm sorry. I was only thinking of my daughter. I didn't consider your son's situation.'

'There are always two sides,' Bev said. 'I'm sorry, I need to get back to work. It's been good to talk with you. I'm not sure why our paths have never crossed more in the past. Feel free to contact me anytime.'

After Bev left, Greta, realising her coffee had gone cold, ordered another along with a brownie. While she was waiting for them to arrive, she noticed an older woman arrive on a green bicycle and unload several boxes from a large basket attached to its rear. The woman called out, 'Sorry I'm late. I got held up.'

As Greta watched, a dark-haired woman, who Greta knew to be Cleo, the manager of the café, came out to help her carry the boxes into the kitchen. Greta recognised the older woman. Ruby Sullivan was well-known locally for her delicious cakes and also for her strangely accurate predictions. Greta wondered what she'd predict for her.

She didn't have to wonder for long. When Ruby reappeared, she fixed Greta with her eyes. 'You worry too much,' she said. 'Things will work out. It may not be all plain sailing but there's always a second chance for those who believe.' Then she wheeled her bicycle out of the café and was gone, leaving Greta staring after her in surprise.

Twenty-two

Leo gazed down at Sydney harbour, one hand clasping his morning coffee, the other grasping the balcony rail. It felt strange to be back in the city again. Despite only having been gone for a short time, he found he missed the peace of Bellbird Bay.

He'd contacted Ken when he arrived the previous evening and arranged to meet with both him and Roy this morning before seeing Roslyn Portelli. Hopefully, they'd be able to tell him more about her and help work out a plan of how to proceed. One thing Leo was sure about was that he wanted the Bellbird Bay hotel more than he'd wanted any of the others he'd purchased over the years. He hadn't stopped to consider why that was – if it was due to Greta, to the memories of the summer spent there, or to the way Bellbird Bay itself had managed to get under his skin. He only knew he wouldn't rest till the purchase was completed.

He turned from the sight of the large expanse of water filled with vessels of every description, from the Sydney Harbour bridge rising majestically in the distance, and sighed, the image of Greta as he'd last seen her floating behind his eyes.

Whatever he'd anticipated when he saw the hotel for sale, he knew now it was the memory of Greta which had driven him to investigate it for himself, rather than sending one of his many minions to do the groundwork. And now he'd met her again, he couldn't wait to return. For the first time in over thirty years, the excitement he felt about the future was due to a person rather than a block of concrete.

*

The meeting with Ken and Roy produced little new information. It appeared the relationship between this Roslyn Portelli and Milton Harris, the owner of the hotel in question, was fairly new, so there was no real indication of why she had been granted power of attorney. At Leo's request, Roy had done some digging and reported the woman had recently undergone surgery, had been married several times, had lived in various parts of the world and, interestingly, her first husband was a retired architect who now lived in Bellbird Bay.

None of this explained why Harris wasn't handling the purchase himself, or why he hadn't instructed his solicitor to do so on his behalf.

It was early afternoon when Leo arrived at the café which Roslyn had nominated. Located close to the harbour in the northern suburb of Waverton, it wasn't one with which Leo was familiar. It was easy to find a parking spot, since several groups who had clearly been there for lunch, were now leaving. He entered the open courtyard and looked around.

A woman around his age was seated at a table in one corner. It must be her. As he approached, he could see her hair was a brassy shade of blonde, she was expensively dressed – he'd learned this from Zoe – and was wearing more makeup than was customary in the middle of the day. As he came closer, he could see it was designed to disguise her raddled appearance and wondered if the hair was a wig. This was a woman who had suffered. Leo recalled Roy's comment regarding recent surgery and assumed it had been serious.

'Leo Carlson,' she said in a coy voice which was at odds with her appearance. She stretched out her hand.

'Ms Portelli.' Leo shook her hand which was soft to the touch.

'Call me Ros,' she purred.

'You wanted to see me regarding the purchase of the hotel in Bellbird Bay, Ros.' Leo took a seat, feeling awkward. He wasn't accustomed to doing business in cafés and there was something about the woman that made him feel uncomfortable. He wished he'd insisted Roy or Ken accompany him.

'Why don't we have coffee first? It's some time since I enjoyed the company of an attractive man.'

Leo drew a hand round the inside of his collar, glad he'd dressed formally for the meeting, unsure how to react.

Ros waved a hand at the young waiter and ordered two coffees, then she gazed intently at Leo. 'So, you're the famous Leo Carlson Milton told me about. I expected someone older,' she chuckled.

For a brief moment, Leo caught a glimpse of the pretty young woman she must once have been, then reality set in. He thought about her relationship with Harris, about the ex-husband living in Bellbird Bay and wondered if there was a connection.

'Do you mind?' She took out a cigarette case.

Leo did but forbore to say.

'I really shouldn't,' she said, lighting up and blowing smoke in Leo's face, 'but life would be pretty boring if we always did the right thing, wouldn't it?' She glanced at him from lowered eyes.

It took all Leo's willpower to remain there. He just wanted to get this over and leave. He wondered how soon they could get down to business.

By the time their coffee arrived, he'd had enough. 'About the purchase of the hotel,' he said. 'It's my understanding Mr Harris has granted you power of attorney regarding this purchase.'

'Milt's a darling,' she said, taking another draw on her cigarette, smirking when Leo coughed. 'Since at the moment, he's not in a position to meet with you himself, he suggested I do so on his behalf. I think he got the idea I might be able to persuade you to make a better deal.' She smiled coyly again.

'It's more customary for our respective solicitors to handle these matters,' Leo couldn't help saying.

'But isn't this much pleasanter?'

Leo squirmed. This encounter was not what he'd expected. 'I just want to get things settled,' he said. 'Harris has a hotel to sell. I'm interested in buying it. I'm prepared to pay the asking price, to sign the contract immediately. My solicitor has a copy.'

'Oh!' Ros's lips formed a round O. 'And here am I thinking you might want to take pity on a poor woman. It's been lonely in Milt's harbourfront apartment since he was locked up.' She pouted, not a good look on someone who'd never see fifty again.

Leo had had enough. He hadn't made the trip from Bellbird Bay to Sydney to be flirted with by this woman who seemed to think she was irresistible to men. Perhaps she had been once. Maybe, even now, there were some men who'd fall prey to her charm. But he wasn't one of them.

'I think we're done here,' he said. 'You can tell Harris he has a sale. If he wants to negotiate further, his solicitor can contact mine.' He drained his cup and left.

*

It was a relief to Leo to board the plane which would take him back to Bellbird Bay. In a call to Ken, he'd given a brief outline of his meeting with Ros, omitting the thinly veiled invitation, and in another to Roy had instructed the company solicitor to proceed with the sale under the terms of the existing contract. He was done playing games. He wondered if Harris knew what his lady friend was up to. Roslyn Portelli seemed to be one of those women who needed to have a man in her life. He'd met a few like her on his travels. As a wealthy hotelier, some saw him as fair game. But few were quite as blatant as she'd been on such a brief acquaintance.

Leo couldn't wait to return to the peace of Bellbird Bay, to see Greta again. The meeting with Roslyn Portelli had left a bad taste in his mouth, reinforcing the realisation of how much it meant to him to have reconnected with his first love. It was as if he'd been waiting all his life to be reunited with her. He hoped she felt the same but was aware he wasn't the only man in her life. There was her ex, and Mick Roberts seemed to believe he had a claim on her.

Bellbird Bay welcomed Leo as he stepped out of the plane into the cool evening air. A flock of black cockatoos flew overhead squawking. He found himself smiling. It was good to be back.

Back in his hotel room, Leo ordered a plate of sandwiches to be brought to his room and opened one of the miniature bottles of scotch from the fridge. A call from Roy confirmed the sale was proceeding; Roslyn Portelli had agreed to sign the contract, only wanting to consult with Harris again first. Leo gave a sigh of relief. He'd been afraid his refusal to succumb to her advances might have scuppered the deal. Unwilling to make another trip to Sydney, he arranged for the contract to be couriered to him for his signature.

Now the only thing he wanted was to hear Greta's voice, to make arrangements to see her again. He picked up his phone and pressed the number which was now on his speed dial, drumming his fingers on the bedside table as he waited for her to answer.

Twenty-three

Greta hadn't been able to stop thinking about Leo all day, wondering what had taken him to Sydney and if he really meant to return. She couldn't help remembering the last time he'd left, the promises he'd made then. What if the business he mentioned was just an excuse? His life was in Sydney, not here in Bellbird Bay. Maybe he'd decide not to buy the hotel and there would be no reason for him to return.

After torturing herself with these thoughts all day, it was a relief when Jo arrived home with the suggestion they go out for dinner.

When they walked into the surf club, the first person Greta saw was Bev, then she realised Jo was staring at Bev's companion. It was Bryan, and holding his hand, was the small girl Greta had seen on the beach.

'It's Miss Roberts,' Mia yelled. 'Look, Daddy!'

Bryan turned, his eyes lighting up at the sight of Jo.

'Hello, Greta,' Bev said. 'Fancy bumping into you. Twice in the one day.'

Jo gave her mother an odd look.

'Hi, Bev.'

Just then an older version of Bryan appeared. 'I've managed to snag a table out on the deck,' he said. Then he hesitated, staring at Greta and Jo.

'Iain this is Greta, a friend of mine,' Bev said, 'and her daughter who's...'

'A friend of *mine*,' Bryan said with a grin.

'And *my* teacher, Grandad,' Mia said proudly.

'Iain is Bryan's dad,' Bev said.

Greta had already worked that out, feeling embarrassed now about her visit to the garden centre earlier in the day. But Bev appeared to take it in her stride.

'Why don't you join us for dinner?' Bryan asked. 'Dad? Bev?'

'Of course,' Iain said.

'And remember you can call me Jo outside school,' Jo said to a delighted Mia, who had dropped her dad's hand and taken hers.

The dinner went smoothly. Both Bev and Iain proved to be excellent company, and Greta was able to see Jo and Bryan together. He certainly seemed genuine, and Mia was a darling and clearly very fond of Jo. Greta began to relax, but she still had a niggling doubt that Bryan was still grieving and wasn't ready for a new relationship. Was Jo? Greta looked across the table at her daughter laughing at something Bryan had said and tried to dismiss her concern.

By the end of the meal, Greta felt she had found a new friend in Bev. She was surprised they hadn't connected before now. But, she reasoned, Bev had been above her at school and always part of the group she strived unsuccessfully to be part of. It was different now they were both older; the age gap didn't seem to matter.

Iain was an interesting man, too. During their conversation, she'd learned he'd been part of an architectural practice in Sydney before moving to Bellbird Bay with Bryan and Mia in an attempt to help them recover from their loss. Iain and Bev made a good couple and appeared to be very happy together. Seeing their affectionate glances, the way their hands touched, made Greta think of Leo, of the way his lips had lingered on hers. She wondered where he was now, what he was doing, and when – if ever – she'd hear from him again.

*

'Wasn't it great – to meet Bryan like that?' Jo asked when they reached home. 'His parents seem lovely, too.' She paused. 'But what did Bev mean about seeing you twice today? I didn't think you two were friends. Is she another of your book club ladies?'

'No.' Greta had hoped Jo hadn't heard Bev's words. She took a breath. 'I went to the garden centre this morning... to see her.'

'You did what? Why?'

'Sit down, sweetheart.' Greta pulled Jo down beside her on the sofa. 'I wanted... needed to be sure of Bryan. I know he recently lost his wife and must still be grieving. It may be too soon for him to form another relationship. I wanted to talk with Bev, to... I just don't want to see you hurt again. You're still my little girl and...'

'Mother! I'm tougher than I look. I've lived on my own for years. I can take care of myself. I don't need looking after.'

Greta was surprised to see the resolve in Jo's expression. She kept forgetting she was an adult, not the vulnerable teenager Greta had fought to protect from the trauma of losing her father. Though to give him his due, Mick had never abandoned his daughter.

Jo hadn't finished. 'I like Bryan... and I think he likes me. It can't have escaped your notice that I'm grieving too, grieving for the child I lost. Maybe we can even help each other. Have you thought of that? And there's Mia.' Her voice softened.

'I'm sorry, honey. You're right. I do need to remind myself you're all grown up, but to me you'll always be my baby. You'll understand when you...' Her voice trailed away remembering the child Jo had lost, the grandchild she'd never have.

How she'd envied Bev tonight, watching her with Mia. The little girl was a delight, exactly the sort of grandchild Greta had imagined having if... She shook her head. There was no sense in tormenting herself with dreams of what might have been. 'You're right,' she said. 'Mia is delightful. Will you be seeing Bryan again?' She tried to sound upbeat.

'Probably. I told him about Dad's whale watching cruises and he thinks Mia would like to go on one. I'm going to talk to Dad about it.'

'Oh!' So Mick would get to meet Bryan, too. Maybe she should talk with him about it, get his opinion. She might sometimes doubt Mick's motives, disapprove of his actions, but she knew he loved Jo as much as she did – and Jo would sometimes listen to her dad's opinion and take his advice. 'That's a good idea. I'm sure Mia would love it.'

Jo wandered off to bed, leaving Greta sitting alone staring into space. She was startled when her phone rang, a wave of relief swamping her when she saw Leo's number.

'Hello?' she said, her stomach churning with excitement. Was he back in Bellbird Bay?

'Greta. I just got back. I can't wait to see you again.'

Twenty-four

It was five days since Leo's phone call and, although they had yet to meet again, he had texted her on every one of them. For Greta, it felt like being eighteen again and she had to keep reminding herself not to become complacent. Bellbird Bay was only a temporary stopping place for Leo, a hiccup in his otherwise busy life, regardless of how exhilarating his texts might be.

But she couldn't stifle the anticipation she felt at the prospect of seeing him again, of having dinner at *The Beach House*, Bellbird Bay's top restaurant. She dressed carefully in a royal blue wool mid-length dress with long sleeves and a high neckline. It was from her latest delivery, more conservative than her usual selections, and she'd brought it home even before Leo's invitation, knowing how well it would suit her.

'You're looking great, Mum,' Jo said, when she walked into the living room, where her daughter was rifling through a bundle of old photographs. 'Wish it was Dad you were having dinner with, though. Look at this one.' She held up a photo of the three of them which had been taken when Jo was twelve. In it, she and Mick had their arms around each other and were grinning at the camera; Jo was standing in front of them holding a ginger cat. 'Remember Ginger?' she said. 'I loved that cat.'

'What are you doing with these old photos?'

'Dad asked me to look out one he wanted.'

'You're having dinner with him tonight.' Greta remembered.

'It's tomorrow we're going out with him whale watching. Mia is really excited about it.'

From the expression on Jo's face, she was excited about it, too. And Greta was sure it wasn't the prospect of seeing whales that put the glow there. 'I don't expect I'll be late,' she said, hearing Leo's car pull up.

'No worries. I plan to stay over at Dad's. I'll go straight out on the boat tomorrow, so I'll see you when you get home from work.'

She still needed to talk with Mick about Jo seeing Bryan. She'd put off contacting him, worried about giving him the impression she'd changed her mind about his suggestion they get back together. But it was something she needed to do. 'Tell your dad I'll be in touch,' she said, to see a glint of pleasure in Jo's eyes.

Once in Leo's car, being whisked off to dinner, Greta was relieved to be able to forget about Jo and Bryan, and Mick, and concentrate on her companion who was looking even more sexy than she remembered. She relaxed into the leather upholstery of the BMW Leo had rented for his stay in Bellbird Bay and allowed her mind to wander. It was almost a surprise when they reached their destination.

As Leo helped Greta out of the car, she looked up at the restaurant's imposing wood and glass structure. This would be the first time Greta had eaten here, though she had heard lots of reports about the amazing view and the delicious food. It was situated on an outcrop of land making it appear as if it stood on top of the ocean. Tonight, the setting sun's rays glinted on the tall glass windows making them seem like jewels. A flock of rosellas screeched their way across the sky, the brilliant colours of their wings adding a touch of magic to the scene.

Inside, the restaurant was just as spectacular as it appeared from the outside. They were shown to a table which overlooked the ocean.

'Not bad for a small town like this,' Leo said. 'It rivals anywhere I've been before, either in Australia or overseas. Have you eaten here often?'

'This is my first time. I've heard the food is good.'

'With a view like this, they could get away with anything.' Leo gestured to the waves which looked as if they were lapping at the foot of the restaurant's windows.

'You're looking very beautiful tonight,' he said, turning away from the view to focus on Greta.

She blushed and looked down at the white linen tablecloth. Then, raising her eyes asked, 'Did your business go okay?'

They were interrupted by the arrival of a waitress with menus. With a glance at Greta for approval, Leo ordered a bottle of champagne before replying to Greta's question.

'It did. I'm able to finalise the hotel purchase. You're looking at the new owner of Harris's hotel. It could have been awkward.' He rubbed his chin. 'The guy has given power of attorney to his lady friend. Seems she has an ex living here, too… a former architect.'

Greta's eyes widened. 'I think I may have met him. Iain Grant.'

Leo raised his eyebrows. 'What's he like?'

'He seems nice. He and Bev Cooper – she owns the garden centre – are together, and Jo is friends with Bryan, his son.'

Leo's eyebrows raised further. 'Roslyn didn't say anything about a son.'

'It's a bit complicated. I don't know the whole story. Iain and his son and granddaughter arrived in Bellbird Bay last year when the son's wife died. Then it came out that Bryan is Bev's long-lost son. I don't know how the woman you met fits into the picture.'

'Hmm. Well, it sounds like they are very different from Roslyn Portelli. She… No, enough said.' His lips tightened. 'Anyway, we're not here to talk about them or my business.' He picked up his menu. 'What would you like to eat?'

After studying the menu, they decided to share the seafood platter. The champagne arrived, and Leo raised his glass. 'To us, to the renewal of our friendship, to keeping promises.'

Greta raised her glass to meet his. It was a good toast, but she wondered what promise he intended to keep this time. She hadn't forgotten how he'd abandoned her before, and even though he'd apologised and explained the reason, the memory still had the power to hurt her.

But tonight, she decided to forget the hurt, to remember the happy times they'd spent together and to hope this time would be different. She couldn't dismiss the knowledge that these days his life was that of a jet-setting hotelier while her future was tied to Bellbird Bay but was determined to enjoy his company while she could and try to ignore the fact that he'd be bound to leave again.

When they left the restaurant, a cool breeze was blowing making Greta shiver. Leo threw an arm around her shoulders and pulled her towards him, sending shivers of a different sort down her spine.

'Better?' he asked.

Greta nodded.

Neither spoke much on the way back. Greta was conscious of the empty house that awaited them, of Jo spending the night with Mick. When the car stopped outside her house, she turned to Leo and seeing the question in his eyes asked, 'Would you like to come in?'

'Your daughter?'

'Jo's staying with her dad tonight.' She realised this was tantamount to an invitation.

Once inside, Leo followed Greta into the kitchen. As she was filling the kettle for tea, he came up behind her and wrapped his arms around her waist. 'Forget the tea. I have a better idea,' he said, his voice thick with desire. Greta turned into his arms as his lips found hers.

It was as if the years fell away. But this time, they were more experienced in the ways of love and, instead of on a deserted beach or in the back of a car, they were alone in a house where there was a comfortable bed. Taking Leo's hand, Greta led him to the bedroom, glad she'd had the foresight to change the sheets and set a bowl of fragrant potpourri on the windowsill.

As they lay side by side afterwards, Greta realised there had been no time to worry about her middle-aged body, the ravages of having given birth. They had both been so eager to satisfy their appetite for each other, a craving as strong as it had been when they were younger. Now, she pulled the doona over her nakedness, only to have Leo turn it back.

'I love your body,' he said. 'I've thought about it so often over the years. I can't believe I've found you again.'

Greta snuggled into him and sighed with pleasure.

Twenty-five

It was over a week since Leo had made love to Greta for the first time in thirty-five years and he could barely believe how the years disappeared when they were together. Sure, they no longer had the bodies of teenagers, but what did it matter? The old spark was still there; the magic they made together hadn't disappeared... and now they were older, the urgency and secrecy were gone; they had time to enjoy each other in ways they never had in the past.

Since that first night, they'd met several times, mostly in his hotel suite where they could be sure they wouldn't be disturbed. But Greta had always insisted on returning home afterwards, refusing to stay the night, no matter how much he pleaded. It had been so wonderful, after their first night together, to wake up next morning to see her lying beside him, to inhale the scent of her – exactly as he remembered – and to have breakfast together.

Today was to be a big day for him. The contract for the hotel was finally going to arrive. There had been a few minor hitches, but yesterday he'd received the news from Roy that it was on its way. The courier should arrive this morning, and once his signature was on the document, the hotel would be his.

As he made his way out of the hotel, Leo greeted the staff members he passed with a smile, before walking to the esplanade for his regular breakfast at *The Bay Café* from where he could see Greta arrive at *Birds of a Feather*. He loved to get this early morning glimpse of her, to watch as she opened the door to her shop and disappeared inside.

Last night, after dinner in the hotel restaurant – he liked to check on the meals and service – they had retired early and watched a movie together before making love. Before she left, explaining as usual that she wanted to keep Jo in the dark about the intimate nature of their relationship, they'd arranged to meet for lunch. Leo couldn't wait to see her again, to tell her he was now the proud owner of the hotel. As he'd explained to Greta last night, all his properties were called *The Leonard* after him. It was a name he'd coined when he opened his first one and it was a tradition he'd continued, even though now it might appear somewhat egotistical. He couldn't wait to see the name emblazoned across the entrance of his hotel in Bellbird Bay.

Leo was tucking into the eggs benedict which had become his favourite breakfast dish when he became aware of a young couple stopping beside him. Looking up he saw Jo Roberts, accompanied by a young man with reddish fair hair. Before he could speak, a small girl ran up to join them, pulling on the man's hand. When she saw him looking at her, she stared at him curiously. 'Hello, Jo,' Leo said with a smile.

'Leo.' She turned to her companion. 'This is Leo Carlson. He knows my mother,' she said awkwardly. 'Leo, this is Bryan and Mia.'

'Hello Bryan and Mia.'

Bryan looked puzzled for a moment, then his face cleared. 'You're the guy who's buying the hotel Milton Harris owned, the one everyone's talking about.'

'Guilty.' Leo held up his hands as if in submission.

'Everyone was glad when he was convicted,' Bryan said bitterly. 'He tried to ruin *Pandanus Weddings*.'

It was Leo's turn to be puzzled, then the penny dropped. 'You're…' he began.

'Bryan Grant. Bev, who owns the garden centre where I work is my mother,' Bryan said. 'She set up *Pandanus Weddings* last year, no thanks to that Harris bloke. Now he's latched on to my other mother, the one who was married to Dad.'

'You… you're Roslyn Portelli's son?'

'How do you know her?'

'It's complex. Why don't the three of you join me? My treat. Were you planning to have breakfast here?'

Bryan and Jo looked at each other, Mia swinging on her dad's arm. 'If you're sure,' Bryan said, seemingly having received a silent communication from Jo.

'Can we have breakfast? I'm hungry,' Mia said, making the adults laugh and answering the question.

By the time they'd arranged the extra chairs, Bryan and Jo had been served with scrambled eggs and bacon and smashed avocado on toast respectively, and Mia was enjoying a plate of pancakes topped with strawberries, chocolate and maple syrup, Leo had missed seeing Greta arrive at her shop.

But it didn't seem to matter. He was delighted to have met Jo again. Even though he now knew she wasn't his daughter; she was Greta's and looked so like her mother, it was as if the years had dropped away.

'Your connection with Ros?' Bryan reminded Leo.

'Yes.' Leo took a drink of coffee – his second cup – while he worked out what to say. 'As you know, I came to Bellbird Bay to check out the possibility of buying the hotel which was owned by Milton Harris. When my legal guy came to check it out, knowing Harris was locked up, he discovered Roslyn Portelli – your mother...' he glanced at Bryan, '... had been granted power of attorney and she was the one we had to deal with.'

Bryan's forehead creased. 'I don't understand,' he said. 'I know they became friends when she was in hospital. She had cancer,' he explained, 'and I took Mia down to Sydney to see her. Harris was there... in the hospital. She was all over him. That was Mum... *is* Mum, I should say. Although I guess the cancer slowed her down some.'

Not a lot. Leo remembered how she had come on to him, how a lesser man might have succumbed to her undoubted charm.

'After that...' Bryan spread his hands, '... who knows?'

'You haven't been in touch with her?' Jo asked.

Bryan shook his head. 'We never did communicate much after she left, only when she wanted something. Dad and I...' he choked, '... we managed pretty well on our own. That's why it was so wonderful when I found Bev. I'd always known I was adopted. Mum and Dad adopted me soon after I was born. Bev is a much better mother... and grandmother...' he glanced down lovingly at Mia who was completely focussed on demolishing her pancakes, her mouth rimmed with chocolate, '... than Mum ever was.'

'That's so sad,' Jo said. This was clearly news to her.

'I'm sorry,' Leo said. He wondered how well Jo knew Bryan, if they were a couple. Mia seemed to be fond of her, he thought, recalling how the little girl had chosen to sit next to her and share her menu.

'It is what it is,' Bryan sighed. 'But how did you come to meet her? Surely the lawyers took care of everything?'

'There were a few hitches and Ros insisted on meeting me face to face to negotiate. I had to travel down to Sydney.'

'Sounds like Mum. She never misses a chance to meet a new man. I thought she was over all that, had settled on this Harris fellow. But I guess now he's locked up...'

'He must trust her a lot... to give her power of attorney over the sale of his hotel,' Jo said.

'She can be very charming... as I'm sure you discovered, Leo.' Bryan dragged a hand through his hair. 'I hope you weren't sucked in.'

'I figured her out pretty quickly. But you're right, she turned on the charm. Unfortunately for her, I was immune to her wiles. My interest lies elsewhere.'

Jo frowned, causing Leo to wonder which part of the conversation upset her. Was she concerned on Bryan's behalf – or did she disapprove of his friendship with her mother? She was such a lovely girl. How he wished she was his daughter... his and Greta's. He liked to imagine any child of theirs would have looked like her.

Having satisfied Bryan's curiosity – and found out more about Roslyn Portelli than he needed – the conversation became more general. It was as they were all leaving, that Jo said to Leo, 'I believe you know my dad, too.'

'Mick Roberts? We've met. Seems like a nice guy.'

'He is. The best. It wouldn't surprise me if he and Mum got back together. They're not like your parents seem to be, Bryan. My mum and dad have always been friends and now they're older and both on their own, it would make so much sense for them to join forces again.' She gave Leo an odd look. 'I suppose you'll be leaving again once the sale goes through?'

Jo's obvious antagonism, so unlike her manner when they first met, or even during breakfast, took Leo by surprise.

'I'm not sure about my plans,' he said in an attempt to mollify her.

'There will be a fair bit to do here to turn the place into part of the Leonard stable. After that…' He spread his hands much as Bryan had done earlier.

Jo seemed about to say more but was distracted by Mia pulling on her hand and whispering in her ear.

'Thanks for breakfast, Leo,' Bryan said, shaking his hand. 'It was good to meet you. I'm sure Dad would like to meet you, too. I think you'd have a lot in common. He's had a bit of involvement with hotels and such in his life as an architect, and I suspect he misses it.'

'No worries, Bryan. It was good to meet you, too, and I would be interested in meeting your dad.' It would be good to chat to the former architect about some of his plans for the hotel, maybe even get some fresh ideas.

Twenty-six

Greta was on cloud nine. Ever since the first evening she and Leo had gone to bed together, her life had taken on a new glow. She felt she was walking around with a smile on her face the whole time. Cass had noticed and begun making wild guesses as to the reason.

'It's got to be a man,' she said, when the pair met for lunch at the surf club. It was Monday. Greta had spent the morning catching up with housework. Leo was busy with some hotel business, and they had arranged to meet that evening for dinner at the surf club, which seemed to be becoming a home from home for him.

'Why is it always a man with you?' Greta asked.

'Well, it usually is, isn't it? So, who is he? It's not Mick, is it?'

Greta shook her head and gave a dismissive laugh.

Cass's eyes widened in delight. Is it Leo Carlson? Didn't you say you and he were…' she winked, '… years ago?'

Greta couldn't recall mentioning her old romance with Leo to Cass, only that she'd known him. Trust Cass to put two and two together and make five. 'It might be,' she said with a grin.

'Do tell.' Cass leant over the table, almost overturning her wine glass. 'Oops, sorry,' she said, righting it again.

'There's nothing to tell,' Greta lied, trying to control the thrill which always engulfed her when she thought about Leo.

'You're blushing!'

Greta put her hands to her cheeks, only to see Cass laugh and realise she'd given herself away. 'Okay, maybe I have been seeing Leo.

So what? We're both free agents. But there's no sense in you reading any more into it. He's only in town for as long as it takes to get the hotel up and running. Then he'll be off. It's what he does.' It was good to remind herself, too, lest she allow herself to become too involved. Who was she kidding? She was involved, hook, line and sinker. Just like before. The difference was that now she was older and wiser, she knew this wasn't for ever. It was only an episode, an episode which she intended to enjoy for as long as it lasted. She'd worry about the fallout when it happened.

'So, what do you hear about the hotel?'

This, at least, was comfortable ground for Greta. 'He's definitely buying it. I'm not sure if the contract is finalised yet. There seemed to be a few hitches.' She wrinkled her brow. 'But Leo is a man who gets what he wants.' She'd come to admire how the young boy she'd known – and loved – had turned into this wealthy entrepreneur who bought hotels like they were mere trifles. 'It'll become part of his international chain – a Leonard hotel.'

'He'll change the name?'

'He says all his hotels are called *The Leonard.*'

'Sounds a bit posh for Bellbird Bay.'

'Not really. Leo intends for it to be a family resort.'

'Then why not call it that? *The Leonard Family Resort?*'

'I'll suggest that to him. Now can we talk about something else?'

'Sure, but before we do. What's happening with Mick?'

'What do you mean?'

'You told me he wants the two of you to get back together. Where does he fit in with the handsome Leo Carlson?'

This time Greta knew she was blushing. She had been trying to forget Mick's declaration. 'Mick says a lot of things. He's all talk. Leo has met him, and they seemed to get on.' But although Greta was playing down Mick's desire for them to be a family again, she knew he was serious about it. He did seem to have turned over a new leaf. She hadn't heard any gossip about him with a woman for some time – and if there was anything, she'd have heard. The Bellbird Bay gossip mill was still alive and kicking.

'Mick's changed,' Cass said as if reading her mind. 'He seems to have settled down.'

'About time. He'll soon be sixty. Maybe he's discovered he's no longer the lothario he was in his youth.'

'He's still an attractive man,' Cass persisted.

'You're welcome to him,' Greta said, but the thought of Mick and Cass getting together sent a sliver of jealousy through her. What was she thinking? She should be pleased if her ex and her best friend got together,

'Not my type.' Cass dismissed the idea. 'But he'll make someone a good partner – or husband.'

'Enough! We didn't come to lunch to talk about my men friends, past or present. What's been happening in your life? You've been suspiciously quiet about it.'

'Nothing much. You seem to be having enough fun for both of us.' She picked up her wine glass and took a sip. 'How's Jo?'

'Good. She seems to have settled back in. She's enjoying teaching and appears to be slowly recovering from what happened to her in London.' Although she'd shared Jo's miscarriage and break up with Cass, to her credit, Cass hadn't mentioned it again. 'I am a bit worried about her though.'

'Oh?'

'She's formed a friendship – relationship – with the father of one of her pupils. Bryan was recently widowed, and I'm not sure it's such a good idea.'

'Bryan? Not Bev Cooper's son?'

Greta should have known Cass would immediately know who she was talking about. She nodded, then took a gulp of wine. Maybe this lunch hadn't been such a good idea.

Their meals arrived at that point. Greta refilled their wine glasses and the conversation stalled as they both tucked into the Caesar salads they'd ordered.

*

Talking with Cass reminded Greta she still hadn't shared her worry about Jo with Mick. Checking the time, she calculated she should be able to reach him before his afternoon cruise began. As she made her way to the harbour, Greta remembered the excitement with which Mick had set up his business. It was soon after their divorce, and she'd been pleased when he decided to break away from his dad and start out on his own. The timing was right, and he'd immediately made a success of the whale watching cruises. Even though they were seasonal, he'd managed to continue offering cruises throughout the year when there were no whales to be seen. His knowledge of the area and his cheery banter ensured the trips around the bay were popular with tourists.

Arriving at the harbour, she could see Mick on the deck of his boat. The passengers for his next trip had yet to arrive. She saw him wave as he caught sight of her and, by the time she reached the edge of the harbour, he had jumped down to meet her.

'Didn't expect to see you here,' he said. 'Is everything all right? Is Jo okay?'

'As far as I know, but it's Jo I want to talk with you about. I thought I might catch you around now.'

'I have an hour before the next lot arrive. Come aboard for a cuppa?'

Gingerly, Greta took his hand and climbed aboard with him. It was years since she'd been on any boat, never mind this one, but the familiar smells and sensations immediately returned, bringing back memories of days spent with Mick on his dad's fishing boat when they first met.

'Okay, what's up with Jo?' Mick asked.

They were seated in his tiny cabin with cups of the strong black tea Mick preferred. 'I may be worrying unnecessarily,' Greta began, then proceeded to tell Mick her worries.

'You're talking about the guy she came out with on the weekend – and his daughter?'

Of course, Mick had met Bryan and Mia. 'Yes, I'd forgotten they went on one of your cruises. What did you think?'

'Jo talked a bit about him when she stayed over. You're right in thinking she might be developing feelings for the pair. She seems fond of the little girl. But I don't think we need to worry too much. It was a pretty busy cruise, but from what I could see, the guy was more interested in making sure his daughter was enjoying herself and wasn't coming to any harm. He seems like a good dad. And the kid was clearly enjoying being with Jo. Looked like they were just good friends having a nice day out.'

'But you said she's developing feelings for him.'

'Feelings of friendship. She told me all about his wife dying, about how he was in a depression, how coming to Bellbird Bay helped him heal. I think they may be helping each other, Greta. Our girl has some healing to do, too.'

Greta felt a weight lift. 'You're right. I've probably been a fool. She keeps telling me I fuss too much. I know she's all grown up, but she'll always be our little girl.' A tear escaped and trickled down Greta's cheek before she could wipe it away.

'Come here.' Mick pulled her into his arms.

As Greta felt his firm body against her face, the old, familiar smell of him, a mixture of saltwater and oil from the boat, she knew it would be so easy to sink back into their old relationship. Mick was right about one thing. They still had a lot in common, not least of it their daughter. And Mick wasn't going to leave town and abandon her.

She pulled away. 'Thanks, Mick. I don't know what came over me. I didn't mean to sob all over you. I haven't changed my mind.'

'It's this Carlson guy, is it? He won't stay around, you know. Guys like him don't. He'll be off to buy up another hotel as soon as he's done here.'

A spurt of anger threatened to spoil the moment with Mick. How dare he pass judgment on Leo, a man he barely knew. But a tiny voice in the back of her mind told Greta Mick had only put her own fears into words.

Twenty-seven

It was a stroke of luck for Leo to meet Iain Grant only a few days after he'd decided he should have a chat with him. He'd just received a call from Roy to tell him the contract had been signed. He was now the owner of what was to become the latest Leonard hotel. He couldn't wait to tell Greta, glad they had arranged to have dinner at the surf club that evening.

Unable to settle to anything, he decided to pay another visit to the art gallery he'd first visited soon after his arrival in town. He remembered the water colours he'd seen there, along with Martin Cooper's photographs of the area, and wanted to pick up a few of each for the hotel foyer. It would be good for guests to be greeted by local scenes, and for the hotel to support local artists at the same time.

On this visit, he noticed the current exhibition featured a number of pen and ink drawings and, taking a closer look, he was able to identify many of the houses and buildings he'd walked past. They were good, more than good. He was just wondering if they were the work of another local, when the owner of the gallery emerged from a back room accompanied by a tall, erect man with cropped grey hair.

'Looks like we have another admirer of your work, Iain,' the owner, who on Leo's last visit had introduced himself as John Baldwin, said.

Leo turned sharply. Iain? Could the creator of the drawings he was admiring be the same Iain who was an architect and the father of Jo Roberts' Bryan? 'They're very good, brilliant,' he said to the man. 'An exact replica. I recognise most of these buildings.'

'Thanks. I'm Iain Grant.'

'Leo Carlson.'

The men shook hands, as John Baldwin discretely moved away.

'I know who you are,' Iain said.

'I suppose all of Bellbird Bay knows about me by now.' Leo chuckled. 'I think I know who you are, too. I met Bryan... your son?'

'That would be right. He mentioned meeting you.'

'I knew you were an architect, but didn't realise you were an artist, too.'

Iain shrugged. 'It keeps me off the streets now I'm retired. With Bryan working, and Mia – my granddaughter – at school, I had to find something to keep me occupied.'

'This is a bit of luck,' Leo said. 'I was hoping to run into you. If you've not completely hung up your architect's hat, I'd like to have a chat, run a few ideas I have for the hotel past you.'

'Always open to a chat. I'm free now. How about a coffee?'

Unable to believe his luck, Leo agreed and, promising the gallery owner he'd be returning to make a purchase, they walked out together.

Half an hour later, Leo was seated opposite Iain in *The Greedy Gecko* outlining his plans for the hotel. 'What do you think?' he asked, when he had made some rough sketches on several paper napkins. 'Is it feasible?'

'I'd have to see the place first, but it looks possible. I'd be happy to draw up plans for you.'

'Oh, I didn't mean... but, if you would, I'd be delighted.' Since meeting Bryan, Leo had googled Iain to discover he had been a partner in Connor Grant Architects and Urban Planners, a well-known and award-winning architectural practice in Sydney. It must have been a wrench for him to leave it to come here.

'What brought you to Bellbird Bay?' he asked, curious to know more about his companion.

'Family. My daughter-in-law was killed in an accident. It tore Bryan apart. I knew we had to do something to bring him out of his depression. Coming here has changed his life. Mine, too.' He chuckled again. 'But I won't bore you with the details. Suffice it to say, it was the best decision I've ever made.'

Leo would love to have asked more but decided to respect the other man's privacy. Perhaps Greta would be able to shed more light on it. It was enough Iain was willing to employ his talent to work on the plans he had for his hotel.

Leo shook Iain's hand again then they rose to go, but not before making arrangements to meet again at the hotel next day. The year was already half over, and he wanted to be ready for the influx of visitors that heralded summer. He had no time to lose.

*

The surf club was busy as usual, when Leo ushered Greta to the top of the stairs and into the restaurant. He hesitated when he saw Will Rankin standing at the bar with his partner, guessing Martin Cooper and his wife wouldn't be far away. He was right. Glancing around he caught sight of the photographer and his wife seated at a table out on the deck and with them… Leo narrowed his eyes to get a better look … was Iain Grant with a slim woman, her faded blonde hair tied loosely back. Of course, she must be Coop's sister, the woman who owned the garden centre.

Leo and Greta made their way to the bar, reaching it just as Will and Cleo left.

'That's Iain Grant sitting out there on the deck.' Greta nudged Leo. 'Bryan Grant's Dad. He's with Bev Cooper.'

'I know. We've met.'

Greta looked at him in surprise.

'Tell you later. We'll have a bottle of champagne,' he said to the barman.

'Champagne… are we celebrating?'

'We are,' Leo said with a grin, taking the bottle and the two glasses the barman handed him and heading for the deck where he chose a table some distance from the one where Will and Martin were now seated.

Once there, Leo opened the bottle and filled the two glasses, laughing as the foam spurted over the table 'To *The Leonard* in Bellbird Bay,' he said, raising his glass.

'Oh, congratulations, Leo. I'm so pleased for you. I know it was what you wanted.' Greta raised her glass to join his, but there was a cloud in her eyes.

'Something the matter?' he asked, only to see her shake her head.

'No, nothing. So, what comes next?'

'As I said, I met Iain Grant. It was completely by chance. I was in *The Bay Gallery* intending to choose some bits and pieces for the hotel foyer, and there he was. I didn't realise he was an artist, too. We got talking, and he's agreed to take a look at the hotel and draw up plans for the changes I'd like to make.'

Greta's face brightened. 'So, you'll be around for a bit longer?'

'Of course I will. I told you, didn't I? I want us to have the chance I threw away last time.'

'You did, but...' Greta twirled her glass, and Leo could see her biting her bottom lip.

'Let's drink to that,' he said in an attempt to reassure her, pleased when she raised her glass to meet his again, a smile on her face.

'Good. Now what will you have to eat?'

They had just ordered their meals – rump steak for Leo and pan-roasted Tasmanian salmon for Greta, both served with salad, when Leo, seeing Bryan Grant join the group at the other table, said, 'That's the guy your daughter is seeing, isn't it?'

Greta turned to see who he was talking about, then nodded. 'Jo says they're just friends, and Mick suggested that they're both grieving in different ways and might be able to help each other. I just worry she's getting too close to him... and his daughter.'

'Mick is probably right,' Leo said, irritated at the information she'd been talking to her ex. 'When I had breakfast with them on Saturday, they seemed like good friends... and the little girl, Mia, seems very fond of your daughter.'

'Yes.' Greta sighed. 'That's part of my problem. She's recently lost her mother and seems to have latched onto Jo. But Jo's her teacher and...' She bit her lip again.

'You feel there's something wrong with the relationship?'

'Not wrong exactly. I don't want to see her being hurt either.'

'I'm sure that won't happen.' Leo had no idea if it would but wanted to reassure Greta, to take away the crease on her brow, to see her smile again.

'You're probably right.' Greta sighed again, then smiled. 'Sorry, we're supposed to be celebrating your purchase of the hotel, not worrying about my daughter. Tell me about these renovations you plan.'

The rest of their meal was taken up by Leo explaining how he intended to transform the upmarket hotel Milton Harris had built into a family resort, more in keeping with the character of Bellbird Bay. As he'd done with Iain Grant, he covered several paper napkins with drawings to demonstrate what he was talking about.

'It looks wonderful,' Greta said, when he had finished describing the pools, playground and crèche areas, 'but why not call it *The Leonard Family Resort?*'

'Because…' Leo started to say that all his hotels were called *The Leonard*, that it was his trademark. Then it occurred to him that they were *his* hotels, and he could call them anything he wanted. He pulled on one ear. *The Leonard Family Resort*. He liked the sound of it. 'You know, that's not a bad idea. I'll take it on board.' And he'd run it past Ken and Roy next time they spoke.

The bottle of champagne had disappeared while they were eating and talking and, when they rose to leave, Leo knew he had drunk too much alcohol to drive.

As she almost tripped going down the stairs, Greta laughed. 'I think perhaps we both need something to sober us up before either of us gets behind a wheel. We can walk to my place. Why don't I make us both coffee?'

'If you're sure? We could take a cab.'

'I'm sure. It's a lovely night and the fresh air will do us good.'

As he threw an arm around Greta's shoulder, Leo looked up into the sky, the stars seeming brighter than ever before. He felt a burst of joy at the realisation this was the first time Greta had invited him home when her daughter would be there. Was this a step forward, a sign she was beginning to consider him a permanent fixture in her life?

Twenty-eight

Her senses dulled by the champagne, Greta hadn't considered Jo would be home. When she and Leo walked into the kitchen, Jo was sitting at the kitchen table. She looked up from her laptop. Her eyes widened. 'Good evening, Mum?' she asked, then, her eyes narrowing as they moved to Greta's companion, 'Hello, again, Leo.'

Greta flinched. She couldn't tell whether Jo was pleased or annoyed with her. What had possessed her to invite Leo back here? They should have taken a cab to the hotel as he suggested. Until now, although Jo knew she was seeing Leo, they had both been able to pretend it wasn't happening... that she wasn't sleeping with him. She knew she'd have to come clean eventually, but how did you share your sex life with your daughter?

'It was lovely, honey. We were celebrating Leo's purchase of the hotel.'

'So I see,' Jo said, as Greta stumbled against the table. 'Shall I make coffee?'

'I can...' But Greta collapsed onto a chair. 'Please.'

'Congratulations on the hotel,' Jo said to Leo, sending a glare in Greta's direction as she set about making coffee.

'Thanks.' Leo pulled out a chair and sat down beside Greta, who was now wishing she hadn't invited him. All she wanted to do was collapse into her bed – alone. She felt the beginning of a headache. How had they managed to demolish an entire bottle of champagne?

'We saw Bryan Grant at the club... with his dad and Bev Cooper.

They were sitting with Will Rankin and Martin Cooper and their partners,' Greta said in an attempt to sound normal.

'I don't know what you have against him,' Jo said, ignoring Leo's presence.

'I haven't. I like him. It's just…' Greta was too tired to argue and didn't want Leo to see her and Jo at odds.

'I think your mother is concerned about you,' Leo said.

Jo turned to face him. 'What would you know about my mother? You swan into town throwing your money around, wanting to pick up where you left off all those years ago, before Dad…'

'Before you were born. When I was a lot younger than you are now,' Greta reminded her.

'About that. How do you know…? How can you be so sure?' She peered at Leo as if she could read the answer in his face.

Leo reddened.

'I told you,' Greta said with a sigh. She didn't want to discuss Jo's paternity here, with Leo present.

'Not in detail. You only said *he*…' she looked pointedly at Leo, '… wasn't my father.'

'Not now, Jo.'

'I think I should probably leave.' Leo stood up. 'I'll call you, Greta. Bye, Jo. I'm sure you and your mum can sort this out. I like your mum a lot. I hope we can be friends.'

Too tired to do more than give Leo a wave, Greta watched him leave. Then she turned to her daughter. 'How could you? I told you Mick was your dad. Why couldn't you be satisfied with my word?'

'It's just… it all seems too pat. You and Leo were together, Dad appeared on the scene back from a gap year, then you suddenly discovered you were pregnant, Dad married you, and I arrived early. A bit of a coincidence.'

Greta could see Jo needed more information. 'Have you said this to your dad?'

Jo shifted uncomfortably in her chair, having given up on making coffee when Leo left and she'd joined Greta at the table. 'He said the same as you, but he would, wouldn't he? You're in cahoots.'

'Why would we both lie to you about something as important as this?'

'I don't know, but Bryan...'

'What does Bryan Grant have to do with it?'

'He was adopted. Oh, he always knew that. But last year he discovered Bev Cooper was his mother and she'd thought he died a few days after he was born. These things happen.'

So that was Bev Cooper's story. Greta filed it away to think about later. 'But you weren't adopted. No one thought you were dead.' Greta couldn't see the connection.

'No, but...' Jo seemed to be floundering for words. 'How do you know for sure?'

Greta sighed again. She could really do with that coffee. 'Do you remember when you were seven and had to go to hospital, when you needed a blood transfusion?'

'When Gran and Gramps came to stay? Yes.'

'Well, that's what put my mind at rest. Until then, I wasn't sure, to be honest. I thought it possible Leo was your father. But when they tested Mick and my blood for a match, they discovered you were type RHnull.'

'I knew that was my blood type, but...'

'Both parents need to have it. Both Mick and I are RHnull, too.'

'But what if Leo has that blood type, too?'

'Jo, fewer than one in six million people have it. The chances of Leo having it too are so improbable it's not worth considering.'

'Oh!' Jo's expression changed. 'But I just don't get why he's come back here to Bellbird Bay. It's not the sort of place he usually chooses for a Leonard Hotel.'

'I don't know either. Maybe the place holds good memories for him.' *Or maybe he hoped to meet me again.* Greta shivered. Could Leo have gone to all the trouble of purchasing a hotel in the hope of seeing her again and rekindling their romance? It was a heady thought and not one she was able to process in her present inebriated state.

'Hmm.'

'Anyway, I'm for bed. We can talk more in the morning.' Greta pushed herself up and made for the bedroom. Hopefully, by morning Jo would have forgotten her concerns, but Greta doubted it. Once her daughter latched onto something, it was difficult to shift her.

*

Greta awoke with a headache, reminding her she was getting too old to consume half a bottle of champagne. But it had been a great night… until they came home. The memory of her conversation with Jo made her wince. Had she been stewing about this all the time? At least now she must accept the fact Leo Carlson wasn't her father.

After a cool shower which managed to reduce the tiny hammers in her head, Greta swallowed a couple of Panadol. Then, dressed immaculately in a pair of black slacks and a tunic gaily patterned with a flower motif, her makeup perfectly applied, she made her way to the kitchen.

Jo was already there. 'Coffee's made,' she said, taking a bite of toast liberally spread with marmalade. 'I thought you might need it this morning.'

'Thanks.' Greta peered at Jo, trying to work out if she'd got over her spat of the night before.

'Sorry about last night, Mum, if I upset you. It was seeing the two of you together, looking so…' She waved a hand in the air. 'But I guess you're right. I'm glad Mick's my real dad.'

Greta gave a sigh of relief, only to be upset again by Jo's next words.

'I think it may be time I found my own place,' she said. 'I can't bludge off you for ever and now it looks like I'm going to stay in Bellbird Bay… I'll start looking around.'

'Oh!' Although Greta knew this day would come, it was still a shock. She resolved to focus on the positive aspect of Jo's decision. 'You intend to stay in Bellbird Bay? Is there a position opening up at the school?'

'There may be, but I can always find something else to do if it doesn't. Bryan says…'

Greta bit her lip to prevent her telling Jo she shouldn't base her decision on Bryan Grant. What did she know about their friendship? 'What does he say, honey?' she asked, pouring herself a coffee and dropping two slices of bread into the toaster.

'He changed his life by coming here, changed careers, too. And he says he's happier than he would have been staying in the city as a reporter. There's more to life than teaching.'

'But you love teaching.' Greta's toast popped up and she took it and her coffee to join Jo at the table. 'Wouldn't you miss it if you had to find something else?'

'Perhaps, but... I'm really beginning to enjoy being back here again, Mum, being able to see you and Dad regularly... and meeting Bryan and Mia. I plan to start surfing again when the weather gets warmer, and I might rejoin the surf lifesavers. I can always work with Nippers, even if I can't teach in school.'

'Seems you've been thinking about this for a while.'

'I've been talking with Bryan... and Mia started in Nippers last year. It got me thinking.'

Bryan Grant again. Greta tried to stifle her ongoing concern about the guy. It could be he was a good influence on Jo. And it seemed to be thanks to him that she was planning to stay around.

'It's a good idea, Jo. And maybe a position at the school will come up. Even if it does, you can still help with Nippers, too.'

'I know. Thanks for being so understanding, Mum.' Jo dropped a kiss on Greta's head as she rose to load her dishes into the dishwasher. 'I may be late home tonight. Don't wait up for me.'

Alone in the kitchen, Greta smiled to herself, her earlier anxiety forgotten. Jo was staying in Bellbird Bay. That was all that mattered.

Twenty-nine

Leo made his way back to the esplanade to pick up a cab, confused by Jo's obvious antagonism towards him, coupled with her questions about her paternity. He could understand her desire to see her mum and dad get back together – well, almost. They had been divorced for years, after all. But this, combined with her still wondering if he was her birth father, didn't make any sense, not to him anyway. But he had no children of his own, and it was a long time since he'd had anything to do with young women of Jo's age – apart from those at work, and that was a different scene altogether.

He thought back to the first time they'd met. Everything seemed fine then. She'd been friendly. Even when he had breakfast with her and Bryan – not to forget Mia – things had gone well. What had been different tonight? Was it the fact he had gone home with Greta? He realised now it might have been a mistake. But at the time it had seemed to be the sensible thing to do. Neither of them was in a fit state to drive. Damn the champagne! What had started out to be an evening of celebration had turned into a fiasco.

On the drive back to the hotel, Leo tried to make sense of the scene in Greta's kitchen, but the more he thought about it, the more he regretted having been the cause of what appeared to be a conflict between Greta and her daughter. Maybe they should cool it, give Jo time to become accustomed to the fact he and her mother were... what? How would he define their relationship? Lovers... yes. More than that? Leo knew that now he'd found Greta again he wanted to

135

remain part of her life. He hadn't been joking when he said he might stay around… in Bellbird Bay. He just had to figure out how he could do that and still run his hotel empire.

*

Everything looked better next morning and by the time he was sipping his coffee and enjoying breakfast at *The Bay Café* – three types of bread with two boiled eggs this morning – he had decided he and Greta needed to talk.

Once they'd cleared the air, he was convinced between them they could come up with a solution unless – the niggle at the back of his mind which had kept him awake half the night surfaced again – unless Greta still had feelings for Mick, or felt she owed it to Jo to make an effort to put her daughter and Mick before her own happiness. Or was this his arrogance talking – the belief Greta preferred him to Mick. He remembered the words of the old woman he'd met on the headland, her reference to his arrogance, her advice not to let it ignore what was in front of him. He wished now he'd asked her what she meant, but he'd been too stunned by her strange pronouncement, then she'd disappeared, leaving him to wonder if he'd dreamt the whole thing.

He was still pondering over how to approach Greta again, when she walked along the esplanade and, instead of heading straight for *Birds of a Feather*, she stopped at his table and slid into the seat opposite.

'I thought I'd catch you here,' she said, breathlessly. 'I don't need to open up just yet. I owe you an apology for Jo's behaviour last night. She was out of order.'

'Greta, how wonderful to see you.' He rose and gave her a kiss on the cheek, marvelling yet again at the softness of her skin – just as he'd remembered. 'Can I get you a coffee?'

'That would be lovely, thanks.' She sat down,

'A… cappuccino?' he raised an eyebrow at Greta, as a waiter appeared.

'Yes, please.'

'There was no need to apologise. She's your daughter. She has a right to be concerned about you. Perhaps it was too soon to have our relationship in her face. Maybe…'

'No, Leo.' Greta put a hand on his arm. 'She's not a child, not even a teenager who needs to be placated. She's a grown woman. She'll soon be thirty-five. She's had relationships of her own. She knows the score.'

'Maybe it's different for her to see her mother in one?'

Greta chuckled. 'You may be right. She probably can't remember what it was like when Mick and I were together. But she'll need to get used to it if...' Her expression turned doubtful.

'I don't intend to let you go this time.' Leo squeezed Greta's hand.

'I'm glad.' She spoke so quietly Leo could barely hear her.

Greta's coffee arrived, and Leo dropped her hand to allow her to pick up her cup. For a moment she stared into the hot beverage, then said, 'All that talk of her paternity, too. I'm sorry if it upset you. There was no need for her to bring it up again. I'd already told her...'

'You told me, too. How can you be so sure?'

Greta sighed. 'Both Mick and I are RHnull. Jo is, too. I presume you're not?'

'No,' Leo said regretfully. He was still sorry not to be Jo's father. 'I'm type O.'

'There you are.'

'You sorted it out with Jo?'

'She now believes me, if that's what you mean. I was still pretty upset when I went to bed, but she was in a better mood this morning and apologised.'

'Good.'

'She's also decided to move out.'

'Not because of me?' Leo said, shocked to think he might have caused a rift between Greta and her daughter.

'No, it seems to have been on her mind for some time. I suspect Bryan Grant has something to do with it. The main thing is, she's decided to stay in Bellbird Bay.'

'I'm glad for you. It's what you wanted, isn't it?'

'Yes, it is.' Greta smiled. 'She was gone for too long. If she moves out, it means...'

He took her hand again. 'We won't be in her face if we go back to your house... once she's moved out, that is.'

'My thoughts exactly. Now, I really must get over and open up or I'll have a line of customers at the door.'

'Will I see you tonight?' Leo grasped Greta's hand as she was leaving.

'Maybe not tonight. I need some time with Jo after… But Saturday?'

'Wonderful. Why don't we eat at the hotel, and I can show you what I plan to do there – much better than my bad drawings on table napkins. And keep Monday free. I know it's your day off. I have a surprise planned for us.'

Greta beamed. 'Sounds lovely, Leo. I love surprises. See you on Saturday.'

Leo watched her walk off, admiring her elegant figure as she made her way across the esplanade to *Birds of a Feather*. He sometimes had to pinch himself to confirm he really had met his Greta again, and she still cared for him.

Thirty

Greta was surprised when a couple of days later, one of the members of her book club walked into *Birds of a Feather*. Libby Walker didn't often patronise the boutique, though she had bought several outfits there when she first moved to Bellbird Bay.

'Lovely to see you, Libby. How can I help you today?'

'I'm not looking for anything to wear, although...' her gaze fell on the new outfits lying on the counter waiting to be priced and hung on the racks, '... I might be tempted by one of these.'

'They are lovely, aren't they,' Greta said, holding up a dusky pink dress with long sleeves and a high neckline, more conservative than many of her other garments. 'You'd look lovely in this one.'

'Mmm. I may just try it while I'm here. It would give Adam and me an excuse to go out to dinner – not that we need one.' She chuckled. 'No, the reason I'm here is I heard on the grapevine your daughter is looking for somewhere to stay.'

'Word gets around fast.' It was only two days since Jo had confided in Greta she planned to move out. But Bellbird Bay was like that. It was difficult to keep anything secret. Greta felt a sudden jolt. Did that apply to her and Leo, too? It probably did.

'Small town. But the thing is, Eddie, who lives next door to me and Adam, recently suffered a stroke. She's on the mend now but still not able to go back home, to live by herself. She's in a nursing home and is going to stay with her sister further up the coast for a bit.' Libby shook her head. 'I'm not sure if she'll ever be well enough to come back home. She's such a lovely person and has been a good neighbour to me.'

Greta was wondering what this had to do with her or Jo, when Libby got to the point.

'The thing is,' she said, 'she doesn't want to sell the house. She's still hoping to get back to it one day. In the meantime, she wants to rent it out, but only to someone she feels she can trust. It's fully furnished, so Jo wouldn't need to buy any furniture. What do you think?'

Greta thought this was all happening too fast, but she said, 'It sounds wonderful. I'm sure Jo will be thrilled. We've always admired those homes on the boardwalk. But won't the rent be a bit steep for her? She's only on a teaching salary and her position is temporary.'

'Not at all. Eddie doesn't need the money. She… her partner left her pretty well off.'

Greta recalled Eddie's partner passing away. Paula had belonged to their book club for a time before she became sick. 'So?'

'She only wants a peppercorn rent. It's more important she has someone who'll look after the place.'

'Jo will certainly do that. I'll tell her about it tonight, then… Who should she contact?'

'I've already spoken to Eddie about her. I have a key to the house. So, if Jo contacts me, I can show her round.'

'Thanks, Libby. I'll tell her. I'm sure she'll call you straight away.'

'Great. Now, I *will* try that dress.'

When Libby left, she was carrying a bag containing not only the dress, but a brightly patterned top she'd been unable to resist and a long scarf which she picked up as Greta was packing her other purchases into the bag.

It wasn't till the door closed behind Libby that Greta remembered. Bryan Grant also lived in one of those renovated shacks on the boardwalk with his dad and his daughter. If Jo moved there, they would practically be neighbours.

*

Greta waited until after dinner before telling Jo about the possibility of renting Eddie Armstrong's house. They had enjoyed the onion tart

Greta brought home from the bakery along with a glass of red wine. Greta was glad Jo seemed to have forgotten her hissy fit when her mother came home with Leo but was taking care not to mention him lest Jo have another meltdown.

'Libby Walker came into the shop today,' she began.

'Your friend from the book club? Shall I make us some tea?'

'Later. She wanted to tell me about a place you could rent.'

'How did she know?' Jo asked, initially looking startled. Then she relaxed. 'Of course, it's Bellbird Bay. How could I have forgotten? So, Mum, where is this place?'

'Next door to her, on the boardwalk. It's Eddie Armstrong's place. I don't know if you remember her?'

Jo shook her head, but her eyes lit up. 'On the boardwalk? One of those lovely, renovated, old beach shacks? It's where Bryan and Mia live.' Then her face fell. 'I could never afford a place like that. I was thinking perhaps a studio apartment or a one-bedder on a back street.'

'That's the thing. She says it's a peppercorn rent because Eddie wants to be sure she lets it to someone who'll take care of it, and she doesn't need the money. It sounds like a good deal.'

'Really? How do I...?'

'You should give Libby a call. I have her number.' She read it out from her phone while Jo entered it into hers.

'Thanks, Mum. It sounds perfect.' Jo looked at Greta again. 'And I really am sorry about the other night. Your sex life is really none of my business. I'll call Libby now.' She disappeared from the kitchen leaving Greta staring after her in surprise.

Since Jo seemed to have forgotten about her offer to make tea, Greta filled the kettle and took a box of teabags from the pantry, choosing peppermint today. She had just dropped one into a mug when an excited Jo returned.

'Oh, Mum, it sounds perfect. She has a key. She says I can see it tomorrow and if I like it, I can move in right away. Just think... a house on the boardwalk.'

Greta's heart dropped. Jo was going to move out. She'd be on her own again. And she couldn't stifle the slight hint of envy at the prospect of Jo moving into one of those shacks which were much sought after. She and Mick had often wished they could afford to live there, but it had been beyond their budget. She looked around her own kitchen and knew she had nothing to be envious of. She loved where she lived, the house she'd grown up in which she'd renovated when she and Jo moved in after her parents died.

'It does sound wonderful,' she said, 'but why the rush?'

Jo came over to Greta and gave her a hug. 'It's not that I don't love you, Mum, but I've been used to being independent. It's been great these past few weeks, being home, spending time with you again. But it's not who I am anymore. I need to make my own way, have my own place. You'll probably be glad to have this place to yourself again, too… without my clutter.' She gestured to her jacket hanging over the back of a chair, her laptop pushed to the side of the table, her briefcase leaning against the wall – and that was just in the kitchen.

'I've enjoyed having you here,' Greta said. 'But I understand you want your own place.'

'I called Bryan, too,' Jo said. 'He knows the house. We'll be practically neighbours. He's going to come to look at it with me tomorrow.'

'Oh!' Greta wished she was the one going to look at the house with Jo but of course she couldn't. She had a shop to open. 'Won't he be working?'

'No, he has weekends off… because of Mia. Maybe I can move in on Sunday. I don't have much; there are all my old books and maybe I'll need a desk. Libby said it's furnished but it'll depend what's there. I guess it might be a tad old-fashioned. Do you think Dad would help?'

'Why don't you wait to see what the place is like?' While it was good to see Jo excited, Greta worried she might be disappointed when she actually saw inside the house.

'Okay, but I can't wait.'

Suddenly tea didn't seem appropriate, and Jo poured them both another glass of wine before they moved into the living room and turned on the television.

But the rerun of *Line of Duty* failed to hold their interest and Jo soon drifted off to her room, muttering about checking out a few things on the internet, leaving Greta to contemplate how her life was about to change again.

Thirty-one

Leo had made arrangements to meet with Iain Grant at the hotel on Saturday morning. Impressed by what he had learned about the former architect, he was looking forward to seeing him again and to showing him around. The man was young to have retired. Leo wondered what had brought him to Bellbird Bay but was grateful to whatever had. It meant he could have access to Iain's expertise right here, without having to employ someone from the city.

He'd told the staff to expect him, too. The day before, after some consideration, he'd called them all together in the room Harris had designated as a conference room. There, he'd explained he was the new owner and about his plans for the future. At the sight of a few downcast expressions, he'd been quick to reassure them no one would lose their job, adding that they would be given leave on full pay during the renovations. At this, there was a loud cheer.

Leo still had to find a new manager, but decided to wait till closer to the completion of the work which he hoped would be finished before the summer tourist season, ready for a grand re-opening.

He whistled as he dressed in a pair of chinos and a long-sleeved denim shirt, pleased that in the more laid-back atmosphere here in Bellbird Bay he didn't need anything more formal. He felt good, looking forward both to the meeting with Iain Grant and to seeing Greta for dinner later. He'd missed her these past few days, and hoped she'd managed to sort things out with her daughter.

'Iain.' Leo shook Iain Grant's hand and led him into the office behind the reception desk. It was the one Harris had used and was more like a living area than an office, the desk dwarfed by a comfortable sofa with matching armchair, a low table and a window overlooking the well-appointed gardens.

'Not a bad place you have here,' Iain said, when Leo had settled him on the sofa with a cup of coffee from the Nespresso machine – one of his first additions to his new purchase.

Leo outlined his plans again, confident Iain understood what he was trying to achieve, then he stood up. 'Let me show you around, then you can tell me what you think, if I'm being too ambitious. As you'll see, the former owner had visions of grandeur. He seemed to want to establish the hotel as a place for wealthy city dwellers to relax. My vision is quite different. I want it to have a family focus. *The Leonard*, Bellbird Bay, will be in keeping with the community, a place for families to relax, activities for both adults and children, even provision for their animals – though I still have to work out that part of it.'

'Sounds interesting. I'm honoured to be involved. Of course I know of your hotel group – everyone in my line of work does. They are renowned for their design, their fixtures and fittings. This appears to be quite a departure from your usual format?' He raised an eyebrow.

'Yeah, I guess so.' Leo grinned. 'It's been suggested I call it *The Leonard Family Resort*.'

'Not a bad idea. But lead on. I'm keen to see the rest.'

'Good. Let's go.'

*

By the time they returned to Leo's office, Iain had taken a raft of photos and made lots of notes on his iPad.

'Well?' Leo asked. 'Am I expecting miracles, or can it be done?'

'It's an ambitious project but certainly doable,' Iain said. 'When were you thinking of starting?'

Leo exhaled, relieved at Iain's response. 'We still have a few guests, but no further bookings. Once they leave in a week's time, I plan to give the staff paid leave till the work is complete. I'll stay on, of course, but apart from me, the building will be empty.'

'Right.' If Iain was surprised at Leo's response, he didn't show it. 'I can get onto the plans right away and… unless you already have people in mind… I can source builders, landscapers etc. There's no reason why the outside work can't start right away – the tennis court, putt putt and children's playground. I assume the existing pool will stay?'

'Yes, but the smaller one I mentioned will need to be dug, along with the paddling pool for toddlers.' He felt a burst of excitement at the prospect of getting his project underway. It was something he experienced with each new project but somehow this one felt more important. It would be hard to cap it with whatever followed. Unexpectedly, a thought crossed his mind – *maybe it was time to slow down*. He immediately dismissed it. Slow down? What would he do without a new project, a new hotel, a new challenge? Leonard Holdings was his life. He could no more stop acquiring new hotels than stop breathing. But the thought didn't immediately disappear.

*

Leo was still buoyed up from his meeting with Iain, when he picked Greta up that evening. He could tell straight away she had something on her mind, but waited till they were seated in *The Firenze* and had placed their orders before asking, 'What's bothering you? Problems with Jo again?'

'Yes and no.' Greta took a sip of the chianti he'd ordered. Then she placed her glass on the table and clasped her hands. 'I told you she said she wanted to move out.'

Leo nodded.

'Well, she's found a place and plans to move in tomorrow.'

'Wow! That was quick.'

'Too quick.' Greta took another sip of wine. 'I thought I'd have at least a few weeks to get used to the idea.'

'It's not because of me, is it?' Leo didn't want to think he might be the cause of Jo wanting to leave home.

'No… at least I don't think so. No,' Greta repeated decisively. 'It's just a coincidence it happened so soon after you came home with me. I know she acted aggressively towards you the other night but… she seems cool with it now. This place just came up... from someone I know, actually. The owner has taken sick and wants to rent it out to someone she can trust. Jo went to look at it today and fell in love with it. It's one of those homes you've probably seen on the boardwalk, and it's only a few houses down from where Bryan Grant lives with his dad. That probably sweetened the deal,' she muttered almost to herself.

Deciding to ignore the last part of her remark, Leo latched onto the reference to Iain Grant. 'Speaking of Iain Grant, I met with him today, at the hotel.'

'Oh, you mentioned he was going to check out what you wanted to do. Was it a productive meeting?' To Leo's relief, Greta seemed happy to change the subject.

'Very. he's going to draw up plans and contact tradesmen. It looks like we can meet my summer deadline.'

'That's good.'

But Leo could tell Greta's attention wasn't on his renovation of the hotel. She was still focussed on her daughter.

'Have you seen where Jo is moving to?' he asked.

'Only from the outside. The house is next door to where a friend from my book club, Libby Walker, lives with her partner, Adam Holland. Eddie Armstrong has lived there for years. It's the most prized location in Bellbird Bay. Bev Cooper lives there, too, and Grace Winter and Ted Crawford.'

'Wait a minute. Did you say Adam Holland? I knew he lived in Bellbird Bay. I didn't realise you knew him.'

'It's really Libby I know, but I have met Adam several times. Let me guess... you're a fan.'

'I love all his books. I just bought the latest from *Bay Books*. I can't believe how many famous people live here.'

'Adam Holland and Martin Cooper... who else?'

'I guess that's it. But I was also blown away by Iain Grant's sketches and the pastels done by Ted Crawford. I never thought of Bellbird Bay as being home to such talent.'

'We're quite an artistic community. Grace writes books, too – for children. And there are a lot of other artistic types living here. Some grew up in the town and have returned, like Martin and Ted, some are newcomers like Grace, Adam and Iain. But we're all one big happy family.'

'So it seems.' Leo pushed a hand through his hair. Bellbird Bay continued to surprise him. He didn't know what he expected when he decided to investigate the hotel for sale, but this wasn't it. Besides being reunited with Greta, in this small coastal town he had found a place where people cared for each other, where there was a sense of community he'd never experienced before. 'What is it about this place?' he asked.

Greta chuckled, her earlier worries seemingly forgotten. 'Some say there's magic in the air, but apart from Ruby Sullivan, I think we make our own magic.'

'I don't believe in magic,' Leo heard himself say, trying to dispel the memory of the old woman, which refused to leave him. Had she been Ruby Sullivan?

'You don't have to believe in it for it to work.' Greta grinned.

'Enough!' Leo held up his hands. 'You do realise, when your daughter moves out, we won't have to skulk around anymore?'

'Is that what we've been doing – skulking?' Greta rolled the word around in her mouth giving it an erotic flavour. She laughed.

Leo was saved from replying by the arrival of their meal. Both had ordered the blackboard special which was *Gnocchi alla Bolognese* – slow-cooked beef Bolognese topped with partigiano, Reggiano cheese and pangrattato.

'Wow, this looks delicious,' Greta said as the waiter refilled their wine glasses.

'To us,' Leo said, raising his glass towards Greta.

After a slight hesitation, Greta raised her glass. 'To us,' she repeated.

With the arrival of their food, the conversation turned to Italian meals they had enjoyed which led to Leo talking about the Leonard hotels in Rome and in Venice.

'I've never been to either,' Greta admitted. 'Never been out of Australia.'

'But you had all those plans.' Leo remembered how they'd lain on the sand talking about all the places they'd visit. Greta's list had been longer than his, but he was the one who'd travelled the world while she remained here in Bellbird Bay.

'That was then. It was a pipe dream. When Jo was born, I knew she meant more to me than any travel. I've been content here... even after *she* chose to travel to the countries I only dreamt about.'

Leo wasn't convinced. Her dreams had been so vivid. But as he gazed across the table at the woman he'd never forgotten, he saw the look of contentment on her face. Maybe Greta had found what eluded him, a sense of being satisfied with what she had. He'd spent his life striving to achieve happiness, while she had found it right here in Bellbird Bay.

Thirty-two

Greta couldn't help but feel a frisson of excitement, albeit tempered with a hint of sadness, as she prepared to visit Jo in her new home. She was sorry she hadn't been able to help her move but was thrilled to be having dinner with her daughter and was looking forward to being shown around.

Mick would be there, too, having helped Jo move her few belongings from Greta's earlier in the day. When Greta asked about Bryan, Jo had shaken her head. 'I want my first meal to be a family dinner – just you and Dad.'

Worried this might be another attempt on Jo's part to push her and Mick together again, Greta almost refused, but curiosity and her pleasure in Jo's invitation won the day. It had meant refusing to see Leo that evening and his expression when he learned Mick would be present had been a surprise. How could he be jealous of her ex-husband, a man she hadn't lived with for over twenty years?

Jo was waiting at the door to greet her, a wide grin on her face.

'Come on in, Mum. This place is amazing. It's so much more modern than I expected.'

'So you said this morning.' At breakfast, Jo had enthused about Eddie's house, so delighted to have been offered the opportunity to rent it, even if it might only be for a short time.

Jo led Greta through the hallway and into a large living area, sparsely furnished in stark primary colours. There were a few cushions on the sofa but apart from them, the furniture was pale blond wood, perfectly suited to the coastal landscape outside. On one wall hung a large photograph of two women smiling at each other.

'It's all exactly what I'd have chosen for myself,' Jo said. Then, seeing Greta's eyes on the photograph, added, 'I guess that must be Eddie and…?'

'Her partner. Paula passed away a few years ago. It was so sad. She was a lovely woman. They both were. Eddie still is.' She stared at the photograph of the two happy women, a shiver running down her spine. Life could throw up so many unexpected incidents. You never knew what lay ahead. All the more reason to grasp happiness while you could. Was that what she was doing with Leo – grasping at happiness before he disappeared again?

'Mum?'

Startled, Greta forced herself back into the moment. 'Sorry, sweetie, I was miles away.'

'Dad's in the kitchen. Come through?'

'Sure.' Greta followed Jo through into the large kitchen which opened out onto a deck and faced the ocean. It was similar to Libby's house which Greta had visited several times, and which she could see from here – just over the hedge. The lights from Libby's kitchen were shining out across the boardwalk, mingling with the glow of the moon reflected on the water.

'Isn't it amazing?' Jo said, folding her arms and gazing out at the view. 'I have to keep pinching myself to make sure it's real, that I'm not dreaming, that I'm really living here.'

'It's beautiful, darling. You're very lucky.'

'Isn't she just? It's a lot better than we started out with.'

Greta hadn't noticed Mick standing there. He came forward to greet her with a kiss on both cheeks and a warm hug.

She felt shaken for a moment, as if she'd travelled back in time. Then everything returned to normal again.

'Good to see you, Greta,' Mick said.

'You, too, Mick. Looks like you got Jo settled in.'

'It didn't take long.' He glanced at Jo. 'We had some help.'

Greta gave Jo a puzzled look.

Jo blushed. 'Bryan and Mia dropped in to see how we were going. They brought lunch.'

'He seems a good lad.'

'He's not a lad, Dad.'

'He is to me, honey. And his daughter is a sweetheart.'

Greta bit her lip. Aching though she was to warn Jo about becoming too involved with the pair, she knew her daughter. She'd already made her views known and any further comments would only alienate Jo. 'What's for dinner?' she asked instead.

'Dad's going to barbecue some steaks. He brought them over earlier, and they've been marinating.' Jo threw a smile at Mick. 'It'll be just like old times.'

Greta stifled the temptation to grimace. It was a long time since they'd enjoyed a family barbecue. She was surprised Jo remembered. Maybe she didn't. Maybe it was all in her imagination.

'Eddie has a top-of-the-range barbie, but it'll take a bit to heat up. How about a glass of wine while we wait?' Mick suggested.

'Good idea.' Greta needed a glass of something to help rid her of the feeling she was being manipulated into something she had no intention of being party to.

'White or red, Mum?' Jo asked. 'I bought a few of both yesterday.'

'White, please.' Greta felt some of the tension leave her as she took a sip of the chilled chardonnay.

'How are you, Greta?' Mick asked, when Jo disappeared to fetch something from the other room. 'I haven't seen much of you lately.'

'I've been good, Mick. Busy.' Greta took another sip of wine.

Mick helped himself to a beer from the fridge and snapped it open, slurping up the liquid that spurted out of the can. 'Still seeing Leo Carlson?'

'What if I am?' Greta bridled. It was none of Mick's business who she was seeing, hadn't been for years. Just as she'd shown no interest in the women he went around with – she'd have been hard put to keep up with the string of women he'd kept company with over the years.

'I'm just concerned for you, Greta. Carlson's way out of your league these days. Maybe once upon a time you and he…' He let his voice trail off. 'But now he's up there with the likes of James Packer, Kerry Stokes, Gerry Harvey.'

'Hardly. He's a hotelier, not a multi-millionaire.' Or was he? Leo didn't parade his wealth, but he did own properties all over the world

– unless he owed a lot of money. Wasn't that what people like him did? They borrowed money to make money. She'd read that somewhere.

'Still, he's not like us.' Mick took a swallow of his beer and burped.

'It's good of you to be concerned, Mick,' Greta said more stiffly than she intended, 'but…'

'Mum! Dad! This is what I wanted to show you. I found it when I was packing my things.' Jo came bounding into the kitchen waving a photograph. 'I must have been about six when this was taken.'

Greta peered over Jo's shoulder at the photo showing the three of them standing beside a gas barbecue in the backyard of their old house.

'Wow, that takes me back.' Mick took the photo from Jo. 'Those were the days, weren't they, Greta?' He nudged her. 'I remember that day. Wasn't it the one…?'

'… where there was a leak in the valve and the flames rose up and set fire to the awning, and we had to call the fire brigade? It was.' How could Greta ever forget the embarrassment of being told there was a fire ban, and they had no business lighting a barbecue that day?

'Wow! Did it really? I don't remember that.' Jo wrinkled her forehead. 'Well, no chance of that happening tonight.'

'No,' Greta said.

Mick handed the photograph back to Jo. 'We were all so happy then,' he said with a sigh. 'What happened to us?'

Greta glared at him. He knew very well what happened… she became tired of finding lipstick on his shirts and handkerchiefs, of the sympathetic glances from other mothers at the school gate, the conversations abruptly curtailed when she appeared. 'We had some good times together,' she said smiling at Jo, 'but it's all in the past. We've all moved on. We are different people now.'

'But we don't have to be,' Mick said. 'Didn't someone once say *it's never too late and you're never too old?*'

Greta flinched at having one of her favourite sayings thrown back at her. It was never meant to refer to reuniting with a former husband.

'Mum? Dad?' Jo said again, staring from one to the other. 'I think the barbie might be ready. Shall I take the steaks out, Dad?'

'Good idea, Jo,' Greta said. *Anything to change this conversation. Had Mick really changed? Could a leopard change his spots? Was this all because Jo had come home, or had he been working up to it and only started talking about it because of Leo?*

Once out on the deck, the steaks sizzling on the barbecue, Greta felt better, able to put the conversation with Mick into perspective. Maybe she was becoming too jumpy, too quick to take offence.

Thirty-three

Greta awoke with a start. Her eyes flew open. She'd been dreaming, but it had been so real. She'd been lying on Dolphin Beach with Leo, both scantily clad, when Mick came running along the sand with a young Jo wearing the outfit she'd been wearing in the photo, and yelling they needed to leave as there was a fire.

Checking the time, she saw it was only three o'clock, but she was too awake to go back to sleep. Rising, she made her way to the kitchen and made herself a mug of hot chocolate before returning to bed. She'd read for a bit, drink her chocolate, then maybe manage another few hours' sleep.

When she awoke again a few hours later, Greta's eyes felt gritty, but the hot chocolate had ensured she fell back to sleep. It was now half-seven, time to get up. She was seeing Leo today and he'd promised her a surprise. After a shower which helped her feel more human, she dressed in a pair of jeans and topped them with a warm tunic in a tropical pattern, finishing off with a long scarf she'd brought home from the boutique. It was similar to the one Libby had bought, but this one was in a brilliant shade of blue which matched the pattern on Greta's top.

The house seemed so quiet without Jo. In the short time she'd been there, Greta had become accustomed to her presence, to the music she always seemed to like to have blaring away, and to her conversation over breakfast. She turned on the radio to break the silence then made coffee and toast, taking both out to the courtyard.

Relaxing to the sound of the pair of kookaburras who often visited at this time of the morning, cackling as they perched on the top of the fence, Greta checked her phone. She smiled at a text from Leo reminding her he'd be picking her up at nine and to dress casually and replied with a smiley emoji. There was one from Jo, too, to say she hoped she wasn't missing her too much and to reiterate how much she liked living at Eddie's. Greta sent a quick reply. Then she saw Mick's name. What did he want?

Sorry if I came on too strong at Jo's. I only want what's best for you. Can we meet up for coffee soon? Mx

Greta snorted. What's best for her, indeed. She knew he meant only if it included Mick Roberts. She didn't reply.

Finishing her coffee, Greta went back inside in time to hear the radio announcer mention something about an earthquake somewhere in Asia, buildings demolished and lives lost. Greta shivered at the thought of those poor people, glad Australia was free of such tragedies. It reminded her of her parents' deaths, and she stopped in her tracks, her eyes moistening at the memory, and the realisation that more families were suffering as she had. Then she forced herself to focus on the day ahead, as she carefully applied a light makeup, tidied her hair, and sprayed herself with her favourite perfume. She'd been wearing Calvin Klein's Obsession since she was eighteen – back then, she'd sneaked her mother's bottle from her dressing table – and it always reminded her of Leo. This morning, she felt a frisson of excitement as she breathed in its familiar fragrance. Mick's words about Leo came back to her. But he was wrong. He had to be. Leo wasn't the tycoon Mick painted him. It was unlike Mick to be jealous.

The radio was announcing the time was nine o'clock when Greta heard Leo's car pull up. A few seconds later, there was a knock at the door, and there he was, looking even more handsome than ever in a pair of neatly pressed jeans and a navy sweater, with the collar of a white shirt peeking out at the neck. As he pulled her into an embrace, Greta inhaled the aroma of soap and an aftershave with which she wasn't familiar, but which smelt expensive.

'Wow, you look lovely,' he murmured into her hair. 'Maybe we should just stay here.'

Greta felt her insides turn over, but before she could reply, Leo grinned. 'No, I have our day planned. I think you'll like what I have in mind.'

As they set off, Leo pressed a button which opened the sunroof. Greta enjoyed the unexpected breeze whipping her hair around, laughing as they drove out of town. This wasn't a cheap car, not like her own small Mazda or even Mick's Toyota Landcruiser. Maybe Mick had a point, but she wouldn't think about it now. It was enough to enjoy the experience of being driven in this lovely car, sitting next to the man who'd stolen her heart, about to spend the day with him.

It didn't come as a surprise when their destination proved to be Dolphin Bay. Greta had housed a suspicion it was where they were headed. It had been their special place back then, the place where...

'Remember?' Leo asked turning to her with a smile.

Greta nodded, too overcome to speak.

Leo helped her out of the car, and they stood together, staring down at the pristine sand, his arm around her waist.

Looking down at the beach, Greta could almost believe they were still the two eighteen-year-olds who had stolen away to spend their days right here. Now, with Leo's arm around her, the memories came flooding back.

'I know a place,' Greta said, when Leo suggested they get away from the others who were engaged in horseplay on Bellbird Bay's main beach. She couldn't believe this hot guy from Sydney wanted to spend time with her, had chosen her out of all the other girls in the group.

She had always been on the outside of the surfing crowd despite belonging to the surf lifesavers and knowing them all from school and, although she'd pined after the heroes, Will Rankin and Martin Cooper, they didn't know she was alive. Only Mick had been friendly to her, and she'd been grateful to attract his notice, to at least be on the periphery of the group she admired. Then he'd gone off on his gap year and she'd been left out again.

Leo Carlson was one of a group of schoolies who'd arrived to spend the summer in Bellbird Bay and effortlessly became part of the crowd that surfed and partied the summer away. But, whereas the others in the group vied with the locals for the popular girls, Leo had chosen Greta, and she couldn't believe her luck.

'Shall we?' Leo's voice pulled Greta back to the present.

'Let's.'

Leo took Greta's hand and led her carefully down to the beach which was as deserted as she remembered. It looked different from when she had brought Jo here all those times as a child, and again recently. Today, it was as if the years had rolled back, and she and Leo were eighteen again… and in love for the first time.

'It was good… back then. We were two innocents,' he said, squeezing Greta's hand tightly.

'Not so innocent,' she chuckled, gazing up at him.

'No.' Leo chuckled, too. Then he pulled her into an embrace. 'I never forgot you… or this place. It's magical.'

Greta allowed herself to be caught up in the moment. If only they could stay here for ever like this, the only two people in the world on a deserted beach.

The moment passed, and they stood, gazing out at the ocean, Leo's arms around Greta's waist as she leant back against him, the only sound the gentle lapping of the waves and the cries of the seagulls.

'It hasn't changed,' Leo said. 'I was afraid it might have. There has been so much development, and for my sins, I've often been part of it.'

'It almost happened here a few years ago,' Greta said, 'but the community fought against it. Will Rankin and others managed to make a case against the developers, something to do with dugongs and seagrass, as I recall.'

'Wow! I'm glad. Dugongs… imagine?' He nuzzled Greta's neck. 'I wanted to come back here with you… to recapture… But…'

'We're not eighteen any longer.'

'Only in our minds.'

They both laughed, then, holding hands, began to walk along the hard packed sand at the water's edge.

They walked for some time, sometimes silent, sometimes recalling times gone by, stopping occasionally to kiss. Greta was in heaven. She wished the day would never end.

Suddenly, Leo stopped and checked his watch. 'We need to go.'

Startled, Greta felt a sense of disappointment. Her expression must have reflected her change of mood, as Leo said, 'I have another surprise for you.'

Back in the car, Greta found her anticipation building as they drove along the clifftop away from the town, only stopping when they reached a long, low building she wasn't familiar with. It was set right on the edge of the cliff and appeared to be a restaurant.

'It's new,' Leo said, answering her unspoken question. 'I heard about it and thought it would be the perfect spot for lunch.'

He was right. As soon as they entered the open-air restaurant and were shown to a table looking out onto the ocean, Greta knew this was indeed the perfect spot. From here, they had a view right down the coast and could see the township of Bellbird Bay in the distance.

As they toasted each other with the sparkling wine Leo ordered, Greta knew without a doubt she had found the love she'd thought lost for ever.

The restaurant was Italian, and she and Leo shared antipasti followed by plates of chilli prawns, linguini with garlic and tomatoes, and spaghetti with herbs and olive oil. They finished their meal with delicious servings of tiramisu accompanied by coffee served in blue rimmed, white mugs.

'That was superb,' Greta said. 'I don't think I want to eat again for a week.'

'It was good, wasn't it?' Leo smiled. 'Lived up to the reviews. I wonder if I can tempt the chef to Bellbird Bay.' He grinned. 'But now...'

'What else have you planned?' Greta couldn't imagine anything which could outdo the beach and the meal they had enjoyed.

Leo gazed at her, and in his eyes she saw a reflection of her own yearning. 'I understand you have an empty house,' he said.

Greta felt a wave of desire such as she hadn't experienced for years. Her tongue stuck to the roof of her mouth. She couldn't speak. Silently, she held out her hand, to have Leo grasp it tightly in his.

'Let's get out of here,' he said hoarsely.

Back at Greta's house, they barely made it through the door before they were in each other's arms. Then Leo picked Greta up and carried her to the bedroom where they wasted no time in releasing the passion which had been building up since they stood together on the beach.

Afterwards, they lay in each other's arms, spent, Leo's lips in Greta's hair. 'I love you, Greta. I've always loved you and I don't intend to leave you ever again.'

'I love you, too, Leo,' Greta said, hoping with all her heart that this time he meant it.

Thirty-four

Leo awoke to the aroma of coffee. He couldn't believe he'd slept for so long, or that he hadn't been aware of Greta rising. Yesterday, they'd made love all afternoon before raiding Greta's fridge and pantry to find cheese, biscuits and other snacks which they took back to bed. Then they had made love again until… until they fell asleep in each other's arms. Leo stretched before leaping out of bed, feeling good, rejuvenated, better than he'd felt in years.

After a quick shower, he dressed in the clothes he'd hurriedly tossed aside the day before and headed to the kitchen.

'Good morning.' Greta was standing by the stove, already dressed for work in one of the brightly patterned garments she favoured, looking good enough to eat. 'Breakfast? I'm making scrambled eggs. I thought you might be hungry after…' She blushed.

'Good morning, beautiful.' Leo took the wooden spoon from her hand and enfolded her in a warm hug. 'Breakfast? *All I need is the air that I breathe and to love you,*' he sang off-key, taking her in his arms and dancing her around the room.

'Leo, don't,' Greta said, but she was laughing.

'Okay, I give in.' He released her. 'Scrambled eggs sounds good, and I smell coffee.'

'Help yourself.' Greta picked up the wooden spoon again and gestured to the coffee machine.

Breakfast was almost over when Greta looked across the table at Leo and said, 'Did you mean it, Leo… what you said yesterday… about not leaving me again?' Her eyes were filled with hope and something else... doubt?

'Of course I did. I know I behaved badly in the past. I let you down. But that was then. I'm no longer that boy. I'm in a position to make my own decisions, and it's my decision to be with you. I promise you, Greta. I mean it.'

Greta's eyes glowed. She reached across the table to link her fingers in his. 'I'm glad. It's what I want, too.'

They sat like that for a few moments, then Greta unlinked her fingers. 'I'm sorry, Leo. I need to open my shop. Can you see yourself out... and...' She gave him a questioning look.

'I'll see you tonight. I can't wait.'

Greta smiled and kissed his cheek. 'Nor me.' She picked up her bag and headed out, leaving a trail of her distinctive perfume behind her.

Leo felt as if he was eighteen again, though he was sure he'd been too young to appreciate Greta properly when he *was* eighteen. He finished his coffee, stacked his dirty dishes in the dishwasher and left for the hotel, whistling as he went. He was full of the joys of life, sure he and Greta had a magnificent future together.

*

Leo's mood lasted till he reached his suite in the hotel and opened his phone – he had turned it off all the time he was with Greta not wanting to be disturbed by hotel business. There were a series of messages and missed calls from Ken.

Cursing silently, irritated his finance controller had seen fit to annoy him with so many attempts to contact him, Leo opened the latest of the messages to read, *Where are you, Leo? Have you seen the news?* Curious, Leo opened his iPad to check, and there in the breaking news was a report of an earthquake in the Philippines. He swallowed. *How could this have happened? How could he not have known?* While he was enjoying time with Greta there had been a devastating event and one of his hotels... He picked up his phone again.

'Ken, what the hell is happening?'

'Hell is right, Leo. It's a disaster. An earthquake of 6.1 magnitude. All the news outlets are reporting on it.'

Leo felt his heart thud in terror. 'The hotel in Manila? Our people?'

'We're still trying to find out. All communications are down. It looks bad.'

Leo's eyes went back to his iPad. On the screen, an ABC journalist was standing among the rubble, looking shocked. The camera panned to where a young boy was being rescued, carried out of the remains of what had once been an apartment building. The commentary continued to describe the devastation wrought by the quake and the subsequent aftershocks. It was difficult to recognise the city, to determine which part was being shown. Leo remembered when he was last there... at the opening of the magnificent building in the centre of the city. He could picture the brightly coloured frescos, the pride on the faces of the staff. He began to shake. He felt numb.

Ken was speaking again. 'I'll keep trying to contact Adan Garcia,' he said, referring to the manager of *The Leonard* in Manila, the young man who had been so proud to be offered the position and who was a brilliant manager, recently married to Carmela, a local artist. 'Also, I've been in touch with our Department of Foreign Affairs, but they seem to be in chaos, too. The phone lines were tied up for ages. I guess the entire Philippine community in Australia are looking for news. I've been trying to contact you.' There was a note of censure in Ken's voice.

Leo dragged a hand through his hair, overcome with guilt. While he had been enjoying himself, reliving his youth with Greta, this had been happening over five thousand kilometres away. 'What can we do to help?'

'At the moment, not a lot. From what I can make out, the army are sending in aid and supplies but there's no way for you or me to get there. I'll keep pushing and let you know if anything changes.'

'Good man. We need to go... *I* need to go, to be there for our people. If the hotel...' he swallowed, '... if the hotel is still standing, we need to have it set up as an evacuation centre. Can you...'

'I'm on it.'

'Thanks.'

Ending the call, Leo gazed bleakly around the room. The hotel suite which, only a few minutes ago, had seemed comfortable and pleasant, now only reminded him of the plight of all those affected by the quake. He switched on the television, flicking from channel to channel only to see the same footage on all of them. Finally, unable to watch any more reports of the devastation and miraculous rescues, he turned it off.

Unable to settle to anything, he paced up and down the room then, despite Ken's warnings, he opened up the Qantas app to try to book a flight to Manila. But his colleague had been correct. All flights to the Philippines had been cancelled till further notice. The same was the case for the neighbouring countries, no doubt due to the risk of further quakes or aftershocks.

He needed to talk to someone, but Greta would be busy in her shop. He needed to… Leo stood still, trying to work out what it was he wanted to do, before realising he needed something to keep his mind occupied, to help dismiss the images he'd seen on the television. He remembered the exhilaration he used to feel out in the surf, how the sense of freedom as he glided across the water forced everything else from his mind. Dragging a pair of board shorts from a drawer, he pulled them on, then, dressed in another pair of shorts and a tee-shirt and throwing a towel over his shoulder, he drove to the beach.

Once there, he was relieved to see Will Rankin's van in its usual position, a flag announcing it was *Bay Surf School and Board Hire.*

'Morning, mate. Don't usually see you down here.' Will grinned.

'No. Need to hire a board.' Leo wasn't in the mood for conversation, and Will seemed to sense it.

'No problem.' Will pulled a board from the van. 'I'm here if you want a yarn when you get back.'

'Thanks.' Leo paid for the board hire and, dropping his gear on the beach, headed into the ocean.

Once out there among the other surfers, sitting on the board waiting for a wave, Leo felt the sense of release he remembered. As the sun beat down on him, the spray of the sea on his face, the scent of the saltwater bringing back memories, he could almost forget the horrific images he'd seen earlier. Almost, but not entirely. They were imprinted on his brain.

'Have a good one, mate?' Will asked when Leo returned the board.

'Thanks, I did.' Leo pushed his dripping hair out of his eyes. 'It's been a while. I'd forgotten what it was like.'

'Nothing like a surf to blow away the cobwebs or… something bothering you?' Will asked.

'Yeah, it's...' Leo couldn't put his worries into words.

'Look, I'm about to take a break, go to the surf club for lunch. How about you join me, tell me what's the matter over a beer?'

Leo only hesitated for a moment. Maybe it would be good to share his concerns with Will. 'Thanks. Sounds good.'

Leo dressed as Will locked up his van, then the two made their way to the surf club.

Having ordered beers and taken them out to a table on the deck, Leo was trying to work out how to unburden himself to Will when Martin Cooper joined them.

'Did you see the news,' Martin said, before he sat down. 'The earthquake in the Philippines... hundreds dead, more missing.'

Leo felt his gut shrivel. It was worse than he'd thought, worse than the earlier reports.

Will's eyes filled with concern. 'You have a hotel there, don't you?' he said to Leo. 'No wonder you looked like death warmed up when you arrived on the beach. Have you had any word?'

Leo shook his head, taking out his phone to check if Ken had sent any updates. There was nothing. 'It's the waiting, the not knowing,' he said, taking a gulp of his beer. '*The Leonard*, Manila could still be standing or could be a heap of rubble... and the staff and guests could be...' He rubbed a hand across his eyes. 'The building doesn't matter, it's the people...'

'Sorry, mate.' Martin put a hand on Leo's shoulder. 'I've had experience in situations like that in a former life when I was commissioned to photograph the damage. It's heartbreaking. Maybe your hotel and people will be safe. It's always difficult to predict what will go and what will survive. You'll go there?'

'As soon as I can. At the moment there are no flights... and we'd only be in the way of the rescue teams, but...'

'Drink up. Worrying about it isn't going to help. I heard there's a rescue mission on its way from Australia and one from the US, too. The best you can do is try to keep positive... and book a flight as soon as you can. I presume...?'

'My finance guy's onto it. He's going to let me know when things change or when he can make contact. At the moment...' he sighed. But it was good to talk to these guys, especially Martin who'd seen the effects of an earthquake firsthand.

All three ordered burgers and chips but Leo couldn't eat, pushing the food around the plate while Martin shared his experiences of being on the scene when an earthquake happened and tried to reassure Leo that his people might be safe.

Back in the hotel, Leo turned on the television again, unable to keep away from the horrific accounts of the disaster and wondering how he could put on a cheerful face for Greta that evening.

Thirty-five

Greta felt like singing all day, remembering the day before and Leo's promise. This time, she knew he meant it. He wasn't going to leave her. She even began to feel more accepting of Jo's friendship with Bryan Grant, realising she may have been overreacting. In the short breaks between customers, she began to imagine what her life with Leo would be like, shivers tickling down her spine at the thought of them living together, of waking up each morning to see his head on the pillow.

She was glad when it came time to close up, aware her mind hadn't been on the job for much of the day. Cass had noticed how distracted Greta was when she brought her in a coffee mid-morning.

'Must have been good,' she said, with a wink.

'What?'

'Your day out with lover boy.'

Greta felt herself blush. 'We had a nice time,' she said, unwilling to share any more.

'Hmm.' But Cass knew better than to pursue it, merely smiling knowingly.

Now, Greta was filled with anticipation as she prepared to cook dinner. She'd decided on a simple meal of steak with baked potatoes and salad, followed by slices of one of Ruby Sullivan's frangipani pear tarts she'd picked up from the *Pandanus Café*. And she'd opened the bottle of Wolf Blass House of the Dragon cabernet sauvignon shiraz she'd been given for Christmas and had been keeping for a special occasion. It would go well with the steak. She imagined Leo might be a bit of a wine buff. If so, this one should satisfy his palate.

Greta hummed to herself as she showered, then dressed in one of her more vibrant outfits – one which matched her mood, applied her makeup and fixed her hair in a loose topknot, allowing several tendrils to fall around her face.

When the steak was marinating, the potatoes were ready to put into the oven and the salad was in the fridge, Greta poured herself a small glass of wine and tried to calm herself. But it was difficult to control the tremors of excitement coursing through her as the time for Leo to arrive grew closer. She'd set the table in the dining room and the candles were ready to be lit. She couldn't wait to see him.

*

As soon as she saw Leo standing at the door, Greta knew something was wrong. His face was pale and drawn. His eyes had the haunted look she'd seen in Jo's when her daughter arrived home from London. *What could have happened between the time he left this morning and now to cause such a transformation?*

'What's wrong?' she asked, sliding out of the embrace that seemed forced, his lips cool on hers.

'I'm sorry, Greta. I'm afraid I won't be good company tonight.'

Greta's heart dropped, her earlier buoyant mood suddenly vanishing. *What had happened to the loving man who'd danced her around the kitchen only that morning?*

'Come through.' She tried to stifle her distress as she led him into the kitchen. She poured two glasses of wine and handed one to Leo. He took it, remaining standing.

'Did you see the news?' he asked.

'I haven't had the television on. What…?'

'There's been an earthquake in Manila. Hundreds dead, injured, missing.' He dragged his free hand through his hair, the wine in his other hand almost spilling over.

'But…?' Greta had a vague recollection of hearing a news item about an earthquake the previous morning, before she left. What did it have to do with them? Then the penny dropped. 'You have a hotel there?'

Leo nodded. '*The Leonard,* Manila. I don't know if it's still standing. We can't get any word…'

'Oh, Leo!' Greta wanted to wrap him in her arms but could see the state he was in; he wouldn't welcome her embrace. 'When did…?'

'When I turned my phone on this morning, I had so many messages and missed calls I knew something was up. A call to Sydney confirmed it.'

'Oh! Those poor people.' Greta felt useless, unable to say anything more in the face of this tragedy, remembering the agony she'd suffered when her parents had died, caught up in the bombing in Bali. Her eyes went to the steak marinating on the benchtop, the potatoes ready for the oven.

Leo's eyes followed hers. 'It looks like you've gone to a lot of trouble,' he said. 'I'm sorry.' He sighed and passed a hand across his face.

Was he close to tears? Greta had never seen a grown man weep.

'If you don't want to stay, I'll understand,' she said.

'No.' Leo reached for Greta's hand. 'I need company… your company. But I don't think I could do justice to the meal you've prepared.'

'No worries. It'll keep,' she said, immediately rejecting all thought of her carefully planned romantic dinner. 'What about some soup with bread and cheese? I can heat up a can of soup and make a sandwich. It won't take any time. When did you last eat?' she asked, noting how tired he appeared to be.

'Lunchtime… No, I think it was the breakfast I had here.' Leo looked around the room, dazed, a shadow of the man who had eaten breakfast here, who had been so full of joy. 'I went to the club with Will and Martin but I couldn't face food. Soup and a sandwich sounds good.' He smiled weakly. 'Thanks, Greta.'

Feeling unsure of what else she could do, Greta busied herself opening a can of soup and putting it on to heat, before slicing cheese and making sandwiches which she decided to toast.

While she was doing this, Leo had taken a seat and was slumped at the table clutching his glass of wine.

When everything was ready, Greta said, 'Let's go somewhere more comfortable. Putting their food on a tray, she led the way to the living room, carefully closing the dining room door on the way. Leo followed, carrying the wine.

'Thanks, Greta. That was good. Sorry again to have spoiled your evening. Thanks for being patient with me.' Leo finished his wine and clasped Greta's hand.

'Of course.' While it hadn't been the romantic evening Greta had anticipated, Leo was looking a little better than he had when he arrived.

'Do you mind if we check the news?'

'Of course not.' She turned on the television to the ABC news channel which was providing continuous coverage of the disaster.

'There's nothing new,' he said dispiritedly, turning it off.

'Tell me about your hotel,' Greta said, in an effort to change Leo's mood.

For several moments he didn't speak. His eyes took on a glazed look.

Maybe it had been a mistake to mention it.

Then he began talking, almost as if reading from a guidebook, '*The Leonard*, Manila is one of our signature hotels... a luxury hotel located close to the centre of the city. The lobby is decked out in gold, gold columns, gold mosaic on the floor with traditional paintings on the walls. The bedrooms continue the gold motif in the carpets and...' he almost broke down before clenching his fist and forcing himself to continue, '... traditional flower paintings there, too. Then there are all the things the tourists expect in our hotels – restaurants, coffee shop, retail outlets, pool, spa, fitness centre... The thought of it all disappearing...' Leo shook his head. 'But it's the staff – over five hundred of them. Most are locals, but we have a number of international staff who've been with us for years and move between our hotels. And the guests... I can't...' This time, he did break down into a torrent of weeping.

Greta, who had been tentative about comforting him earlier, now didn't hesitate. She took him in her arms, rubbing his back like she had Jo's, when her daughter was a small child and needed comforting.

For several minutes, the only sound in the room was Leo's sobs. Then he took a deep breath and eased himself out of her embrace. 'Sorry.' He knuckled his eyes. 'I don't know what came over me. I don't usually... Sorry,' he repeated.

'It's okay. I understand.' She did, and she loved him even more for his concern over the fate of his employees and guests.

'Do you want to stay... or go back to the hotel?' Greta had no idea how to handle the situation.

'Can I stay? I don't expect to get much sleep, but it would be good to know you were there.'

'Of course you can.'

*

Greta awoke in the middle of the night to an empty spot in the bed where Leo had been lying, curled up beside her. He was standing, staring out the window, shoulders hunched.

Greta went up to Leo, wound her arms around his waist and leant into him, wishing there was something she could do to ease his pain. He turned, took her in his arms, his head on her shoulder. 'Thanks, sweetheart,' he said in answer to her unspoken words of sympathy. 'I'm glad you're here, but there's nothing you can do to help, nothing anyone can do... until we can get there.'

Greta felt a huge chasm open up between them. He was going to go away again, leave her again, putting himself in danger. She thought again of her parents, how their lives had been cut short so suddenly, their lights extinguished. What if Leo died, too? While she could understand his desire to go to Manila, to see the damage to his hotel, to do what he could for his people, it pierced her to the quick. The thought of the devastation he was going to find there brought back memories of that day twenty years earlier when her world had collapsed.

Yesterday, when one of the television reporters had likened the sights in Manila to a bomb blast, it almost tore Greta apart as she remembered that other day, the footage of the destruction in Bali and the realisation she'd never see her parents again. It had come when she and Mick were talking of divorce and, despite their differences, he'd been there for her... for her and Jo. It had been days before they finally learnt the extent of the disaster, much longer for her to recover, to accept what had happened. She had been distraught, grateful to Mick for being there for Jo. Now there were families in Manila experiencing similar uncertainty and grief. It was unbearable.

Thirty-six

Leo was still feeling dazed when he returned to the hotel, despite drinking two mugs of coffee before he left Greta's and forcing down a slice of toast. He could see the worry in her eyes when he left her but there was nothing he could do to put her mind at rest. He was sorry he'd spoiled what she'd expected to be a romantic evening, but he was still trying to come to terms with the extent of the devastation he'd seen on the news.

As soon as he reached his suite, he turned the television on again, but it was still difficult to pinpoint exactly where the footage was being shot. He called Ken.

'Sorry, Leo. There's still no word. But I have my contact at Foreign Affairs trying to get news and I'm hopeful we can get someone on one of the planes which will be taking in aid as soon as they're able to land.'

'I'll go,' Leo said without hesitation. 'I need to see the damage for myself. And maybe I can be of some help. Is there anything else we can offer?'

'Leave it with me. I'll get back to you when I have anything else to report.'

Leo spent the rest of the morning alternately watching reruns of the same news footage and pacing the room, impatient to do something, while knowing there was nothing he could do... not yet. Finally, knowing he'd go mad imagining the worst if he stayed there any longer, he switched off the television and picked up his phone. Luckily, he'd exchanged numbers with Will and Martin the other day.

He dialled Martin Cooper's number. Martin had been in an earthquake zone. Maybe he could answer some of the questions whirling around in Leo's head.

*

'Thanks for coming.' Leo shook Martin's hand.

'You okay? You're looking pretty rough.'

Leo passed a hand over his chin, realising that although he'd had a shower before leaving Greta's, he hadn't taken time to shave. 'Not really. I need to… I want to pick your brain. Just how bad could it be?'

The two men were seated with coffee at one of the sun-bleached tables outside *The Bay Café* where Leo normally ate breakfast. Today, everything was as usual. The sun was shining. There were people sitting enjoying coffee around them, others wandering past intent on shopping, shrieks of happiness coming from the beach across the way. But, for Leo, it was all a blur. His mind was filled with the horror he'd seen on the screen and his imaginings of what might be happening to the people he knew in Manila.

'It depends…' Martin said cautiously, '… depends where the epicentre was, the severity of the quake, the aftershocks. I know your main concern must be your hotel. I'm guessing it's fairly new, built to withstand some degree of earth movement?'

'To some extent, but it's not like those Japanese structures with their reinforced piping and stuff. But it's not just the building I'm worried about. I'm responsible for more than five hundred people – and that's only my employees. It could more than double if we count the guests. I can't imagine…' But he could. Lying awake, he'd envisioned people trapped in the wreckage of his hotel, in anguish, crying out for help.

'Most people are injured or die from falling buildings, debris and fires,' Martin said. 'If the earthquake causes a tsunami, many of the deaths are from drowning, but so far there haven't been any reports of a tsunami warning.' He glanced at Leo, before continuing, 'When a major earthquake occurs, it's possible the violent shaking can fracture structures. Weak building facades may collapse onto the streets. Glass windows and panels may shatter, and roof tiles may dislodge. Once weakened, buildings can collapse and trap or kill people inside.'

Leo winced, his worst fears realised. But he wanted to hear the rest. 'Go on,' he said, his lips tight.

'You sure?'

Leo nodded, his coffee forgotten.

'Okay.' Martin took a gulp of his coffee before continuing, 'Electricity, water and gas may fail or be switched off. Earthquakes often damage water, gas and electricity lines. Ruptured gas lines can ignite, especially if the earthquake has dislodged or exposed electrical wiring. Fallen powerlines may be a hazard, sprinkler systems and fire alarms may trigger. Without running water and electricity, sanitation is an issue. Waterborne infectious diseases, including cholera, are common. I'm sorry to say it, but it really is utter chaos, mate.' He drew a hand through his hair. 'As you're already aware, the phone systems will shut down – both landlines and mobile services. No internet access. Then there are the aftershocks. They can occur in the minutes, days, weeks and even months after the earthquake. These may be stronger than the first tremor.'

Hell, it was even worse than he'd imagined. He had to get there to see for himself.

Martin glanced across the table at Leo. 'You intend to go there, don't you?'

'As soon as I can.'

'It won't be easy.'

'I know, but I may be able to get on one of the aid planes.'

'Good luck, mate. I hope you find...' Martin didn't seem to know what to say. 'Just be prepared. Okay?'

'Okay... and thanks. I appreciate you taking the time to talk with me.' He could see from Martin's expression that talking about it had brought it all back for his friend. As he was describing the effects of a quake, Martin's expression had changed, his eyes clouding over, his lips tightening. 'It can't have been easy.'

'No.' He paused. 'Let me know before you leave. I may be able to give you a few more tips.'

'Thanks.' He shook Martin's hand, and they went their separate ways, Leo deciding to visit *Birds of a Feather*. He had a strong urge to see Greta, to inject some sense of reality into a day which seemed to be becoming more surreal by the minute. Now he had more facts, the pictures in his head were more horrendous than before.

Thirty-seven

Greta didn't know how she made it through the morning. Every time she thought about Leo and what was happening in the Philippines, she got a lump in her throat and she could feel the tears start. Only the fear of breaking down in front of her customers prevented her from having a complete meltdown. Besides Leo, there was the thought of all the people in Manila… dead, injured, homeless. While she'd watched the unfolding of tragedies before, none had affected her like this. Leo's involvement, his distress, brought home to her how fragile life could be in the face of such a natural disaster. It was as if she was experiencing her parents' death all over again.

'What's the matter?' Cass asked, when she popped in with coffees late morning. 'I thought you and your hotel magnate were having a romantic dinner last night. You look as if you've lost a shilling and found a penny, as my old grandma would say.'

'I've no idea what you mean.' Greta managed a smile which didn't travel to her eyes. 'But if you want to know what's wrong, you only need to look at the news.'

'The news?' Cass took a sip of her coffee. 'The upcoming local elections, youth crime, the latest instance of domestic violence, the… Oh, the earthquake. Does he have interests there?'

'*The Leonard*, Manila.' Greta nodded. 'Leo doesn't know if it's still standing or what's happened to the staff and guests. He's a wreck. And he wants to go there.'

Cass's eyes widened. 'But surely he can't do that. I mean, isn't travel restricted to… I don't know… official bods?'

'He thinks he can get a seat on one of the aid planes,' Greta sniffed, the fears she'd been holding at bay resurfacing. 'He's going away again, Cass, and this time he's going to an earthquake zone. He's going into danger.'

'I'm sorry, Greta. I can see it's no use telling you not to worry, but worrying never does any good. Maybe he won't be able to get there,' she said hopefully.

'He's the sort who gets what he wants. He wasn't always like that.' Greta remembered the gentle boy she'd fallen in love with who had turned into this entrepreneur who seemed to have a host of staff willing to do his bidding. Mick's words came back to her. 'But deep down, where it counts, he's still the same person he was when we first met,' she added, more to convince herself than Cass. *He was concerned about his staff, wasn't he?*

'If you say so.' Cass sounded doubtful. 'Oh, speak of the devil…'

Greta looked up to see Leo in the doorway.

'I'll be off.' Cass scurried away, only turning at the door to give Greta a thumbs-up.

'Leo!' Greta couldn't believe her eyes. He was the last person she'd expected to see in *Birds of a Feather*. She'd thought he'd be busy making arrangements to leave. His face was still drawn and there was an expression in his eyes that hadn't been there before.

'I couldn't settle to do anything,' he said. 'There was no news, and watching the continual newsfeed was doing my head in. I called Martin Cooper. He has experience of being in an earthquake – when he was working as a photographer. I wanted him to tell me what it was like.'

'And did he?' Greta asked, her heart in her mouth.

'It's worse than I thought. It's killing me not knowing what's happening.'

'Mmm.' There was nothing she could say. She just wanted to wrap her arms around him and tell him everything would be okay. But she couldn't and it wouldn't – or it might not be. But nothing he'd said explained why he was here in *Birds of a Feather* in the middle of the day.

'I remember you saying you sometimes closed for lunch. I thought… maybe… we could have it together?'

Greta felt a warm glow that, in the midst of all his angst, Leo wanted to spend time with her. 'Of course. What did you have in mind?'

'Well, if I drink any more coffee, I think I may take off. How about we get a couple of sandwiches and some sparkling water and take it to one of the benches by the beach?'

'That sounds lovely. I just need to finish up here. It'll only take a couple of minutes.'

'Great. Why don't I pick up the sandwiches and drinks while you do that? I can meet you over there.' He pointed to the benches strategically placed for tourists to take in the view. 'What would you like?'

'You choose.'

Greta felt more light-hearted than she had since she saw Leo in her doorway the night before. They were still good together. Nothing had changed. She had to hang on to that, despite the fact he was intent on travelling to Manila, to the site of an earthquake, the very thought of which sent shivers down her spine.

Greta was feeling more composed by the time she joined Leo on the seafront.

'I got ham and cheese, and egg and lettuce,' he said. 'That okay?'

'Fine.' She didn't care what she ate. It was enough to be with him. To know he'd sought out her company after what must have been a difficult talk with Martin Cooper. *Why had he chosen to put himself through that? If he did manage to get a flight, he'd find out soon enough. But maybe he wanted to be prepared.*

They didn't talk much while they ate. Greta didn't know what to say, and Leo was deep in thought.

Finally, she risked asking, 'Do you know when you'll be leaving?'

'No.' Leo dragged a hand through his hair. 'I have to wait till… Hell, I don't really know what the holdup is, but Ken, my go-to guy who handles all the finance stuff for the company, is working on it. He has contacts who he thinks can help. I just have to wait,' he repeated.

'I'm sorry.' Greta felt she'd been saying those words so often she must sound like a stuck record.

'I know.' Leo squeezed her hand. 'You don't know how much it means to me to know you're here… and you'll be waiting for me.'

A warm glow started at Greta's toes and began to move through her. 'I will be. Always.'

He squeezed her hand tighter. 'Thanks.'

They finished their lunch in silence, but it was a comfortable silence, neither feeling the need to talk, to add anything to what had already been said.

Leo walked back to the boutique with Greta, his hand clasping hers. When they reached the door, they stopped.

Greta looked up at him, at the man who now meant everything to her.

'Can I see you tonight? I can come round at seven. Don't go to any trouble.'

'I can cook the meal we were going to have last night.' Greta held her breath.

Leo gave a crooked smile. 'That sounds good. I may still not be good company, but I promise to try.'

Greta stood on tiptoe to kiss him on the cheek. His words, his promise, were good enough for her.

Thirty-eight

Leo had only just left Greta and was walking back to where he'd parked his car when his phone rang. Grabbing it quickly, hoping it was Ken with news of a flight, he was disappointed to see Iain Grant's number.

'Iain,' he said, trying to inject some enthusiasm into his voice.

'I've finished the plans. Can we meet so you can approve them before I submit them to the council? I understand the building committee is meeting tomorrow so we might be able to get a head start on the project.'

In the worry about what was happening in Manila, the Bellbird Bay project had slipped to the back of Leo's mind. Iain's words brought it back to the forefront. After a moment's hesitation, during which he wondered about the wisdom of planning a new hotel when people's lives were in danger, he said, 'Sure. I'm free all afternoon.'

'Great. Shall I see you at the hotel? Around three?'

'Sure,' Leo said again. It would give him time to check the news and contact Ken for any updates.

*

By the time Iain arrived, Leo had talked with Ken to discover there was still nothing happening, and communication lines were still down. The only information getting out from the stricken area seemed to be on the news channels and it was on a repetitive loop. He was still no further forward.

When he received a message Iain Grant was at reception, Leo decided to go down to meet him there and have coffee in the office. At least it would get him away from the television screen which was beginning to hold a grisly fascination for him.

Iain was waiting for him with a roll of papers. Evidently not everything was on the computer these days. 'Hey,' Iain said. 'Everything okay?'

Leo realised he must look strange. This was the second time he'd been asked this today, and last time he'd looked in the mirror he'd been shocked to see how grey his face was and the lines which seemed to have deepened overnight.

'Not exactly,' he said grimly.

'Oh, hell. The earthquake. You have a hotel there.' Iain's expression changed. 'Is everyone okay?'

'We don't know. There's no word.'

'I'm so sorry. It must be a worrying time for you. Are you sure you want to do this?' He held up the roll of plans.

'Might as well. There's nothing else I can do right now.'

'Okay.' Iain gave him a searching look.

Leo ushered Iain into the office and to a seat by the low table, and fixed coffee, making up his mind to try to concentrate on what the architect had come to discuss.

The plans were brilliant, exactly what Leo had envisaged. 'These are great. Thanks so much. And you think you can get them through the council tomorrow?'

'So I've been told. You've met Will Rankin, haven't you? He's been a great help and, after the debacle we had with the previous owner here, I understand the committee will be keen to approve the new plans. There shouldn't be any problem.'

Good old Will. Who'd have thought, all those years ago, he'd become a respected member of the community, a local councillor predicted to become the next mayor, and he'd be in a position to ease the plans for a new hotel of Leo's through the council planning process?

'Right, if that's all?' Leo was anxious to get back to his suite. Maybe there was some news, maybe Ken had managed to arrange a flight for him.

'Sure,' Iain began to pack up. 'I'll take these over to the council now and fill in the appropriate forms.' His expression changed, became more serious. 'And I hope you have good news soon.'

'So do I, Iain, so do I.'

*

Back in his suite, Leo couldn't resist turning on the television again. This time, there was footage of more rescues and cheers as a young mother and her baby were pulled from the rubble of what had been a multistorey apartment complex. His fears for the fate of his hotel grew as he watched, trying without success to identify the location of the shots.

Making a decision to focus instead on something he could control, Leo switched off the television. He unrolled the copies of the plans for what he was now calling *The Leonard Family Resort*, Bellbird Bay, which Iain had left with him, and spread them out on the coffee table. But it was no use. His eyes blurred as the images from the television interposed themselves between him and the plans.

He was on what must have been his fourth cup of coffee when his phone rang. Grabbing it anxiously, his stomach churned when he saw Ken's number. 'Ken, have you heard anything? The television…'

Ken's voice sounded more upbeat than earlier. 'Do you want the good news or the bad news?'

Leo groaned. It was at times like this he wished he was a smoker. 'What? Don't mess me about.'

'The good news is the hotel is still standing and appears to be undamaged. Adan managed to get through to me with the help of a television crew who are camping out in the foyer.'

Leo had a vision of the ornate golden foyer, crammed with television crews.

'He tells me power is still out and there's no water. The hotel was half-filled with guests, most of them international travellers who are stuck there until flights recommence. Some are helping with the rescue work.'

As I should be. Leo seethed with impatience but forced himself to listen.

'As regards flights, I've managed to get you on one, but not till next week, that's the bad news.'

Leo groaned with annoyance. Another week of doing nothing.

'Steady on, Leo. You're lucky to get one even then. Adan wanted to know if you have any instructions for him. It would seem most of the staff are safe, but there are still some he can't contact. If they were off duty at the time the earthquake struck, I guess they could be taking refuge somewhere.'

Or lying dead.

'Adan's family?' he found himself saying.

'All safe. I asked him about them. Evidently, they were with him at the hotel. What do you want me to tell him?'

'The hotel must become an evacuation centre. There's lots of room. It sounds as if some people are already utilising it, if the television crews are there. It's normally a bit rich for their budget. Can you ask him what else we can do to help from this end and let him know I'll be there as soon as I can.'

'Are you sure, Leo? I'm not sure what you can do.'

'I'm sure. I can't sit here in comfort when my people need me, and in a situation like that, the more hands the better. I do have some first-aid experience and can at least talk with people. I've heard how sometimes that helps in a disaster.'

'Okay, I'll pass it on.'

'And be sure to let him know my thoughts are with him and with everyone in Manila.'

'Will do. I'll be back in touch when there's more news.'

'Right.' Leo ended the call reluctantly. While pleased the hotel had survived along with most of the staff and guests, it didn't change the fact that the city itself was still a disaster zone... and he was stuck here in Bellbird Bay for another week.

Thirty-nine

Greta was feeling a little more cheerful as she prepared dinner that evening. She'd decided against the candles and had set the table in the kitchen, feeling it would be more appropriate to Leo's mood and the situation. She'd turned on the television for a few minutes when she got home, shocked to see the scenes of devastation, and worried about Leo's determination to go there. It was madness, but she knew there was no way she could dissuade him. She could only hope his anticipated flight didn't eventuate.

By the time she heard his knock on the door, Greta had almost persuaded herself Leo wouldn't be able to leave, but as soon as she saw his face, she knew she was wrong.

'You're looking more cheerful,' she said, extricating herself from an embrace that was warmer than the one the previous evening. 'Good news?'

'The best.' He grinned, then his expression changed. 'But not for most of the people in Manila. *The Leonard*, Manila has survived the earthquake, as have most of the staff. And, Ken is arranging a flight for me.'

Greta's heart fell, her stomach roiling at the prospect of Leo flying into danger. 'When?' she stammered, almost too afraid to ask.

'Not for another week, dammit.' His face fell.

Greta felt a small flicker of relief. Anything could happen in a week. 'I thought we'd eat in the kitchen,' she said, leading him through.

'Suits me. I hope I can do justice to the meal tonight. Last night...' Leo ran a hand through his hair.

'I know. I'm glad your people are safe.'

'There are still some who can't be contacted – those who weren't on duty. They may be…'

'Shh.' Greta put a finger to his lips. 'Try not to think about them. I know it must be difficult. I watched the news when I got home. It looks to be such a mess. Are you sure you…' She stopped at the sight of Leo's expression. 'Sorry, of course you must do what you think's best, but I'll be a nervous wreck all the time you're gone.' She bit her lip.

'You're a darling. The fact you're here waiting for me will help me get through whatever I find there. I know it won't be easy, but think of what it's like for all those people living there, those who have lost their homes, their families. I have a home to come back to… and you waiting for me. I *will* come back this time, Greta.'

'I know.' She didn't doubt Leo meant every word, but who knew what might happen once he reached Manila? Even *he* couldn't be sure he'd be safe.

They enjoyed their meal and the wine she'd purchased, splashing out on another bottle of the Wolf Blass House of the Dragon cabernet sauvignon shiraz she was sure Leo hadn't taken time to appreciate the previous evening. When they had finished eating, they took their glasses into the living room and curled up together on the sofa.

'You're so restful to be with,' Leo said, stroking Greta's hair and sending shivers down her spine. 'It's been quite a day. It's so good to relax here, with you.'

Greta murmured her appreciation.

After a few minutes, Leo said, 'Iain Grant came to see me today.'

Greta twisted around to look at Leo's face. 'What did he want?'

'He wanted to show me the plans he's drawn up for *The Leonard Family Resort*, here in Bellbird Bay. He's submitting them to the council today.'

'You're going ahead with the renovation?' Greta had imagined he'd have delayed till he returned from Manila.

'It seems so. Iain heard the committee that deals with approvals is meeting tomorrow and got the heads up it would go through. It appears Will Rankin may have had a hand in it.'

'He's a good guy – our next mayor, all going well.'

'So I've heard. He's come a long way from the rough surfer I remember.'

'We all have. It was a long time ago, Leo.'

'Mmm. And yet, sometimes, when I'm with you, it only seems like yesterday.' He pulled Greta into an embrace, their lips meeting.

They were interrupted by Greta's phone ringing.

'Damn! I should have turned it off.' About to reject the call, she glanced at the screen to see Jo's face smiling out at her. 'Sorry, it's Jo. I'd better answer. It's not like her to call me at this time. It may be important.'

She moved out of Leo's arms and pressed to accept the call. 'Jo, darling, what's up? Is everything okay?'

'Everything's perfect, Mum. This house is so great. I've decided to have a housewarming on Saturday, just a few friends, and I hope you can come.'

Greta didn't answer immediately. She looked at Leo who was regarding her with a puzzled expression. Normally, she wouldn't hesitate to accept. She loved her daughter, and the idea of a housewarming in Eddie's house was a sure sign Jo was well on the way to recovering from her grief but... She gazed at Leo. They would only have a few more evenings together before he left. *Could she bear to lose even one of them by going to Jo's housewarming?*

Jo seemed to understand. 'I heard about the earthquake, Mum. Leo must be in a panic. If you want to bring him along, it's okay with me.'

'Are you sure?' She mouthed *Jo's inviting us to her housewarming on Saturday* to Leo, who nodded his agreement and squeezed her shoulder. 'Okay, thanks, sweetheart. We'd both love to come. Can I bring anything?'

'Some of your famous cheesy dip would be great.'

Greta chuckled. The dip was from an old recipe – a creamy cheese and spinach dip served in a cob loaf. It had been handed down by her mother who got it from *her* mother. It was a family favourite which had graced all their special occasions when she, Mick and Jo were together as a family. 'No problem. Around what time?'

'Seven.' Jo paused. 'Bryan will be there... with Mia and a few other people you know.'

'So, I'm going to be treated as one of the family?' Leo hugged Greta when the call ended.

'She must have decided to get over her disapproval of our friendship,'

Greta said. 'And I suppose I have to get over mine regarding Bryan.'

'He's a nice guy.'

'Yes,' Greta sighed, not completely convinced he was right for Jo, but willing to make an effort for her daughter's sake. As Bev said, they were both vulnerable and Bryan was as susceptible to being hurt as Jo was.

That night their lovemaking was gentle, with none of the wild passion which had been a feature of their previous encounters. It signified a new phase in their relationship, their ability to provide comfort to each other. They fell asleep curled up together, only awakening when the sound of the resident kookaburras heralded the dawn.

Forty

Saturday came around almost too quickly. For Greta, it was as if the days until Leo's departure for Manila were flying past. Even though they spent each night together, it was never enough, as she tried to savour every minute of pleasure from their time with each other.

Dressing in one of her favourite outfits – a kaftan patterned with tropical flowers – Greta tried to subdue the butterflies careering around in her stomach. Last night, Leo had told her he had a flight arranged. He was to fly out to Manila on Wednesday, heading to Sydney on Tuesday. That gave them only three more nights together. She was glad she didn't have to work on Monday when they planned a picnic on Dolphin Beach, the beach which figured in all her memories. But the fact she had no idea when she'd see him again once he left weighed heavily on her.

Luckily *Birds of a Feather* had been busy all day, giving her little time to think. But now, alone in her house, all her fears for Leo's safety re-emerged, the worry he might be injured, even die. Telling herself her fears were groundless, she took a deep breath and carefully applied her makeup, determined to enjoy what time they had left and to hide her concerns from Leo. It was Jo's housewarming, and she needed to put on a brave face for her daughter.

'Ready?' Leo stood in the doorway, looking as handsome and sexy as ever in a pink button-down shirt and black cord jacket over a pair of black jeans. Now he had a date for leaving, the worry lines on his face seemed to have lessened and he was more like the man who had arrived in Bellbird Bay to buy a hotel.

'I am now,' Greta said, pulling out of Leo's arms and patting down her hair which had become dishevelled in his embrace. 'You're looking very smart tonight.'

'And you're looking as lovely as ever. Great outfit.' Leo grinned.

Damn the man! How could he even contemplate flying off to an earthquake zone when everything between them was going so well? Greta pasted a smile on her face. She picked up the special cob cheesy dip which she'd placed in one of her old Tupperware containers. 'Shall we go?'

It only took a few minutes to drive to Jo's new home. As they parked, they could already hear voices echoing through the open front door. Jo had said a small group of friends. It sounded more like a large gathering.

Greta knocked on the door and called, 'Hello, Jo?' Getting no reply, she took Leo's hand and led him in the direction of the voices, only to be greeted by two young girls and two dogs, one small and one large and of indeterminate breed. 'Hello, Milo,' she said, leaning down to pat the head of the larger one she recognised as belonging to Libby.

'Mum, you're here.' Jo appeared, a glass of wine in one hand. Tonight, her daughter was glowing, her eyes bright with pleasure. There was no sign of the despondent woman who'd arrived home from London.

'Hello, darling.' Greta handed over the dip and hugged her daughter.

'Thanks, Mum,' Jo said. 'Hi, Leo. Good to see you, too.'

'Jo.' Leo smiled and gave her a peck on the cheek.

Greta exhaled. *Was this a turning point for them? Had Jo finally accepted that Leo was part of her mother's life?* Then the familiar pain stabbed her, as she remembered he was leaving in a few days.

'Everyone's outside,' Jo said. 'Let me get you a drink and we can join them. Careful,' she admonished the two young girls trying to catch up with the dogs. 'They're so excited to be allowed to stay up past their bedtime,' she laughed. 'Mia,' she said to one of the girls, 'come and meet my mum. Mum, this is Mia, Bryan's daughter.'

'Hello, Mia,' Greta said.

The little girl looked up at her for a moment, then asked, 'Are you a grandma?'

Greta's heart clenched. Her eyes moistened. She must look old to this young girl, old enough to be a grandma. But she wasn't. 'No, my darling, I'm not. Is your grandma here today?' she asked, remembering Bev was one of Mia's grandmothers, the *new* grandmother Jo had mentioned.

'I have two grandmothers,' Mia said in a voice filled with pride. 'My grandma doesn't live here but my nana does… and she's here with Dad and Grandad. This is Holly,' she said, picking up the small dog.

'Isn't she sweet,' Jo said, as Mia bounced off. 'She's such a good kid, too, and bright.'

Carrying their drinks, Greta and Leo followed Jo outside where they greeted Bev and Iain, Leo immediately being drawn into a conversation with Iain about his plans for the hotel, while Greta and Bev chatted.

'Your daughter seems lovely,' Bev said. 'Mia is very fond of her… Bryan, too, I think. He has really come out of himself since meeting Jo. I don't think you have anything to worry about.' She patted Greta's arm reassuringly. Greta smiled, now embarrassed about her trip to the garden centre. But it had brought her and Bev closer, so might not have been such a bad thing.

During a break in their conversation, she glanced around to see Libby and Adam talking to Grace and Ted. A little way apart from them were a younger group in which Greta was able to identify Libby's daughter, Emma, and her partner, Nick. Clancy was Emma's daughter and seemed to be a good friend of Mia's. The others in the group were Mel, Grace's daughter, along with her partner, Aaron, who was also Ted's son. It seemed the residents of the homes on the boardwalk were all out in force. She also recognised Neil Simpson, who was now running *Bay Books* with his dad. He was with an elegant woman Greta knew to be Adam Holland's sister. Bellbird Bay was really such a small place.

Then Greta caught sight of a face she should have expected. Of course, Jo would have invited her dad. Mick was strolling over in their direction. Greta pulled on Leo's arm but didn't have time to warn him before Mick bowled up.

'Isn't this lovely,' he said to Greta, before turning to Leo. 'I thought you were heading off to be a hero.'

There was a stunned silence, then Greta said, 'Leo is flying to the Philippines next week to do what he can for the rescue effort. He has a hotel there, and people he's concerned about.'

Mick had the grace to look embarrassed. 'The hotel's still standing?'

'It is,' Leo said, 'but so many other structures aren't. We're lucky we can provide an evacuation centre for those who've been displaced or injured... or both.'

'I'm sorry.'

Greta glanced at Mick and, to his credit, he did appear apologetic. 'You should be,' she said, before turning her back on him and, taking Leo's arm led him away to join the group around Libby.

For the rest of the evening, she tried to make sure she and Leo kept out of Mick's way. But it seemed that, everywhere they went, Mick was there, too, like a shadow, making her cling more closely to Leo's side as they moved around. She couldn't wait for the evening to end so she could be alone again with Leo, feel his arms around her, his lips on hers and try to forget he was leaving in two days' time.

As the evening progressed, Greta became even more aware of Mick's presence, but it wasn't till they were laughing with Jo over the cheesy dip she'd brought, that it came to a head.

'Brings back memories, doesn't it?' Mick asked, suddenly appearing at her shoulder, and reaching over to dip a cracker into the thick cheese sauce. 'It was your standard dish for every one of Jo's birthdays, and whenever you were asked to take a plate to an event. Why I can even remember when...'

'That's enough, Mick.' Greta pulled on Leo's arm, eager to move away.

But Mick was persistent. He wasn't prepared to give up easily. 'We had good times together, you, me and Jo. It's not too late to re... re... recapture them.' He slurred his words.

Greta wondered how much he'd had to drink. This behaviour was intolerable, even for Mick.

'She'll come back to me, you know,' he said to Leo. 'Greta and I belong together. We...'

Greta did the only thing she could think of to stem Mick's words. She reached up to kiss a surprised Leo on the lips. When they drew apart, Mick was nowhere to be seen.

Forty-one

When Greta awoke on Tuesday morning, curled up beside Leo, it took her a few moments to remember this was the day he was leaving.

'Morning, sweetheart. Why so sad?' Leo kissed her on the forehead.

'I wish you weren't going,' she said, stroking his cheek and gazing at him to imprint his image on her mind – as if she could ever forget.

Last night had been special. Leo had pulled out all the stops to make it a night to remember. In an effort to take her mind off his imminent departure, he'd booked a table at *The Beach House* then, after a delicious meal accompanied by glasses of champagne, they'd driven out to Dolphin Beach again. Luckily, the tide was out, and they'd walked along the wet sand at the edge of the water in the moonlight. Leo said it was to lay down memories he could recapture when he was far away, but Greta felt it was more than that. It was to give her memories in the event he didn't return.

'You know I have to go.' He stroked her hair back from her face and kissed her lips. 'But I'll be back.'

Greta bit back the temptation to remind him he'd said that last time. She knew this time he meant it. The situation was completely different. He was going on a mercy flight to help the earthquake victims, and while she was proud of his determination to help in the rescue effort, she couldn't help wishing he wasn't leaving. She couldn't bear to lose Leo when they had just found each other again.

'I'll make breakfast,' she said, and slid out of bed before she could say something she might regret or burst into tears.

'Sounds good. You do know I love you, Greta? Nothing will keep me away from you this time. Believe me.'

'I do.' She was enveloped in a glow of certainty. This time nothing could come between them. Leo would go to Manila, do what he had to do there, and come back to Bellbird Bay, back to her. She had to keep telling herself that. Anything else was too frightening to contemplate.

When Leo walked into the kitchen, dressed in a pair of cargo pants and a denim shirt, his hair damp from the shower, Greta felt her stomach lurch. In only a few hours, he'd be on the plane to Sydney. Then, tomorrow, along with firefighters and medical workers, he'd board the RAAF flight stocked with supplies, which would take him to Manila. Then her worries really would begin.

To her surprise, Greta managed to put on a brave face during breakfast, even managing to make conversation which didn't make reference to his trip. But when they'd finished the scrambled eggs and smoked salmon, Leo had drunk two cups of coffee, Greta had finished her usual lemon and ginger tea, and it was time for him to leave, she felt her eyes moisten. 'I wish I could come to the airport with you.'

'It's best you don't. You have the shop to open, and I have to drop off my rental car. There's no sense in it sitting here while I'm away. I'll organise another when I get back, maybe even buy one. I want to remember you here, where we've been so happy, not in an airport with crowds of other people. Okay?'

'Okay,' Greta sniffed, trying to smile. She didn't want Leo's last image of her to be one of her in tears.

'Come here,' Leo pulled her into his arms, his lips on hers sweeter than ever.

How could she let him go?

'I need to go now,' he said, picking up the small bag he'd brought with him the day before – space was limited on the plane. 'I'll be in touch when I can but try not to worry if you don't hear from me.'

'I'll try.' But Greta knew it would be impossible. She'd worry all the time he was gone, imagining all sorts of situations he might be in. 'Take care. I love you.'

'I love you, too.' They made their way to the door and with one last hug, he was gone.

Back inside, Greta stared around in a daze. Hanging on the back of a chair was the sweater Leo had worn yesterday. *Had he forgotten to pack it, or had he left it there deliberately... as a sign he intended to return?* Greta picked it up and put it to her nose; it still smelt of him. A tear trickled down her cheek.

*

The day passed slowly for Greta. Each time she looked at her watch, she pictured where Leo would be... now at the airport, then on the plane, arriving in Sydney, at his office... From there the picture was less clear, presumably at some stage he'd go home, to the harbourside apartment he'd been so scathing about, saying it wasn't really a home. Then, tomorrow, he'd fly off to Manila.

She had just arrived home when she received a call from Jo.

'It's today Leo is leaving, isn't it? Want some company?'

Company was exactly what Greta needed. She'd been dreading this, her first night alone... without Leo. And, despite her apparent disapproval of their relationship, Jo seemed to understand. 'Thanks, honey. I'd love to see you.'

'Why don't I bring over a large bag of *Golden Gaytime Bites?*'

Greta managed a smile. *Golden Gaytime* paddle pops had always been a favourite of theirs when Jo was small. It was the treat she'd always craved when she was upset. Now the confection was available in bite sized morsels, and Greta was aware Jo always kept some in the fridge to be consumed on special occasions or when she was feeling down. 'That'd be lovely, Jo. Have you eaten?'

'What's on offer?'

Greta had no idea what she'd intended to cook. She'd been too upset to plan a meal. But she knew there were several pre-cooked meals in the freezer. 'I'll find something in the freezer,' she said, trying to pull herself together. Just because Leo had left, was no reason to fall into despair and let things go.

'Great. See you soon.'

Now she had some purpose, Greta searched in the freezer, finding a quiche she'd bought several days earlier. Taking it out, she turned on the oven, then headed to have a shower before Jo arrived.

She had opened a bottle of wine and was putting together the ingredients for a salad when Jo walked in carrying Greta's Tupperware container and a bag of *Golden Gaytime Bites*.

'Hi Mum.' She put down the container and gave Greta a hug. 'Something smells good.'

'Just a quiche.'

'I'll put these in the freezer for later.' Jo waved the bright yellow and brown bag in the air. 'And I'll have a glass of wine, too.' She put the ice cream in the freezer and poured herself a glass of wine before taking a seat and peering at Greta. 'You really like him, Mum?'

'Yes, Jo. I do, and I can't bear to think of him putting himself at risk this way.'

'Trying to be a hero.'

Jo sounded just like her dad. Greta felt her hackles rise. 'Leo's not like that,' she said defensively. 'He wants to help.'

'What can he do to help? He's not a medico or a rescue worker. He'll probably just be in the way. He'd have been better…'

'Stop right there!' Greta held up her hand. 'If you've come here just to put Leo down, you can go home again. I'm upset enough that Leo's gone. I don't need you – or your dad –bad-mouthing him and what he's trying to do.'

'I was just saying…'

'Well, don't. I'm glad you rang and I'm glad you're here, Jo. I've missed you since you moved out. But let's have a nice evening together without you bagging Leo.'

'Okay.' Seeming chastened, Jo took a sip of wine.

During their meal, Greta and Jo stuck to safe topics of conversation – the upcoming local election, Will Rankin's prospect of becoming mayor, the small touches Jo was adding to Eddie's house, and her renewed interest in surfing. They were enjoying the *Golden Gaytime Bites*, which Jo had emptied into a bowl, when she asked, 'What did you think of Bryan, Mum, when you met him at my housewarming?'

Greta took a drink of wine before replying. 'He seems like a nice man… and Mia is a delightful little girl. You're becoming close to them?' She held her breath.

Jo twirled the stem of her glass, bit into another of the *Golden Gaytime Bites* then said, 'Would it worry you if I was?'

Surprised to be asked, Greta thought for a moment. 'When you first mentioned him, I was worried… for you. I knew he'd recently lost his wife and I was concerned you were in danger of being hurt again.'

'But now?' Jo asked, her face alight.

'Now I've seen you together, I can see how…'

'We get on so well, Mum,' Jo interrupted. 'He's not like Damien. He's been hurt, yes… and he's grieving. But we… somehow, we… we're on the same page. And Mia… she's… she's like the daughter I'd love to have.'

'Are you sure it's not Mia who's the attraction?'

'What?' Jo looked surprised. 'No, Mum. I like Bryan, too. He's… I really like him a lot. But I… we're in no rush. We just enjoy spending time together. He's told me about his wife… and I've told him about Damien… and the baby. And if I stay in Bellbird Bay, who knows…?'

'I'm happy for you, Jo.' To Greta's surprise, she really was. She was glad Jo had found someone she enjoyed spending time with, someone who understood what she'd been through, who had suffered too and who was able to comfort her. None of them knew what the future had in store; it was enough to enjoy the present.

When Jo had left, and Greta was preparing for her lonely bed, she thought back over the conversation with her daughter and decided she should take her own advice. Instead of worrying about what might happen to Leo, to their relationship, she would concentrate on what they had and try to be content knowing he was doing good work. It wouldn't be easy, but she'd try.

Forty-two

Leo had been in Manila for a week and he'd found things a lot worse than he anticipated. Everything was chaotic, and rescue efforts were hampered by the lack of power and water. From day one, he'd been able to help with the rescue mission despite his lack of experience. It seemed every able-bodied man – and some not so able – was being put to use in one way or another.

There had been little time to think about Greta, or what he'd left behind in Australia. He could only hope Greta knew he loved her, and that he'd contact her when he could. In the meantime, hers was the face he saw in his mind's eye when he collapsed, exhausted, onto his makeshift bed at the end of each day. He hadn't deemed it appropriate to take up a room when there were so many others in need of accommodation.

The renovations on the hotel back in Bellbird Bay would be proceeding as planned. He'd left everything in Iain Grant's capable hands. The man seemed to know what he was doing and had been glad to have something to keep him occupied, and before he left, Leo had put him in touch with Ken. The two men had his authority to go ahead with bringing *The Leonard Family Resort*, Bellbird Bay, into being.

Today, he returned to the hotel as usual after helping pull people out of the wreckage. He pulled off the hard hat he now regularly wore and passed a hand over his face which was ingrained with dirt and sweat. What he'd give for a beer, but there was no chance of getting one. At least they had managed to restore the water supply to the hotel so he could slake his thirst with a glass of water, but he doubted there would be any to wash with.

Among the people huddled in the foyer as he walked through, was a face he recognised. Her normally immaculate dark hair was a mess, there were cuts oozing blood on her face and she was curled up as if in pain. 'Zoe?' he asked in amazement. 'What are you doing here? I thought you were in Thailand with…' He couldn't remember the name of her latest fling.

'As you can see, I'm no longer in Thailand. Joel and I came here a few weeks ago. He wanted to check out some of the traditional artwork. He…' She gazed around as if seeking something or someone.

'He's not here?'

'We became separated. I was brought here. He… You have to find him, Leo.' She clutched at Leo's arm, then gave a yelp of pain.

'What's the matter?'

'I've done something to my ribs… when I fell.'

'You weren't staying here?' he asked, puzzled.

'Here? How could we afford to stay here on the pittance your finance guy pays out?'

Leo winced. He'd been generous. More than generous. But it seemed that even in this dishevelled state, clearly in pain from her injuries, in the midst of the aftermath of an earthquake, Zoe could still manage to needle him about money.

'Sir!' Leo turned to see Adan trying to catch his attention.

'I have to go, Zoe.' He released her hands.

'But… Joel…' She grasped him again, her hand like a claw.

'I'm sorry, Zoe. There are others who need me. I'll get back to you when I can.' He freed himself from her to join Adan who was looking anxious. 'What's up?' he asked his manager when they were out of earshot of Zoe.

'More aftershocks out at sea and reports of the possibility of a tsunami,' Adan said, his face grim.

'Hell!' Leo groaned and dragged a hand through his hair. He wasn't prepared for this. He looked around at the groups of people crowded into the foyer, knowing every other corner of the hotel was the same. Once it was known *The Leonard* was an evacuation centre, it had been inundated with people fleeing from the devastation. Most had nowhere else to go and had set up home here with such belongings as they were able to save, some even bringing their animals. Children were running around among them, seemingly oblivious to the danger outside.

'Would it reach us here? What should we do?'

'There were hundreds of lives lost in the one in Indonesia in 2004. I was a boy at the time, but I remember my parents talking about it and what they'd do if it happened here. The waves were huge, and it moved fast. You need to move to high ground but with all the people here...' Adan looked around and shook his head.

'We'll just have to hope the reports are wrong, then.' Leo patted Adan's shoulder and tried to inject more confidence into his voice than he was feeling. For the first time he understood Greta's fears for him. *Had it been a foolhardy decision to come here, to put himself in danger? How much help had he really been? And how would Greta cope if he died here?*

*

The days flew past, each one busier than the last, leaving Leo little time to think about Greta or Bellbird Bay. It was only when he closed his eyes that the image of her face appeared, looking as calm and beautiful as ever, and he longed to see her again. But he knew there was work to be done here before he could even contemplate returning to Australia.

Zoe continued to be a problem for him. To date, there had been no sign of Joel, although she went out every day, checking in at various centres and, he suspected, wandering the streets in an attempt to locate him. She didn't want to believe he could be dead.

The breakthrough came when there was a shout of excitement from what had been the office of the hotel. It was where Adan still maintained a desk, and where several of the journalists had set themselves up.

Leo had just returned from yet another day of hard labour when he heard it and immediately hurried to see what was happening.

'Another planeload of supplies has landed,' Adan told him when he reached the office, 'with a couple of politicians from Australia. Now, maybe we'll see more action.'

'Good news,' Leo replied, 'but it won't change much on the ground.

There will still be the hundreds who've been dispossessed, who have lost their homes, their families, who...'

'We also have more water,' Adan said, 'so you can have a shower. It will be cold, but...'

'A shower?' Leo couldn't believe how much the thought of standing under a spray of cold water excited him. He'd felt filthy for so long, it had become second nature to him to fall into his makeshift bed still covered in the grime and sweat of the day. The guys in his Sydney office wouldn't recognise him if they could see him now.

Maybe Adan was right, and things were about to turn around. Maybe he could soon go back to Australia... but what was he to do about Zoe?

Forty-three

Greta was missing Leo so much. Every night when she went to bed, she cuddled into his sweater, imagining him in it, his body close to hers, his lips seeking hers, his… But it was no good. He wasn't there. There was no warm body to snuggle into, no arms to hold her. She was alone.

Leo had been gone for over two weeks now, and apart from a brief message he'd managed to send with the help of one of the journalists, she hadn't heard from him. She didn't know if he was alive or dead, though she was sure she'd sense it if he was dead. This belief was the only thing keeping her sane, this and *Birds of a Feather* where she spent most of her days.

But today was Monday, and the boutique was closed, giving Greta more time to think about Leo and to worry. Taking her breakfast tea and toast through to the living room, Greta turned on the television. She'd become addicted to the news bulletins from the Philippines, hoping one day she might catch sight of Leo in one of them, even though she knew there was little chance of it happening. The news was bad, but at least the threat of a tsunami had been averted. Greta just wanted Leo to come home. She knew Bellbird Bay wasn't really home for him but, given what he'd been saying about staying around, she'd begun to think that maybe it would become his home.

Wondering what to do with her day, and unwilling to spend it sitting alone, Greta pulled on a pair of jeans and one of her multicolour tops in an attempt to cheer herself up and set out, unsure where she intended to go.

She headed for the esplanade, then began to make her way up the boardwalk, past Eddie's house which was now Jo's home. It was a beautiful spot, one of the best locations in Bellbird Bay, she thought, admiring the homes on one side and gazing down to the beach on the other. Today there was enough of a breeze to whip up the waves. Greta was glad she wasn't out on the ocean on a day like this. The sea looked angry.

Turning back before she reached the headland, unwilling to risk being waylaid by Ruby Sullivan who lived in the house on the point, she was surprised by a large dog.

'Milo, where's your mistress?' she asked, even though she knew the dog couldn't speak back. But he must have understood, because he hung his head before turning back the way he'd come.

'Milo!' Libby appeared, panting. 'Oh, hello, Greta. The damned dog ran off when I opened the gate. It's unlike him to go off like that. We'd just been for our walk along the beach.'

'It looks wild out there today.'

'It is.' Libby pushed her windblown hair back from her face. 'Well, I need a cup of tea after that. Will you join me?'

Greta didn't need to be asked twice. She realised Libby's comforting company was exactly what she needed. Had it been her subconscious need for company which had led her up here... and had Milo sensed it, too? Telling herself not to be so fanciful, she followed Libby through her gate and into the house which was almost a mirror of the one next door, the one in which Jo was living.

'That's better,' Libby said, when they were seated in a sheltered spot on her deck with cups of peppermint tea and a plate of Tim Tams. Milo, chewing on a biscuit, had settled at their feet. 'I'm getting too old to be racing around like that, especially after a long walk. Adam's busy writing,' she said in response to Greta's unasked question. 'I took his tea in to him. When he's on a roll, he doesn't like to take a break.'

'Right.' Greta knew nothing about the habits of writers. She supposed they became so engrossed in the world they were creating, the real world disappeared. She'd read a couple of Adam Holland's books, but they weren't her favourite genre. She preferred books with characters she could relate to, stories of families, people like herself... and Libby.

'Now, tell me what you've been doing with yourself,' Libby said. 'I know Leo Carlson has gone to help in the rescue mission in Manila. You must miss him.'

For a moment, Greta was taken aback. *Did everyone know about her and Leo?* Then she remembered they'd all been at Jo's housewarming. 'Yes,' she said. Then, as Libby gave her a sympathetic look, Greta found herself pouring out all her fears and worry, ending up in tears. 'I'm sorry, Libby. Whatever must you think of me? I don't normally behave like this.'

Libby handed Greta a box of tissues, and she wiped her eyes.

'I think we need something a little stronger than tea,' Libby said, disappearing and returning with two small glasses. 'Sherry,' she said. 'I keep it for medicinal purposes… and for times like this.'

'Thanks.' Greta took a small sip, the warm liquid sending a glow right down to her toes.

'What's this? Drinking at this time of day?'

Greta looked up to see Adam Holland in the doorway, an amused smile on his face.

'Adam, I thought you were busy.'

'Obviously. Is this what you get up to when I'm writing?' he joked.

'Greta was telling me about Leo… Leo Carlson. He's in Manila. He went to offer what help he could. His hotel there has been set up as an evacuation centre.'

'Of course.' Adam immediately became more serious. 'It was a brave thing to do. I got caught up in a quake once… when I was a correspondent. It's no fun. But he should be safe,' he added, clearly seeing Greta's fearful expression. 'So, you ladies are having a glass of…' he picked up Libby's glass and sniffed, '… the best sherry?'

Libby nodded. 'Would you like some?'

'No. I didn't realise we had company. I've come to a grinding halt and thought we might go out to lunch. Why don't you join us, Greta?'

'Oh, I couldn't.' While Greta knew Libby from the book club, she'd only met Adam a couple of times and was in awe of the famous author.

'Nonsense, of course you must,' Libby said. 'Surf club?' she asked, looking at Adam.

'Where else?'

Greta felt obligated to agree and, as they walked down the

boardwalk together, she reflected that this wasn't how she expected her day to turn out.

Once in the surf club, seated on the deck with the sun on her face and a breeze ruffling her hair, Greta began to feel better. Sitting in these peaceful surroundings, it was difficult to believe such terrible destruction was happening elsewhere in the world.

Greta had always felt comfortable with Libby, finding the older woman always willing to offer an opinion but never to force it on others when they met at the book club. And Adam proved to be an interesting companion, regaling them with tales of his time as a political correspondent when he travelled to all parts of the world, stories she imagined Libby had already heard, but which were new to Greta. Reports of his exploits took her mind off Leo, which she was sure was his intention.

They had finished their meals and progressed to coffee, when they heard a commotion in the club and the door to the deck opened to reveal Will Rankin accompanied by several young people carrying banners reading *Rankin for Mayor*.

'Will!' Adam stood to shake Will's hand. 'I know the local election is imminent, but isn't the mayor voted in by other councillors?'

'You're right,' Will laughed. 'But these guys...' he gestured to his companions, who Greta now recognised as Will's son and his friends, '... want to give the other councillors a nudge – or a hefty shove.' He laughed again.

'I've heard you're a shoo-in,' Adam said, sitting down again. 'Can I buy you a beer? And what about your entourage?'

'Oh, they'll be off soon. Nate's shift starts shortly, and Owen and Bronte have work to get back to. It's their idea of a joke. That's enough, guys,' he said to the group of young people who, as Will spoke, had begun to check their phones.

'See you later, Dad,' said the one who looked like a younger version of Will, with his blond hair tied up in a bun and wearing a pair of disreputable shorts and a tee shirt bearing the slogan *Bay Surfboards*.

'Owen's business still going well?' Adam asked when the group had left.

'My word. I tell him he'll be able to keep me in my old age if it continues to grow the way it has in the past few months. Adding

Bronte to the mix was an act of genius,' he said, referring to the girl who'd arrived in Bellbird Bay, had joined Owen in the business and was now living with him and others in a share house.

'Neil says she's found her calling,' Adam said with a grin.

'Of course, I forgot. Ali's your sister and her and Bronte's father...' He nodded.

Greta listened, smiling. Bellbird Bay was such a small community. Everyone was connected in some way. She remembered Ali visiting *Birds of a Feather* several times and had heard she'd connected with Neil Simpson of *Bay Books*.

While Adam and Will went to the bar, Greta said to Libby, 'Thanks so much for inviting me to lunch. I seem to have been on my own so much since Leo left, apart from seeing Jo... and Cass. It's been good to see some fresh faces.'

'I'm glad.' Libby put her hand on Greta's. 'And, before the men come back, let me just say that anytime you want to talk... about anything at all. I'm a good listener and I never repeat confidences.'

'Thanks, Libby. I appreciate that.'

The two men reappeared at that point, carrying beers and two glasses of white wine, and the ensuing conversation focussed on the upcoming council elections, Will's forthcoming marriage to Cleo, who managed *The Pandanus Café*, and young Owen's latest venture into online marketing of surfing videos, in conjunction with Martin Cooper who was providing the footage. It was all a world away from earthquake torn Manila and strangely comforting.

*

Greta was on her way home when her phone rang. Seeing an unfamiliar number, she hesitated. But it was a local one so, curious, she accepted the call.

'Hello?'

'Mrs Roberts?'

'Yes.' Greta rarely called herself Mrs Roberts these days, preferring Greta Roberts, or Ms Roberts for anything more official.

'I'm so glad to have reached you. This is Catherine from *Bellbird Bay Hospital*. We have your husband here in Emergency.'

Her husband? Greta wasn't married, hadn't been for years. It must be some mistake, unless... 'Do you mean Mick Roberts?'

'Yes. He was brought in by ambulance this morning with a suspected heart attack. He had his daughter down as next-of-kin, but we've been unable to reach her. A colleague suggested we contact you. She knew your number from...'

Greta didn't allow her to finish. It didn't matter how they got her number. She knew Jo turned her phone off at school. All she could think about was Mick... another heart attack... and he'd been being so careful. 'I'll be right there.'

It took Greta another fifteen minutes to reach home, a few more to call Jo's number and leave a message, another few to open the garage and start the car. Then she was on her way.

Walking into the hospital brought back so many memories – happy ones of when Jo was born, more worrying ones when she'd fallen off her bike and broken her arm... and the last time, when she'd visited Mick here after he suffered a heart attack six years earlier.

Today, as she headed into Emergency, she clearly recalled that earlier time. She'd been disbelieving when she received the message. Mick had always been fit. Maybe he hadn't always eaten healthily, but he'd never stopped exercising and his work on the boat kept him in good shape. It was a wake-up call for both of them, though Greta had never changed her habits. Mick had. It didn't seem fair for him to have suffered another attack. He didn't smoke and rarely drank.

'Mick Roberts?' she asked at reception.

'And you are?'

'Greta Roberts.'

'His wife?'

Greta nodded rather than try to explain.

'He's in a cubicle through there.' She pointed to an opening close by.

Walking through, into an area where several cubicles were curtained off, Greta peered into each one till she saw Mick, hooked up to a series of gadgets, his face pale. He was still wearing his normal work outfit of shorts and a tee-shirt. When he saw her, he lifted one hand. 'Greta.'

'Mick.' Despite their years apart, Greta felt her eyes mist over. He looked so vulnerable lying there. It was difficult to equate him with the lively man she knew, who she had seen so recently – and tried her best to avoid.

'You came.'

'The hospital called me. Jo would have her phone turned off. I left her a message. I'm sure she'll be here as soon as she can.'

Mick nodded. He seemed to be finding speech difficult.

'Mrs Roberts?'

Greta turned to see a doctor in blue scrubs.

'I'm treating your husband today. He has suffered from a heart attack. I understand he suffered one…' he checked the computer by the bedside, '… six years ago, and has been on medication, and advised to change his lifestyle.' He looked up.

'He has done, as far as I'm aware. We are no longer together.'

'Right.' The young man – he must be younger than Jo – appeared embarrassed. 'A second attack is always more serious. We're considering surgery.'

'Again?' Greta knew Mick had had a stent inserted last time.

'This time the blockage is in another artery.'

'Oh!' Greta hadn't realised this could happen.

Mick reached out for Greta's hand. Automatically, she took it and gave it a squeeze.

'We'll be taking him down to theatre shortly. Then he'll be taken to a ward.'

'Jo,' Mick mumbled.

'I'll let her know.'

Once Mick had gone to theatre, there was nothing for Greta to do. She made her way to the cafeteria she remembered from previous visits and ordered coffee. Then she sent another text to Jo and prepared to wait, wishing she'd thought to pop her Kindle into her bag. As it was, there were copies of the local paper, *The Bellbird Bugle*, and old copies of *The Australian Women's Weekly* and *New Idea*. She settled down for a long wait.

*

'Mum, where is he?' Jo rushed in, hair flying. 'Is he…?'

Greta rose and gave her daughter a warm hug. 'Calm down, sweetie. Your dad's in surgery. The doctor said someone would call me when he was back in a ward.'

'Why do they need to do surgery? Didn't they put a stent in last time?' When Mick had his last heart attack, Jo had been in Europe, and had rushed home. It was the last time she'd been in Bellbird Bay… till now. 'A second attack's more serious, isn't it?'

'I think so.' Greta bit her lip. 'But your dad's a fighter… and he's in good shape.' *Could you really say that about someone who'd just had his second heart attack?* 'I'm sure he'll be fine.' She hugged Jo again. 'Shall I get you a coffee?'

'No.' Jo shook her head. 'I just want to see him. He's got to get better. I want…'

Greta's phone rang.

'Yes?'

'Mick is back in the ward – ward six in the cardiac unit. You can see him there. He'll be a bit groggy.'

'Thanks.'

'Is he?'

'We can see him. He's on a ward.'

Mick was indeed groggy when they entered the single room. Jo went immediately to his bedside. 'Dad!' She bent over to give him a kiss.

Mick smiled weakly. 'My Jo.'

Greta stood some distance from the bed, feeling superfluous. Maybe now Jo was here, she could leave. It seemed Mick was going to recover. There was no need for her to be there any longer, but something made her want to stay. 'I…' she began.

'You can't go, Mum. Dad needs us… both of us.' She turned back to Mick. 'We'll look after you, Dad.'

'Greta.' Mick stretched out his hand.

Greta took it, surprised by the wave of compassion which flooded her. They might be divorced, she might be in love with Leo, but Mick would always have a place in her heart.

It was sometime later, and Mick was falling asleep, when Greta and Jo left the hospital. 'Come back home with me,' Greta said. 'We can have my famous pesto pasta. You need to eat, and I'm sure you don't feel like cooking.'

'And you do?'

'I know we both need something in our stomachs. Your grandma – my mother – always said everything looks better once you've eaten.'

'Hmm.' But Jo nodded and followed Greta home.

Once there, Greta opened a packet of spiral pasta and emptied it into a pot of water, before unscrewing the jar of pesto sauce and pouring it into another, smaller pot. While she was doing this, Jo poured them both a glass of wine. 'I'll only have one,' she said. 'I have to drive home… and teach tomorrow. Though I'll worry about Dad until I can see him again.'

'I'm sure he'll be fine, honey.' Greta joined her at the table and took a gulp of her wine, glad she didn't need to drive anywhere. 'Why don't you stay here tonight? You can go home first thing and change then. It would be good to have some company tonight – for both of us. She knew Jo would imagine she was worried about Mick, and she was, but she was also worried that she hadn't heard from Leo for some time.

All through their meal, and afterwards, until they went to bed, Jo talked about Mick, about how much she regretted staying away from home for so long, about when he had his first attack, and how much she wanted to see her parents back together again.

It was difficult for Greta to keep from telling her it was never going to happen.

'What happened last time?' Jo asked at last. 'When he got out of hospital, after I went back to Europe.'

Greta bit her lip. 'I dropped round to check on him every night after I closed up. It was only for a week or so, until he could go back to work.'

'You could do that again…' she peered at Greta, '… or I could. I finish earlier. Or maybe he could stay with me for a bit.'

'I think he'd like that, honey.' Greta was glad Jo had come up with a solution.

'The doctor talked about inserting a stent. Didn't they do that last time?' Jo asked.

'They did. He had a blocked artery. But we all have more than one artery, and it appears a different one was blocked this time.'

'But…'

'It seemed your dad hadn't changed his habits. I thought he was eating more healthily and taking his medication…' Greta let her voice trail off.

'Well, now I'm back, I'll make sure he does.' Jo glanced across at Greta as if to imply she should have continued to check up on him. *As if anyone had ever been able to tell Mick what to do.*

'Good luck with that, Jo. But he should be home from hospital in a couple of days. It's quite a straightforward procedure.'

'You don't seem worried, Mum. This is Dad we're talking about.'

'Yes, and he's getting the best of care. Think of all those poor people who've lost everything in the earthquake. Many of them are in makeshift hospitals and…' Her eyes moistened again as her concern for Leo started to overflow. 'Sorry, Jo. You're right to be concerned about your dad, but I'm sure he'll be fine.'

After wishing Jo goodnight and seeing her settled in her old bedroom, Greta went to her own room and closed the door. With all the fuss about Mick, she'd missed the daily news report from Manila. She opened her iPad to check. But nothing had changed. The reporter was still standing in the midst of ruined buildings, talking about the possibility of more aftershocks and the miracle rescues. She turned it off, determined to try to get some sleep, comforted in the knowledge her daughter was again under her roof and was sleeping in the next room.

Forty-four

Leo was suffering from exhaustion from day after day spent working to help move huge slabs of concrete in an attempt to discover if any survivors were trapped under them. Each evening, when he returned to the hotel, he'd been forced to spend time trying to comfort a distraught Zoe. He'd been unable to devote any time to searching for Joel as Zoe demanded, but he knew she'd been around all the evacuation centres and Red Cross venues in an attempt to find him. All her efforts had so far proved fruitless, and Leo suspected he was dead, buried under a heap of masonry somewhere close to where he'd been when the earthquake struck. It had been sheer luck Zoe had survived and wasn't buried with him.

But Zoe refused to give up, becoming more and more anguished as each day passed. Leo wished he could do something for her. Although his feelings for her had long since died, he'd loved her once and he hated to see the smart, elegant woman he'd known turn into this fragile creature. She had become a mere shadow of the woman who had argued with him over lunch in Café Sydney before he went to Bellbird Bay. It had only been a few months ago, but so much had happened since then, it seemed like another life. Sometimes he wondered if he'd ever get back there, to Greta and the plans he'd made for their life together.

What was Greta doing now? Did she still think of him? If she was following the news reports, it would be easy for her to imagine the worst had happened, and he was dead. How he wished he was able to contact her. Now some form of communication had been restored, perhaps he could get another message through. The first time had been sheer luck. Maybe he could contact the office through one of the officials who were here. They could get a message to her, tell her he was fine – though that might be an exaggeration, given how he felt. He was sure he looked like a scarecrow, too. He hadn't checked himself in a mirror lately, too scared of what he might see.

'Leo, what am I going to do?' Zoe's hand grasped his as he walked by, intending to find someone who could send a message to Australia for him. 'I can't stay here.' She gazed around in disgust at the groups of families who had made this their home. 'And where's Joel?' she wailed.

'I don't know, Zoe,' Leo said, answering her second question first. 'But you may have to accept that we may not find him. If…'

'He can't be dead!' she yelled, causing those nearest to stare at her. All of them had lost someone; some had lost their entire family. Leo could understand how, to them, the sight of the privileged Australian in tears was just one more victim of the disaster.

Leo pulled her into a hug in an attempt to calm her. 'We don't know yet,' he said. 'But it's been weeks since you last saw him, so it's unlikely…'

Zoe began to weep, taking great gulps. 'What about me?' she wailed again. 'What will I do?'

Leo sighed. It was always about Zoe, though this time he did have some sympathy for her. 'You can come back to Australia with me,' he said without thinking. As soon as the words left his mouth, he regretted them, but what else could he do? She needed medical care, better care than she would get here, where there were many more urgent demands on the meagre resources. Once back in Australia, he hoped she could recover and revert to her normal self.

*

Leo wished he could eat his words again several days later, when word came that all non-essential Australian personnel were to be airlifted out of the Philippines and put on flights to Australia. And, despite his protestations, he discovered he was deemed to be part of that group.

Given his promise to Zoe, it seemed he was to be given responsibility for her, and they would travel together.

'We're really going home?' Zoe asked, when Leo gave her the news. 'To Sydney?'

Leo cleared his throat. 'We have places on an RAAF jet which will take us to Brisbane, with a connecting flight to Bellbird Bay.'

'Where the hell is Bellbird Bay?' Zoe suddenly sounded more like her old self. 'I don't know anyone in Bellbird Bay.'

Leo didn't want her there, either, but had no choice in the matter. 'It's a small coastal town north of Brisbane. I've bought a hotel there. It's only temporary, till you're fully recovered.'

'And then?'

'You can go back to Sydney.' *And hopefully out of my hair. Zoe would no doubt quickly find another like Joel to latch onto and would come back begging for money, but it was a small price to pay for his peace of mind.*

Zoe appeared happier at this piece of news, but her pretty face still held a bullish expression. 'Joel?' she asked.

'The authorities have his details. They'll let us know if they find him. There's nothing more we can do here.'

'I suppose not,' Zoe sniffed. 'Do you think he's…'

'Until we hear otherwise, there's always hope.' But Leo feared the worst.

Forty-five

Greta couldn't believe it. Leo was coming home. She felt like shouting it to the rooftops, but contented herself with telling Cass when she brought in their morning coffees.

'You must be pleased,' Cass said, smiling. 'When's the big day?'

'Thursday. His plane gets in at two. I can close early and meet him.'

'You'd close *Birds of a Feather*?'

Greta had never closed the boutique before, not even when Jo flew off on the first leg of her overseas trip, or when Mick came out of hospital the first time. 'He's important to me, Cass. I'm just so happy he's okay.' She blinked as her eyes misted over.

'I'm happy for you.' Cass gave her a hug.

'I wish you could meet someone, too.' She hugged Cass back.

'One day,' Cass said optimistically. 'I'm not holding my breath.' She chuckled. 'If it's meant to be, it'll happen.'

They were interrupted by a flood of customers, and Cass disappeared as Greta moved forward to serve them.

The rest of the day passed swiftly but between customers Greta couldn't help thinking of the message she'd received that morning. It would have been better if she'd heard Leo's voice, but the message was relayed by an anonymous woman from his Sydney office who said she'd been instructed to pass it on. So, all she knew was the time of the flight. But it was enough.

Greta spent that evening and the next preparing for Leo's return. She put fresh sheets on the bed, refreshed the potpourri and looked out her fluffiest towels. She planned to cook a special meal and had the champagne on ice.

She'd called Jo to let her know and, as she'd expected, her daughter's reception of the news was lukewarm.

'What about Dad?' Jo asked. 'You've been helping take care of him.'

Greta had hesitated, knowing it was true. After Mick was discharged, she'd joined her daughter at Mick's most evenings where the three of them ate together before both she and Jo went to their respective homes. On the weekend, she and Mick had been left alone, when Jo spent time with Bryan. Everyone in both Jo and Bryan's families now regarded the two as a couple, and Greta had happily put aside her earlier concerns and accepted their relationship.

'Your dad's almost back to normal now,' she said. 'He's been agitating to get back to the boat. It's lucky this happened off-season, but he's anxious to get things ready for the start of the summer tourist trade.'

'I know.' Jo sighed. 'But we'll miss you.'

'You'll be fine, both of you. You knew I wasn't going to do it for ever.'

Jo hadn't replied, making Greta believe she'd thought her mother would be there for him, that there was still a chance of them getting back together. It was just as well Leo was returning, and life could go back to normal.

*

Butterflies were turning somersaults in Greta's stomach as she prepared to see Leo again. She felt as if she was about to go on her first date, as she dressed in a calf-length dress patterned in tropical birds. She hoped it wasn't too bright, but it mirrored her emotions. The weather did, too, the sun shining brightly as she drove to the airport. She couldn't wait to see Leo, to feel his arms around her again, his lips on hers.

The plane was late.

Standing in the airport lounge among groups of other people waiting to meet their loved ones, Greta was sure none of them were as anxious as she was. *Would Leo still look the same? After the trauma he'd been through would the kind, gentle man she loved have become hardened?*

She reminded herself that he hadn't changed in the thirty-five years they'd been apart, so why should he have in the past few weeks?

Suddenly, there was a ripple of movement in the crowd, and the announcement of the arrival of the flight from Brisbane. She joined the surge forward towards the gate, her eyes peeled for her first sight of him.

Then she caught sight of Leo, head and shoulders above the other passengers. He was here!

Greta was so pleased to see Leo back safe and sound, she ran up to him and threw her arms around him, oblivious to all the other travellers. 'Leo, you're back!' In her excitement, she didn't notice the figure behind him, the slim dark-haired woman.

Extricating himself from Greta's embrace, Leo turned towards the woman. 'This is Zoe, Greta, she...'

Greta stared at the woman in surprise. *Zoe? Wasn't that the name of...?* 'Your wife?' she asked in a voice which suddenly sounded croaky.

'Ex-wife,' Leo said, as the woman stretched a hand to meet Greta's.

'Hello, you must be Greta,' she said. 'Leo has mentioned you.'

Mentioned? Leo had mentioned her? What the...? What had gone on in Manila? Why was she here? Were they back together? An icy chill ran down Greta's spine. She felt faint. *This couldn't be happening.*

Zoe's face held an amused expression.

She was enjoying this.

'It's good to meet you at last,' Zoe said, smiling sweetly. Then she gazed around. 'So, this is Bellbird Bay. You didn't tell me it was so... small,' she said to Leo.

'Let's get out of here,' Leo said, roughly pushing past the two women.

'I have my car,' Greta began. 'I can...'

'The office arranged a rental car for me,' Leo said, then, more gently, 'I didn't expect you to meet me, Greta. I'm sorry Zoe was a shock. I can explain.'

Looking at Leo more closely, Greta could see he was exhausted, his face grey with fatigue, his eyes clouded with the sights he had no doubt seen, lines on his face where they hadn't been before. She wanted to hug him again, to stroke away the worry, but...

'How long are we going to stand here? I need to lie down... in a proper bed,' Zoe said, clutching at Leo's arm.

'I'm sorry, Greta. We'll go straight to the hotel. I'll catch up with you later, when we're rested.'

Greta stared at him open-mouthed. This wasn't the reunion she'd planned, dreamt of, the image of him which had kept her alive during his absence. *How could she have been so stupid as to believe his promises again?*

Greta watched Leo and Zoe walk away in the direction of the rental car desk, then turned and made her way back to her car, tears streaming down her face. Once there, she sat for what seemed like ages, unable to move. Then she drove home to her empty house and her empty bed.

Forty-six

Leo couldn't get the expression on Greta's face out of his head. He winced every time he thought of it. He'd planned to break the news about Zoe to her gently, to explain why he had no option but to bring her back with him.

He had never expected Greta to be at the airport to meet him.

As soon as he reached his hotel suite, he called Greta but there was no reply. He sent a text suggesting they meet then, exhausted, fell into bed.

Once ensconced in the second-best suite in *The Leonard Family Resort*, which was comfortable despite the renovations which had begun in his absence – Iain Grant had been as good as his word – Zoe had reverted to type. It had only taken a hot bath, a healthy meal, some proper medical treatment and a good night's sleep in a comfortable bed for her habitual behaviour to reassert itself.

The hotel restaurant was closed due to the renovations so, seeing no reason to change the habit he'd developed here in Bellbird Bay, he took Zoe to *The Bay Café* for breakfast, greeting the waitress by name and ordering his usual eggs benedict with a black coffee. Zoe, after turning up her nose at the menu, opted for smashed avocado on sour dough toast with a chai latte.

'So that was Greta at the airport,' Zoe said while they were waiting for their meals. 'She seemed surprised to see me.'

'Yes.' Leo had been stunned to see the two women together. He'd intended to go to see Greta to tell her about Zoe, maybe even enlist her help. His ex-wife would need new clothes. She only had the ones she was wearing, which had been given to her by the Red Cross. 'She's…' He paused. How did he describe the love of his life to Zoe in a way that wouldn't encourage her to mock him for his sentimentality. She'd always enjoyed mocking him, even when they were married. She'd have a ball if she knew Greta was his first love, knew they'd met right here in Bellbird Bay when they were both eighteen. 'She's important to me.'

'Well, it seemed you're important to her, too… or you were… till she saw me.' She grinned, and Leo felt a shiver of not fear exactly, but of a dread of how Zoe might try to manipulate the situation for her own benefit. Now she was no longer the sad waif, sheltering from the aftermath of the earthquake, she could be a force to be reconned with – as he well knew. 'Oh, don't worry, Leo. I have no intention of spoiling your new romance – it is a romance, isn't it? I thought so,' she said as he turned red. 'But I will need some help in getting myself set up again, if Joel…' Her eyes filled with tears before she brushed then away. 'I lost everything in Manila, Joel had most of our money with him. And the Sydney house is rented for the rest of the year.'

Leo sighed. Nothing had changed. With Zoe, it was always about money. 'I'll contact Ken, and he'll see you right when you get back to Sydney. But you should stay here till you're fully recovered. The doctor said…'

'I know what the doctor said – post traumatic stress, cracked ribs, abrasions, yadda, yadda, yadda. There's nothing wrong with me that can't be fixed with a good injection of city life – not staying here in this dump.' She gazed around disparagingly at what Leo considered to be a slice of paradise.

Breakfast over, Zoe looked down at the jeans and shirt she was wearing. 'I need clothes,' she said. 'I can't go around looking like a tramp. Does this place have anywhere I can find something decent to wear?'

Leo saw Greta making her way towards her boutique.

Zoe's eyes followed his. 'Isn't that your *friend*? *Birds of a Feather*. At a guess, I'd say it's a boutique. Come on, Leo. I hope you have your credit card with you. Let's see if she has anything I'd be willing to be seen in.'

*

Greta's head ached. Her eyes felt gritty. She hadn't slept. What was she going to say to Cass who'd be all agog for news about her reunion with Leo? *How could he bring his ex-wife here... to Bellbird Bay, after all his declarations of love, all his promises?*

As soon as Greta walked into *Birds of a Feather*, the ambiance of the shop she'd created wrapped around her like a favourite blanket. This was her place, her haven. No one could take this away from her. She breathed in the scent of the new clothes and the residual fragrance of the scented candle she'd lit the day before, allowing it to fill her senses with its familiar aroma.

Greta had barely put down her bag and set up her computer ready for the day, when the door opened and in walked Leo. Behind him was the woman who had been with him at the airport – Zoe, his ex-wife. Greta almost gasped out loud, her heart suddenly racing.

The woman, dressed as she had been the day before, but looking fractionally more elegant, made a beeline for the rack containing Greta's newest lines and started rifling through them.

Forcing herself to appear calm, Greta pasted a polite smile on her face and, ignoring Leo, she went towards her, as she would to any prospective customer. 'Can I help you?' she said, hating that her voice came out too high-pitched.

'I need some new outfits. Everything I owned has been lost. Some of these might do for the time being.' She pulled several garments from the rail, held them up, and grimaced.

'The fitting room is over there.' Greta pointed to the far corner of the shop.

'Thanks.'

Leo moved closer to Greta, so close she could smell his aftershave. 'I can explain...'

'You don't need to explain. You don't owe me anything. I just wish you'd chosen some other shop to take your wife to.'

'She's...'

But Greta turned her back on him and walked across to serve a couple of women who had just entered. How dare he come in here expecting her to play nice, to listen to him while he told her he and his ex were back together, that he was sorry, that… She had no intention of giving him the opportunity to explain anything. The sooner the pair of them left Bellbird Bay, the better.

All the time Greta was serving the new arrivals, she was aware of Leo standing there, but she determinedly ignored him. She knew that if she looked at him, if their eyes met, she'd be unable to stem the tears which threatened to overwhelm her.

When Zoe appeared at the counter carrying a pair of wide-legged pants and matching top in bright yellow, patterned with white daisies, and a green dress covered in a geometric design, it was difficult for Greta to maintain a professional attitude. But she smiled as she folded the garments and popped them into one of her special bags.

'Your card, Leo?' Zoe turned to him with a smile.

Out of the corner of her eye, Greta saw Leo hand Zoe his credit card. She processed the sale, handed back the card and heaved a sigh of relief. But it wasn't over.

'I'll call you,' Leo said, as he took back the card.

Greta kept her eyes downcast, only raising them again when she heard the door close behind them.

It was a busy morning, and to Greta's relief, Cass didn't appear till almost lunchtime. But when she did, her expression told Greta she'd seen Leo and Zoe together.

Cass waited till they had taken their lunches outside and were seated on one of the benches facing the beach to ask, 'What gives? I had Leo in Sassy's this morning with a woman who acted as if she owned him – and he was paying her bill.'

'It's his wife – ex-wife. He brought her back from Manila with him.'

'What?' Cass's eyes widened. 'How…'

'Don't ask. I don't want to know.'

'But… there might be a perfectly reasonable explanation. You've spoken to him?'

'Not really.' For the first time, Greta wondered if she'd been too hasty in her assessment of the situation. Then she remembered the way the woman had clung on to Leo, the way he'd readily handed over his credit card to pay for her purchases. What explanation could there be other than that they had met in Manila and hooked up again? She tried to remember what he'd said about his ex-wife, but all she could recall was his insistence he hadn't felt for her what he did for Greta, and that she'd refused to have children.

'I thought he was the love of your life, that the two of you were going to ride off into the sunset together.'

'So did I, Cass. So did I,' Greta said, her voice breaking.

Forty-seven

Leo couldn't understand why Greta ignored him, why she refused to let him explain Zoe's presence in Bellbird Bay and why she hadn't replied to his text messages. Surely, once she knew what had happened, how he'd found Zoe, lost and alone, she'd understand? He had to talk to her... without Zoe hanging onto him. The woman seemed unable to be alone for five minutes.

He tried to call Greta, but each time, it went to voicemail, and this wasn't something about which he could leave a message.

It was next day before he finally managed to shake Zoe off, persuading her to go for a swim to christen the new beach gear he'd been coerced into purchasing for her as soon as she saw the display in the window of Sassy's. It was a shop he'd never noticed before but when he walked in with Zoe, he recognised the owner as being a friend of Greta's and saw her eyes widen in astonishment.

No doubt she'd have scurried to check with Greta as soon as they left.

Now, he picked up a couple of sandwiches and two bottles of sparkling water from *The Bay Café* and headed to *Birds of a Feather*. It was lunchtime, and he hoped to persuade Greta to join him on one of the benches where they'd sat before... before he went to Manila... before he brought Zoe back to Bellbird Bay... before there was any need to explain why his ex-wife was in town.

To Leo's relief, Greta was alone when he walked in. 'I thought we could have lunch together. We need to talk.' He motioned towards the beach side of the esplanade with the bag of sandwiches. For an awful moment, he thought Greta was going to refuse, then, flicking her hair back in a nervous gesture, she nodded.

'Okay. Give me a minute.' Greta disappeared into the back shop.

It was a long ten minutes before she reappeared, making Leo wonder what she had been doing. When she did join him, he noticed she had tidied her hair and renewed her makeup. *Was that a good sign?*

Without speaking, they walked across the road to sit on the bench – the same one they had sat on before he left, when everything had been going so well. This time, he was almost afraid to speak. Silently, he handed Greta a packet of sandwiches and a bottle of sparkling water.

'It's not what you think,' he said, breaking the silence.

'How do you know what I think?'

Leo tried again. 'It's not what it looks like. Zoe and I... we're not together.'

'You could have fooled me.' Greta carefully placed her unopened sandwich and the bottle of water on the bench between them. 'What happened in Manila, Leo? You were gone for so long. I didn't hear from you. I watched the news footage every day trying to understand what was happening, terrified, hoping to see you. You could have died over there, and I'd never have known.' Her voice broke.

Leo took a slug from his bottle of water before replying. 'It was hell, Greta, unimaginable. The news broadcasts couldn't convey the heat, the smells, the destruction, the misery and despair in people's eyes, people who had lost everything – their homes, their loved ones, all their possessions. They had nowhere to go, nothing to live for.' He paused, remembering. Then he gave himself a mental shake. 'Zoe was one of them.'

He heard Greta's intake of breath before she said, 'Oh, the poor woman.'

Leo continued, 'She and her partner had travelled to the Philippines only a few weeks before the earthquake struck. I found her in the foyer of my hotel, huddled there with other refugees from the quake. She and her guy had become separated. She'd been injured. I had to help her. She spent days wandering around searching for him but...' he shook his head, '... it was a pointless exercise. He was gone, like so many others. When the powers that be decided Australians should be evacuated, she had nowhere else to go. What else could I do? I had to bring her with me.' He spread his arms, knowing if there had been any way to avoid bringing Zoe to Bellbird Bay, he'd have taken it.

'Oh!'

Was that all she could say? What had happened to the warm, loving woman he'd left here, the woman who'd promised to be here waiting for him?

'So, what happens now?' Greta asked, her voice tight with an emotion Leo didn't recognise.

'Now?' He dragged a hand through his hair. 'As soon as I can arrange it, she'll be going back to Sydney. There's no way I want her here, no way she'd want to stay here in what she considers to be the middle of nowhere.'

'You're sure about that? She seemed very attached to you.'

'Very attached to my money. That's always what it's been about with Zoe. I'm only useful to her for what she can screw out of me.'

'Oh,' Greta said again, but she seemed to be thawing slightly.

What more could he say to persuade her Zoe meant nothing to him, that he was still in love with her, Greta, always had been, always would be?

'You're still the only one for me, Greta. You have to believe me.'

'I want to,' Greta said after a long pause, 'but, when I saw her at the airport, then again in the boutique, it made me realise there's a whole part of your life I know nothing about. Maybe we...' she took a breath, '... maybe we got carried away trying to recapture the past.'

Leo felt something shrivel inside. *This couldn't be happening.* 'Can't we go back to where we were? How about I drop round tonight? I can...'

'I need time,' Greta gazed out at the ocean, at the never-ending motion of the waves which Leo used to find soothing. Today, it merely served to emphasise the chasm which had opened between them.

'For what?' Leo didn't understand. He'd gone through hell and survived, only to come back to discover he'd lost the one thing he treasured more than life itself.

'To decide. I'm sorry, Leo. I can't just go back, not after I've seen you with...'

It was as if she couldn't bear to say Zoe's name. Greta was jealous, jealous of the woman who meant nothing to him, the woman he wished he'd never seen again, never met in Manila, never felt obligated to help. But Zoe had been his wife, and he still felt some responsibility for her. Despite her demanding and manipulative ways, she was vulnerable and needed his support to make a fresh start.

'I'm sorry,' Greta repeated. 'Thanks for lunch.' She walked off leaving the unopened sandwich and the bottle of water lying on the bench.

Leo looked at his own sandwich in disgust. He'd lost his appetite. Then he became aware of two women sitting nearby. They were talking loudly enough for him to hear. They were talking about Mick Roberts. Leo pricked up his ears.

'The poor guy… a second heart attack. Lucky for him his wife was there for him. I hear she rushed to the hospital to be at this side.'

'Ex-wife.'

'Whatever. My daughter works in Emergency and saw her come in. It may bring them back together. It often happens, you know. It can take something like that to bring home what you've thrown away. It happened to my…'

Leo stopped listening. He drained his water and left, his ears ringing with what he'd heard. Was this what it was about… why Greta was being so cagey? Was she using Zoe's presence as an excuse? While he was working his butt off trying to help in the rescue mission in Manila, Greta was playing nursemaid to Mick, to the man she professed to have no feelings for. And she had the hide to blame him for helping Zoe out.

Leo was still fuming when he returned to the hotel to find Iain Grant waiting for him.

*

Unaware of Leo's mood, Iain greeted him with a wide smile. 'Good to see you back in one piece. I've been watching the news. It looked pretty bad. You're a better man than I am, spending time in that hell hole. Did you find your hotel in one piece?'

'It's still standing,' Leo said grimly, 'unlike most of the city. We did what we could, but it wasn't enough. It could never be enough. Then they shipped us out.'

'You must be glad to be back.' Iain paused for a few moments. 'Have you had a chance to check out what we've achieved here while you've been gone?'

Leo stared at him. His eyes glazed over. *What was the man talking about?* It took him a few moments to realise Iain was referring to the program of renovation he'd been left in charge of. 'Some,' he said, dragging a hand through his hair. 'My mind's been on other things since I got here.'

'You've heard, then?'

'Heard what?' Leo knew he sounded brusque, but he was still smarting from his conversation with Greta, followed by what he'd overheard.

'I'm not sure if...'

'Spit it out, Iain.'

'Well... as you may know... my son, Bryan, has been seeing a lot of Jo, Greta's daughter, and... I may have got it wrong, but it seemed both Jo and Greta were spending a lot of time at Mick's. Sorry, mate.' Iain appeared apologetic.

Leo exhaled. Best he knew now, rather than giving up everything for what was no more than a pipedream, an image of the future conjured up by the magic of this place. Bellbird Bay had got to him, just like it had back when he was eighteen and he'd thought... he'd been planning to spend the rest of his life here. *How wrong could he be?*

'Can we do this another time, Iain? I need...' He needed to re-evaluate his entire future. *What was the point of spending time and money renovating this hotel if Greta wanted nothing more to do with him, if she was back with Mick Roberts? Had she intended to go back to him all the time? Had the relationship with Leo been a last fling before she renewed her marriage vows?* He remembered Mick's glowering looks, his jealous taunts. There was no doubt he was still in love with Greta... and they had a daughter together, a daughter who, according to Greta, wanted them to get back together. Well, good luck to them. Suddenly, the prospect of going back to Sydney and forgetting all about Bellbird Bay seemed very attractive.

Forty-eight

Greta wasn't sure if she could believe Leo's explanation of how Zoe came to be in Bellbird Bay, but realised she had no idea of the conditions in Manila. Perhaps he was telling the truth, but the woman had seemed so… so at ease with him, it was difficult to accept they meant nothing to each other. But, she reminded herself, they had been married for ten years, and had just shared a horrendous experience in Manila. Perhaps she was being too hard on Zoe and should try to be more understanding.

As soon as she closed up the shop on Saturday, Greta headed to cast her vote in the council election. She had planned to do it at lunchtime, then Leo had walked in and distracted her. It had been weird seeing him again in the same spot where they'd lunched together before he left, when she had believed him when he said she was the only one for him, that he'd never stopped loving her. Had he said that to Zoe, too? She flinched when the woman's name popped into her head.

The school where the voting was taking place was busy with last-minute voters when Greta made her way across the playground towards the main building.

'Hope I can count on your vote, Greta,' Will Rankin said, appearing from nowhere and flourishing a *How to vote* flier in her face.

'Of course, Will. Bellbird Bay needs you as our next mayor.'

'I hope you're right. I'd be honoured to serve the community in that way.'

'We're all behind you, Dad.' Will's son, Owen, appeared at his shoulder accompanied by his three friends.

'It's not up to you guys,' Will chuckled. 'But thanks for the vote of confidence. Kids!' he said to Greta, shaking his head when the group had moved on to hand out fliers to other voters.

Her vote cast, Greta went back to her car. She wasn't feeling sociable. All she wanted to do was go home, have a glass of wine and fall asleep, in the hope things would look better in the morning. Instead, she had a barbecue to attend. Now she was settled in, and Mick was on the road to recovery, Jo had decided to have a barbecue to celebrate.

It had been arranged when Leo was still in Manila and Jo had agreed that if he returned in time, he'd be welcome to attend with Greta. No chance of that now. Maybe Jo and Mick had been right all along.

She had intended to go home to change before going to Jo's, but the thought of her empty house was so daunting, she drove straight to her daughter's instead, surprised to see Mick's Toyota Landcruiser parked at the kerb. She hadn't thought he was up to driving again and was pleased to see she'd been wrong.

'Here she is,' Mick said, as soon as Greta walked in. 'I told you your mother would come straight here.'

'I voted first… and I hope you did, too,' Greta said.

'Did a postal vote a week ago,' Mick said virtuously. 'And Jo was helping out at one of the polling booths this morning.'

'Mum.' Jo came to give Greta a hug. 'How are you?' She peered at Greta. 'I heard about Leo… that he brought a woman back with him. The bastard!'

'I told you not to trust him,' Mick said complacently. 'These types are always on the lookout for someone new. Met her over there, did he?'

'She's his ex-wife,' Greta said shortly, her innate sense of fair play forcing her to defend Leo, though she couldn't imagine how identifying the woman was defending him. 'Evidently she was caught up in the earthquake.'

Jo raised her eyebrows.

'I heard his hotel was still standing, which is a lot better than others over there have. That must be a relief at least,' Mick said.

'It must, Mum. Wine?' Jo asked. 'Dad's not permitted to have any, but there's nothing to stop us. You don't mind, Dad, do you?'

'Go for your life, sweetheart. I'll just enjoy my glass of sparkling water and pretend.'

The reference to sparkling water reminded Greta of the bottle of water Leo had bought her, the one she had left untouched on the bench, along with the sandwich. But she'd found it impossible to eat or drink anything. She'd felt sick when Leo talked about Zoe, about how he clearly felt some responsibility for her, even though he vowed he still loved Greta.

'Wine sounds lovely, Jo,' she said. It was exactly what she needed to take away the memory of her day.

'Guess what?' Jo said with an excited grin, as she was pouring Greta a generous glass. 'I've been offered a permanent position at the school as of next term. So, I'll be staying in Bellbird Bay.'

'That's wonderful, darling.' Greta gave Jo a warm hug, feeling her mood rise. At least one thing was going right.

'Good for you, sweetheart,' Mick said.

'Now, I'd better circulate. You two be nice to each other.' She gave Greta and Mick a grin before disappearing.

Forcing herself to enter into the spirit of the evening, Greta began to move around the yard. She knew most of the people there, apart from Jo's colleagues from school. Bev and Iain, Libby and Adam were there, of course, along with Bryan and Mia, and Clancy and her parents. Tonight, the dogs had been left at home.

It was a happy evening or would have been for Greta if she could forget Leo. Seeing Bev and Iain together only reminded her of what she had lost. It would be much simpler for everyone if she and Mick were a couple again. But she no longer had feelings for him; meeting Leo again had highlighted that.

Greta had never seen Jo look so happy. She was positively glowing. And Bryan, laughing with his dad, seemed to have thrown off the sadness which Bev said had been dogging him since he arrived in Bellbird Bay. It was good to see the younger couple together, and now Bryan seemed to be recovering from the loss of his wife, it appeared to Greta that Jo's feelings for him were reciprocated, and he intended her to be part of his future – his and Mia's.

Mia was a charming child. At one point during the evening, she ran up to Greta and announced she had decided that, as Jo's mother, she deserved to have a special name. To Greta's delight. Mia had chosen to call her, Gigi, saying, 'You're not my grandma, but you're like a grandma.' It made Greta feel very special, and with the way things were progressing between Jo and Bryan, she entertained the hope she would indeed become Mia's grandmother, and maybe in the future there would be another little one to call her Gigi, too.

At the end of the evening, Greta found herself with Mick and Jo, most of the other guests having already left. She was almost sorry when he rose to leave, too. 'Have to get my beauty sleep,' he joked, then became more serious. 'It's time for my medication so I need to get back. It's been a good night, Jo,' he said to their daughter. Good to spend time with you, too, Greta. Don't forget what I said.'

How could she? She was sure Mick's repeated references to old times had been a deliberate ploy in an attempt to recapture the early days of their marriage. They had been good times, but for Greta they had been overshadowed by what came later, by his serial infidelity.

'Goodnight, Mick. Take care,' she said, turning her head to avoid the kiss he tried to plant on her lips. 'I should go, too, Jo.'

'Oh, stay for a bit longer, Mum, now everyone's gone. Bryan had to take Mia home to bed. I'll just see Dad out, then make us some tea,' Jo said.

'So, you and Leo Carlson, Mum,' Jo said when they were seated in her living room with mugs of peppermint tea. Jo hadn't closed the blinds and they could see out to the ocean and the dark sky. Tonight, the clouds hid the stars, and the moon shone dimly, the mist giving it an ethereal glow. 'What's happening?'

Greta twisted her mug in her hands. 'I don't know any more, Jo. Before he left for Manila, I was sure we were a couple, that we were going to spend the rest of our lives together. But now... this woman... his ex... I know he's explained how it happened, and it all sounds perfectly plausible, but what if...' All the doubts and fears which had been building up ever since she met him at the airport re-emerged.

'Sounds as if you don't trust him.' Jo tipped her head to one side.

'It's not that, but...' *Was it a matter of trust? Or was she remembering how he'd let her down before? Was she afraid it was going to happen again? Was her hesitation a way of protecting herself against being hurt?* 'Maybe I'm too old for all this. I was happy before Leo came to town. I have the boutique… and now I have you, and you look like staying around. I guess Bryan Grant has something to do with that?'

Jo blushed. 'And you have Dad,' she said.

Greta winced. 'Oh, my darling. That's never going to happen. Even if Leo Carlson didn't exist, there's no way your dad and I would be getting back together again. Those sort of feelings I had for him died long ago. He's good company, a good friend. It was fun to spend time with him tonight, but we can't turn back the clock. We'll never be more than friends, no matter what your dad thinks.'

'I didn't realise.' Jo appeared downcast. 'But you're not too old, Mum. Look at Bryan's dad and Bev Cooper. They're your age and they seem to have managed to…' She blushed, perhaps at the idea of her mother having an intimate relationship. 'But, Leo Carlson, are you sure it's not going to happen with him?'

Greta shook her head, her eyes moistening. She knew her attitude at lunchtime had surprised him, but once Leo had time to consider it, she was sure he'd come to the same conclusion as she had. Things were best left as they were. He was still in Bellbird Bay. There was still the hotel to renovate and the grand opening he'd planned. But there was no need for them to see each other again. It would be better if they didn't. Then he'd be off back to Sydney… with Zoe… just as he'd always intended. It was best Greta remember their time together as another magical interlude which wasn't part of her real life.

Forty-nine

Leo felt as if his world had been turned upside down. It was two days since he'd spoken with Greta, since he'd heard the two women gossiping about her, followed by Iain's confirmation that she and Mick were back together.

Today, he'd agreed to meet with Iain again. He'd followed him round the hotel in a daze, trying to come to terms with what he'd been told. One part of him wanted to go back to *Birds of a Feather*, to storm in and ask Greta if it was true. Then he remembered her caginess during their last meeting. Was it due to the fact she didn't want to tell him about her and Mick? It was difficult to believe she had changed during the time he was in Manila, but these things happened.

Had he just been a distraction for Greta? A... what was the word the woman had used to the George Clooney character in the movie he'd watched on the plane? A parenthesis, that was it. Is that what he'd been for Greta? It didn't feel good.

When he arrived in Bellbird Bay, he'd hoped Greta might still be there, but had no intention of rekindling their lost love... or had he? *Had he been the one to make the running? Had Greta really been as invested in their relationship as he was?* Try as he might, he couldn't believe she didn't love him. But what other reason might she have for going back to Mick?

It would be a different matter if she'd only turned to Mick *after* she saw him with Zoe. But according to Iain – who was a more reputable source of information than the two gossiping women he'd overheard by the beach – she had been spending time with her ex long before that. Sure, he was sorry the guy had suffered a heart attack, but surely there were others who could take care of him? He stifled the thought that Greta was a naturally caring person who would provide comfort and care to any friend in need.

He got little sleep that night, awakening early from what rest he did manage to achieve with a sore head, bleary eyes and a bad temper. The call from Ken when he was having breakfast in *The Bay Café* did nothing to improve his mood.

'This may not be the right time,' Ken began.

'What?' Leo wasn't in the mood to indulge his colleague.

'We've had an offer.'

'What do you mean we've had an offer? An offer for what from whom?' He didn't have time for this… and he could see Zoe sauntering towards him. He didn't have time for her either this morning.

'An offer for the hotels. Remember me telling you *Sun Resorts* were sniffing around? They've finally made an offer. It's a generous one, one you might want to consider.'

'What the hell are you talking about, Ken? I have no intention of selling. In fact…' he made a sudden decision, '… I'm planning to come back to Sydney as soon as I can arrange a flight.'

There was a stunned silence, then, 'Right, Leo. I'll have Philippa organise a flight for you.' He cleared his throat. 'What about Zoe? She's still with you?'

Leo looked at the dark-haired figure making her way towards him across the esplanade. Now dressed in one of the outfits she… he had purchased in *Birds of a Feather*, she had regained her former elegance. 'You'd better arrange a ticket for her, too,' he said, before ending the call.

'Good morning,' Zoe greeted him, taking a seat at his table as if she belonged there.

'Is it?' he grunted.

'Who got out of the wrong side of bed this morning?' Zoe asked, seemingly in a better mood than she had been since she'd arrived in Bellbird Bay.

'Don't you start.'

'Sorry. When can I go back to Sydney?' she asked. 'I'm feeling a lot better and will feel better still once I leave this ungodly place.' She glanced around her disdainfully.

'Maybe tomorrow. I've asked Ken to book our flight.'

Zoe's eyes widened. She clearly hadn't expected this response. 'You have? Good. You plan to go, too? What about your...?' Her eyes moved towards where *Birds of a Feather* sat, still empty at this hour on a Sunday morning.

Trust Zoe to have worked out something had happened between him and Greta. 'For both of us,' he said shortly. 'You can take the spare room in my apartment till you get yourself sorted out.' It was the last thing he wanted – Zoe around in his harbourside pad, but it would keep her happy until she found her own place – or another man to latch onto, whichever came first. And he didn't intend to be there. Now might be a good time to do the tour of his hotels he'd always promised himself. That would take his mind off Bellbird Bay... and Greta. As for the hotel in Bellbird Bay... he'd decide what to do with it later.

*

Leo's mind was in a turmoil as he waited to hear their flights had been organised. He knew going back to Sydney was the right thing to do, even though it went against the grain to give up on Greta. But he couldn't bear the thought of staying here and seeing her and Mick together.

By the time the call came, he had changed his mind about ten times, but as soon as he heard Philippa's calm voice giving him details of a flight to Sydney, his doubts disappeared.

'Was that...?' Zoe asked, appearing at his shoulder.

'We're on a flight this afternoon.'

Zoe's worried expression cleared, then she frowned again. 'And Joel?'

'Still no word. I'm sorry. Zoe. Maybe...'

'No! I won't believe he's dead. He can't be. I know you don't think much of him, but he's...' Her eyes moistened.

Leo pulled her into a hug. 'I'm sorry, Zoe, but we may never know what happened to him. Why don't you put your things together and we can go to the airport?'

Brushing the tears from her eyes, Zoe walked off, and Leo made his way to his suite to pack his own belongings.

Neither spoke much on the way to the airport or on the flight. Leo was still thinking of Greta, wondering how he could have got it so wrong. In an attempt to take his mind off her, he opened his laptop and began to plan the itinerary for his tour of the Leonard hotels.

'What are you doing?' Zoe asked, coming out of the cone of silence she'd been in since they left Bellbird Bay.

'Planning a trip. I won't be in Sydney for long. It's time I toured my hotels. So, don't worry, I won't be in your way.'

'Oh! I plan to contact the Red Cross in Sydney. They may have news of Joel.'

Leo didn't reply, only squeezing her hand. Zoe clearly didn't want to believe Joel was dead, lying under a pile of rubble somewhere in Manila, that his body, like so many others, might never be found. He didn't blame her. It must be very difficult to accept.

*

Back in Bellbird Bay, Greta was trying to come to grips with the fact Leo had left. The Bellbird Bay gossip mill being what it was, it had taken no time for Cass to tell her that Leo and a dark-haired woman had been seen heading to the airport. The news had come shortly after a text from Leo which had expressed his regret things couldn't work out between them and to wish her well for the future.

Greta deleted it immediately, upset with Leo and irritated that Mick had been right about him. She wondered what would happen to the hotel. Perhaps he'd sell it again. One thing she was sure of, if Leo Carlson dared to show his face here in Bellbird Bay again, she'd keep out of his way.

Fifty

Leo had been back in Sydney for almost a week, and the arrangements for his trip were close to being finalised. It was strange to be back in the city again, and to be sharing his apartment with Zoe. He'd forgotten what it was like to share living space with her and couldn't wait to be off.

This morning, he was standing out on the balcony with his coffee before going to the office. Since his return, he'd been finding the office claustrophobic, no doubt a reaction to being in the city after the fresh air and the scent of the sea he'd become accustomed to in Bellbird Bay. He missed his regular breakfasts in *The Bay Café* and… yes, he missed Greta.

He wished things could have been different, then remembered a favourite saying of his grandmother – *if wishes were horses, beggars would ride.* He gave a wry grin.

Hearing a sound from inside the apartment, he glanced to where Zoe was seated at the dining table, her phone clasped to one ear, tears streaming down her cheeks. Seeing him, she waved the phone in the air, then spoke into it again before closing it. 'It's Joel,' she said, running out to join him and throwing her arms around his neck. 'He's alive!'

Leo extricated himself and, taking her by the arm, led her to the sofa where he sat her down. 'Now, tell me,' he said.

Zoe smiled through her tears, then the words tumbled out of her. 'I just had a call from the Red Cross in Manila. They've found Joel. He was being cared for by family living in the ruins of an old building on the outskirts of the city. He had no idea of how he got there, or who he was. It wasn't till the Red Cross guys found him and took him to one of the evacuation centres that he was recognised. It seems he's still disoriented and in poor shape... but he's alive!' Her voice rose in excitement, making Leo realise she cared more for Joel than he'd imagined.

'I'm happy for you, Zoe.'

'Thanks, Leo. I know I've made things difficult for you... with Greta. I didn't mean to, but... it was hard to see you happy when Joel... Anyway, he'll be flown back to Sydney, so I can see him there. Can we...' she gave Leo a pleading look.

'You can both stay here till you get yourselves sorted out. It sounds as if he may need medical care.'

'I can look after him.'

Looking at the determined expression on Zoe's face, Leo believed she could. He didn't envy any authority, medical or otherwise who dared to disagree with her. At least his planned trip would keep him out of their hair and hopefully, by the time he returned, Joel would have recovered, and they'd have moved on.

*

Despite Leo's best efforts there were a few hiccups in his plans, and he still hadn't set off when Zoe received the news that Joel would be arriving in Sydney in two days' time.

Zoe was beside herself with excitement, but disappointed Joel would have to spend some time in hospital before he could join her. 'The woman I spoke to was most firm – almost rude,' she said, pouting. 'But I suppose they know what's best for him. The good news is that I can be at the airport to meet him and travel to the hospital with him. I plan to spend every day there till they let him come home.'

Pleased with Zoe's good news, when he arrived in the office, Leo was in a better frame of mind than he had been since he returned to Sydney, only to have it crushed when Ken greeted him.

'Bad news on the Bellbird Bay acquisition, Leo,' he said, frowning.

Leo's heart plummeted. 'What's happened? I thought you and Iain had everything in hand.'

'We did... but...' Ken pulled on one ear, 'it seems there's been a glitch with the builders... and Iain's plans. He'd like you there to sort it out.'

Leo felt his stomach churn. Bellbird Bay was the last place he wanted to be.

*

The sun was shining when Leo stepped off the plane in Bellbird Bay, and he felt as if he was coming home. But this time, there was no Greta there to greet him. He wondered if she knew he was back but was aware it would be unwise to try to see her. No doubt by now, she and Mick might have set up home together again.

Renting a car – a more modest model than before – Leo drove straight to the hotel where he'd arranged to meet Iain. With a bit of luck, this could be sorted out quickly and he'd be back in Sydney before anyone knew he was here.

'Glad you could make it, Leo.' Iain greeted him in the foyer. 'I was afraid you might already have left the country.'

For a moment, Leo wished he had. Being back here brought back too many memories. 'I almost had. Can we get this sorted quickly, Iain?'

'I hope so. It's through here...' Iain led the way to where the builder was poring over the new plan for what had been the ballroom and Leo wanted turned into a children's play area.

At their arrival, the man turned round.

'What's the problem?' Leo asked, only to be bombarded by a torrent of words, the main gist of which was the additional time and costs incurred if the plan was followed. The builder had agreed to a fixed price contract which was now going to blow out. He looked across at Iain who was standing with his arms folded, and wished this could have been dealt with by phone.

'I've tried to explain,' Iain said.

Leo waved him away. 'How much?'

At the amount involved, his eyes widened. But he had no desire to stay here wrangling over a few thousand dollars. 'Do it,' he said. 'I'll get Ken to redraw the contract.'

'Thanks, Leo. Perhaps I overreacted, but a contract is a contract, and I was concerned on your behalf. I know how keen you were to have the play area completed.

'Thanks, Iain.'

'Time for a coffee?'

'Sorry, I'm booked on the afternoon flight back to Sydney.'

'Okay. Thanks again for making the trip. We'll see you around.'

Leo nodded, with no intention of coming back. He still hadn't decided what to do about the hotel once the renovations were complete.

He was on his way out of the hotel when he almost knocked over a tall blonde woman in the doorway.

'Jo!' he said in surprise. *What was Greta's daughter doing here?*

'Leo, thank goodness. I heard you were back, but I wasn't sure I'd find you here.'

'You almost didn't. I was about to leave.'

'Can we talk?' She gazed around the foyer, filled with building materials.

He checked his watch. 'Here? I don't have much time. I was on my way to the airport. He was curious to hear what Greta's daughter might have to say to him – but talking with her might make him miss his plane. Maybe she wanted to tell him about her parents' reunion. If so, she was too late.

'Here will do. Is there somewhere we can sit?'

Leo led Jo into the office which had remained relatively untouched. *What could be so urgent?*

Once inside, he took a seat, and she perched on the edge of another.

'It's Mum,' she said.

'If it's about her and your dad getting together again, I already know. I'll be going back to Sydney again, so she doesn't need to worry about me.'

'No!' Jo said in a strangled voice. 'It's not... they're not... I'd hoped they would, but Mum finally set me straight. You're the one she cares for.'

Leo stared at Jo, his thoughts going around in circles. 'But...' he hesitated to say he'd listened to gossip, '... I heard she was there when he took sick... and when he came home from hospital.'

'That's all true, but the hospital only called her because my phone was turned off. And...' she looked shamefaced, '... when he got home... that was my doing... plus Mum's natural caring nature. I thought it might bring them back together. But I was wrong.' She sighed. 'Mum told me at my barbecue. She never had any intention of getting back with him. It was all Dad's idea... and mine.'

'But she said...' Leo was trying to process what Jo was telling him. *How could he have got things so wrong?*

'I don't know what she told you, but I do know that seeing you with your ex knocked her for six. She was a wreck while you were away and was looking forward to your return so much... I didn't realise how much,' she muttered, almost to herself. 'Then, when you did come back, you weren't alone. She told me about how you and your ex-wife came into *Birds of a Feather* and the woman acted as if you were still married.'

'How...?' But Leo remembered the scene. Zoe had always treated Leo as if they were still a couple... and him paying for her purchases probably hadn't helped. He wondered if Greta had even listened to his explanation of how Zoe came to be here in Bellbird Bay or if she'd already made up her mind about the situation.

'It's partly my fault,' Jo continued. 'I was trying to push her and Dad together. I took his side and told her it would never work with you. I'm sorry.'

Leo stared at her.

'She's in *Birds of a Feather* now,' Jo said helpfully.

Fifty-one

Greta was tired. She hadn't slept well since Leo had returned to Sydney, and the morning had been busy, culminating with a woman who must have tried on half the shop, before finally settling on the first outfit she'd picked. She was about to replace the discarded garments on the rails, when the door burst open, and Leo walked in.

Greta's stomach began to churn. 'What…' she started to say, when he locked the door and turned the sign on it to CLOSED.

'What are you doing here?' Greta gripped the edge of the counter behind her, her hands sliding over the discarded garments.

'Jo came to see me,' Leo said.

'Jo?' Greta was shocked. *What had Jo been doing going to see Leo?*

'She told me you and Mick weren't getting back together.'

Greta's eyes widened. What was he talking about? 'What… who…?' she stammered.

'It was something I heard. I thought it explained your coldness… when you said you needed time.'

'I meant exactly what I said. It was a shock to see you with…' she swallowed, '… your ex-wife, after your protestations of love. I needed time to adjust, to work out if I could believe you. Surely you can understand that?'

'I can now. I've been a fool, Greta. I thought…' He dragged a hand through his hair. 'Hell, I don't know what I thought. Zoe means nothing to me, but I've always been consumed with guilt at the way I allowed my obsession with the hotels to fill my time. It's why I've always given in to her demands… mostly for money. Seeing her in Manila, reduced to the status of a refugee… I felt responsible. I couldn't leave her there. But it's you I love. You're the one I want to grow old with.'

Greta felt herself weaken, the churning in her stomach beginning to slow. Could she believe him? 'But… what if you go off again… if *Zoe* needs you again?'

'I won't… she won't. Her… Joel has been found. I…' His eyes flickered as if suddenly making a decision. 'I've had an offer for the hotels. I can accept it – all except the one here in Bellbird Bay. Doesn't that prove I mean what I say?'

Greta stared at Leo again. *He'd do this… for her?*

Taking advantage of her hesitation, Leo moved closer, pulling her into an embrace.

It felt good to feel his arms around her again, to breathe in his familiar scent. Then his lips were on hers and everything else faded away as she became lost in a tumult of desire.

But… Greta pulled away. *How could she be sure? Leo had let her down before. Was his apparent change of heart real or just another false promise?*

'I'm sorry, Leo. I can't process all this right now.' She stared at him, the sight of the face she had thought about for years, thought never to see again, filling her with hope. But she was aware of how easily everything could change again, leaving her to lick her wounds alone.

Leo seemed to sense her unease. 'What can I do, say, to make you believe me?'

Greta was tempted to throw her arms around him, to tell him she did believe him, that everything would be all right. But something, some innate sense of preservation held her back.

'How about I drop round tonight?'

Greta hesitated.

'No need to go to any trouble. I'll bring a pizza.'

'Okay.' It was the least she could do. Maybe by then she'd have come to some resolution.

Leo leant forward to give her a kiss on her forehead, before walking towards the door, where he changed the sign to OPEN again before leaving.

It was close to closing time when Cass popped her head in. 'I heard Leo was back,' she said.

Greta stared at her.

'I heard Leo Carlson was seen driving in from the airport.'

'How...?'

'Don't ask. So, how are things with lover boy? All sorted?'

'Oh, Cass. I don't know. Leo was here earlier, telling me I was the love of his life, that he plans to sell his other hotels and settle here in Bellbird Bay. But...'

'You don't believe him?'

'I don't know if I dare.'

'Well, far be it from me to offer advice – I've never done too well in the man department – but it sounds as if the poor guy is turning his life around for you.'

'He's not...' Greta was about to say, 'He's not a poor guy,' when she remembered the pleading expression in Leo's eyes.

'Maybe it's time you took him at his word. It is what you want, isn't it?'

'Of course it is.' Greta was sure about that.

'Well then. What's holding you back? Is it fear or pride?'

Greta considered for a few moments before replying. 'I'm just afraid of being hurt again.'

But as she made her way home Cass's words were in Greta's head, reinforced by the call from Jo.

'Did Leo come to see you, Mum? I'm sorry I took against him at first. I can see now that he means a lot to you – and you do to him. I just want you to be happy.'

Oddly enough, it was Jo's last remark that got through to her. Greta wanted to be happy, too. She was tired of being alone, and Leo' reappearance in her life had seemed as if life was giving her a second chance. Would it be mad to allow it to pass her by because of some misguided fear of being hurt again?

By the time she heard Leo at the door, Greta was still undecided. Dressed in her brightest outfit, chosen to give her confidence, she opened the door to see the man she knew beyond any doubt she loved with all of her heart. Throwing caution – and her doubts – to the wind, she smiled and reached towards him.

*

'What shall we do today?'

Greta opened her eyes at the sound of Leo's voice in her ear, glad it was Monday and there was no need to jump up, no shop to open. Last night, the pizza momentarily forgotten, they'd gone straight to bed. It didn't matter that the sheets were no longer in the pristine condition she'd prepared ready for his return. They didn't notice, only resurfacing much later to drink the champagne which was still in the fridge and feast on the cold pizza, followed by some of Greta's favourite chocolate brownies.

Now, they had a whole day to spend together.

'I know somewhere I'd like to go,' she said. 'Can you guess?'

'Dolphin Bay, our special place.' Leo smiled and pulled her into his arms, his lips travelling from her forehead, across her eyelids and down to meet hers.

'Our special place,' Greta agreed, when she was able to speak.

After breakfast, Leo left her for a few moments, citing the need to make a call. When he returned, he had a self-satisfied expression. 'That's done,' he said.

'What?'

'I just told my financial controller to accept the offer on the hotels. So, you'd better not change your mind now.'

'Never.' How could she ever have doubted him?

'Ready?'

Greta picked up her bag with a smile.

They were strolling along the soft sand, the only people on Dolphin Beach, Leo's arm around Greta's shoulders, when she asked, 'What's happening with Zoe?' It took a moment for her to say the woman's name after the trouble her presence had created.

Leo checked his watch. 'Right now, she's back in Sydney sitting at Joel's bedside. He's the guy she was travelling with, the one we feared dead. Sydney's where I should be, too. I was booked on a flight yesterday.'

Greta's breath caught at the knowledge of how close she'd come to losing him, all because of her own stupidity – and local gossip. She hugged closer to Leo, grateful to her daughter for seeing what she couldn't, and for putting Greta's happiness before her own desire to see her mum and dad back together. 'I'm glad Jo went to speak to you. It never occurred to me she would.'

'How do you think she'll like having a stepfather?' Leo asked, as if it was the most natural thing in the world and rendering Greta almost speechless.

Did he mean? 'Do you mean… are you asking me to marry you?'

'Do you want me to go down on one knee? You did agree when I did that… a long time ago.'

Greta remembered that day. The sun had been shining just as it was today. They had been here on Dolphin Beach. She had been wearing her favourite dress – pink and white stripes with tiny shoestring straps – and Leo had been wearing a pair of red, white and blue board shorts. He had gone down on one knee, had placed the ring from a drinks can on her finger and vowed to love her for ever. She had kept that ring for such a long time, a reminder of what had been the most beautiful day in her life. 'I remember,' she said softly, 'and my answer's still the same.'

At her words, Leo picked her up and whirled her around and around till she was dizzy. Then he gently let her down to allow her feet to sink back into the sand, and kissed her, holding her as if he would never let her go.

Fifty-two

It was the Saturday of the October long weekend, and the sun was already beating down on Bellbird Bay with the promise of a perfect summer day. Everything was in place for the grand opening of *The Leonard Family Resort*. The official opening wouldn't take place till six o'clock, but for Greta and Leo, the celebrations had already begun.

'Happy?' Leo whispered in Greta's ear as she slowly opened her eyes, a sense of wellbeing filling her with delight.

'Mmm.' Her mouth curled up in the smile that was never far away these days. Ever since Leo had burst into *Birds of a Feather* and forced her to listen to him, she'd been on cloud nine. Everyone had noticed the difference in her, Cass misquoting the classic line from *Harry meets Sally* – 'Wish I could have a chunk of what you're having.' Even Mick had come to accept her and Leo as a couple, while Jo was taking credit for helping them reconcile.

Greta had closed *Birds of a Feather* for the day to allow her to spend it with Leo. Jo was coming along, together with Bryan – and Mia, of course – to help with the picnic for their close friends at Dolphin Beach where, as Leo proudly told everyone who would listen, it had all begun. He didn't, of course, go into details – only Greta knew those. Then, they'd all go to the hotel to finish hanging the streamers they'd started on last night and take delivery of the fresh flowers which were to decorate the foyer.

The first guests wouldn't be arriving till next day, but the hotel was fully booked through to early February, with bookings now coming in for the Easter holidays. Many were people who had stayed at the old hotel and were interested to see the changes Leo had made, but most were new guests, lured by the magic of Bellbird Bay and the news reports of *The Leonard Family Resort*.

To Greta's delight, once Leo had made the decision to stay in Bellbird Bay and manage the hotel himself, the community had rallied around him with both Martin Cooper and Adam Holland using their contacts to publicise the hotel both in Australia and overseas.

Now it was all set to come to fruition.

'Welcome, everyone.' Leo looked more handsome than ever, Greta thought, as he stood in the foyer of the renovated hotel to greet those invited to share the grand opening. 'It's been a journey not without its challenges, but I'm happy to have made it to tonight, to be able to share with you the vision I had when I stepped into this building several months ago. When I read about a hotel for sale in Bellbird Bay, it evoked memories of a magical summer I spent here, a summer where I met a wonderful girl...' he smiled across at Greta.

She smiled back, a warm glow coursing through her.

'... the girl who has agreed to become my wife.'

There was a loud cheer from a group containing Will Rankin and Martin Cooper. Everyone laughed.

'That aside, as soon as I returned to the town, it enfolded me in its warmth, in the same magical atmosphere I remembered, with the same friendly people. I knew it was the right place for me. And the more I became involved with the town, the more I realised that, not only did I want to own a hotel here, I wanted to make my life here, too, in this special community which first accepted me as one of a group of schoolies...'

Everyone laughed again.

'... then as a so-called hotel magnate. I know, at first, several of you had concerns regarding what I might do with the hotel. I hope I have managed to allay those concerns and *The Leonard Family Resort* will become something for Bellbird Bay to be proud of. Now, I'd like to pass over to the new mayor of Bellbird Bay, Will Rankin, to perform the formal opening.'

There were cheers and catcalls as Will took the microphone.

'There's not much more I can say,' Will said. grinning. 'I was one of those surfers who, after a lot of jibes, accepted the group of schoolies, more years ago than I care to mention. And I have to admit I was one of those who expressed concern when I heard Leonard Holdings were planning to buy this hotel in our small community. But Leo Carlson proved to be a man after my own heart. He has not only put my concerns to rest, he has exceeded my expectations of what this hotel could be, what it could offer visitors to our town, and for that he is to be commended. I'm now happy to count him among my friends, and to declare *The Leonard Family Resort* well and truly open.'

There was a loud cheer as waiters began to circulate with trays of champagne and everyone tried to reach Leo to congratulate him.

Greta watched from a distance as Leo shook hands and smiled, hugging the knowledge he belonged to her.

Finally, when all the well-wishers began drifting off towards the tables piled with food, Leo made it back to her side. 'I'm glad that's over,' he said, running a hand inside the collar of the smart cream shirt Greta had helped him choose, telling him it complemented his eyes. 'I can't wait till everyone's gone and we're on our own. You're looking wonderful tonight, my darling. I still can't believe I found you again.'

Greta looked down at the bright blue dress patterned with peacocks she was wearing and the sparkling ring on the third finger of her left hand, then up at the man she'd never stopped loving, not even when there seemed to be no future for them. She turned her gaze to the magnificent cake baked for them by Ruby Sullivan. The old woman had been right when she told her everything would work out, and although there had been a few bumps along the way, she and Leo had found their second chance right here in Bellbird Bay where it all began.

The End

If you've enjoyed Greta and Leo's story, a way you can say thank you to me is to leave a review on Amazon and/or Goodreads. A few words will suffice, no need for a lengthy review. It will mean a lot to me and help other readers find my books.

The next book in the series, *Celebrations in Bellbird Bay*, features two new characters. Sandy Elliott and Rob Andrews, and those of you familiar with the series will find all of your old friends there too. It's book eight in this series but, like all my other books, it can be read and enjoyed as a standalone novel.

Sandy Elliot is devastated when a fire destroys her new business and doesn't know how she can go on. When she receives a call from her grandmother's old friend seeking her help, a trip to Bellbird Bay seems like the answer to a prayer.

Rob Andrews is proud of what he has achieved with *Bay Bikes*, the business he set up when he returned from Afghanistan. But the memory of his time there still plagues him and has always prevented him from forming any close relationships, afraid his deep-seated guilt and recurrent nightmares would scare off any woman foolish enough to become involved with him.

Upon meeting, it's certainly not love at first sight. Sandy hates his beard and tattoos while Rob, though attracted to Sandy, doesn't believe he deserves to find happiness.

But Bellbird Bay is a small town, and their paths continue to cross, making it impossible for them to ignore each other or to deny the attraction between them.

With the festive season approaching, can Sandy and Rob overcome their pasts and enjoy a celebration of their own?

You can order it here https://mybook.to/CelebrationsinBB

From the Author

Dear Reader,

First, I'd like to thank you for choosing to read *Second Chances in Bellbird Bay*. I hope you've enjoyed this trip to Bellbird Bay as much as I've enjoyed writing it.

I'm really enjoying writing about my fictional town in the part of Queensland where I live and populating it with characters who I hope you will come to love. I'm thrilled at the number of my readers who tell me they want to live there. It's the seventh book in this series, but like the others, can be read as a standalone.

If you'd like to stay up to date with my new releases and special offers you can sign up to my reader's group.

You can sign up here

https://mailchi.mp/f5cbde96a5e6/maggiechristensensreadersgroup

I'll never share your email address, and you can unsubscribe at any time. You can also contact me via Facebook, Twitter or by email. I love hearing from my readers and will always reply.

Thanks again.

MaggieC

Acknowledgements

As always, this book could not have been written without the help and advice of a number of people.

Firstly, my husband Jim for listening to my plotlines without complaint, for his patience and insights as I discuss my characters and storyline with him, for his patience and help with difficult passages and advice on my male dialogue, and for being there when I need him.

John Hudspith, editor extraordinaire for his ideas, suggestions, encouragement and attention to detail, and for helping me make this book better.

Jane Dixon-Smith for her patience and for working her magic on my beautiful cover and interior.

My thanks also to early readers of this book – Helen, Maggie and Louise for their helpful comments and advice. Also, to Annie of *Annie's books at Peregian* and Graeme of *The Bookshop at Caloundra* for their ongoing support.

And to all of my readers, reviewers and bloggers. Your support and comments make it all worthwhile.

About the Author

After a career in education, Maggie Christensen began writing contemporary women's fiction portraying mature women facing life-changing situations, and historical fiction set in her native Scotland. Her travels inspire her writing, be it her trips to visit family in Scotland, in Oregon, USA or her home on Queensland's beautiful Sunshine Coast. Maggie writes of mature heroines coming to terms with changes in their lives and the heroes worthy of them. Maggie has been called *the queen of mature age fiction* and her writing has been described by one reviewer as *like a nice warm cup of tea. It is warm, nourishing, comforting and embracing.*

From the small town in Scotland where she grew up, Maggie was lured to Australia by the call to 'Come and teach in the sun'. Once there, she worked as a primary school teacher, university lecturer and in educational management. Now living with her husband of over thirty years on Queensland's Sunshine Coast, she loves walking on the deserted beach in the early mornings and having coffee by the river on weekends. Her days are spent surrounded by books, either reading or writing them – her idea of heaven!

Maggie can be found on Facebook, Twitter, Goodreads, Instagram, Bookbub or on her website.

https://www.facebook.com/maggiechristensenauthor
https://twitter.com/MaggieChriste33
https://www.goodreads.com/author/show/8120020.Maggie_Christensen
https://www.instagram.com/maggiechriste33/
https://www.bookbub.com/profile/maggie-christensen
https://maggiechristensenauthor.com/

www.ingramcontent.com/pod-product-compliance
Lightning Source LLC
Chambersburg PA
CBHW030619120726
47904CB00006B/1956